A writer digging for secrets may be digging her own grave...

Who saw her die?
"I," said the fly,
"With my little eye,
I saw her die."

Touch of Evil

Let sleeping dogs lie, Sophia had said.

She had also said that Tess had brought evil to the house at one time.

Evil.

Maybe now the evil is inside you, came a voice from deep within.

Tess stopped at the car door, hands shaking, and fumbled for her keys. She hadn't locked the car—it was seldom necessary in a small town. It was so dark she had to feel for them within her bag. After a clumsy grapple, she dropped them to the pavement and stooped over to pick them up.

Suddenly Tess felt a thud, as if someone's fist were striking her from behind. Her knees buckled. At the same time, she heard what sounded like the crinkling of paper. Reaching her right hand underneath her left arm and back around as far as she could, Tess felt, unbelievably, first a piece of paper, and then the handle of a knife . . .

DEADLINE

Diamond Books by D. F. Mills

**DARKROOM
SPELLBOUND
DEADLINE**

DEAD LINE

D.F. MILLS

DIAMOND BOOKS, NEW YORK

DEADLINE

A Diamond Book / published by arrangement with
the author

PRINTING HISTORY
Diamond edition / October 1991

All rights reserved.
Copyright © 1991 by Deanie Francis Mills.
This book may not be reproduced in whole or in part,
by mimeograph or any other means, without permission.
For information address: The Berkley Publishing Group,
200 Madison Avenue, New York, New York 10016.

ISBN: 1-55773-593-X

Diamond Books are published by The Berkley Publishing
Group, 200 Madison Avenue, New York, New York 10016.
The name "DIAMOND" and its logo are trademarks
belonging to Charter Communications, Inc.

PRINTED IN THE UNITED STATES OF AMERICA

10 9 8 7 6 5 4 3 2 1

*For my beautiful sisters,
Jeanne and Amy,
who have honored me with
their friendship.*

ACKNOWLEDGMENTS

IT WOULD BE impossible to write crime novels of any kind without the expert assistance of many professionals who take time out of incredibly busy schedules to offer their support and the benefit of years in the field. I'd like to thank a few of them here.

As usual, I owe a debt of gratitude to my longtime friend Ray Robbins, coauthor of *Introduction to Criminal Evidence and Court Procedure* and my professor for the criminal justice course of the same name at Western Texas College. I can never learn enough from him.

Deepest appreciation goes to the Honorable Judge Joe Kendall, 195th District Court, Dallas, for allowing me unlimited access to his courtroom smack in the middle of a murder trial. I couldn't have learned nearly as much as I did without the cooperation of Deputy Chief Assistant District Attorney Jerry Simms; she has my thanks, my respect, and my affection. Thanks, also, to her very able assistant, ADA John Withers.

I would also like to thank Assistant District Attorney Dana Cooley, Snyder, Texas, for reading the manuscript in progress and offering her expertise toward its accuracy.

None of this would have been possible without the hand-up I got from my very dear friend Ken Carden, former Deputy Chief Assistant District Attorney, Dallas. He has taught me not only about law but about life, and I sincerely hope he will be the first paraplegic to sail around the world.

I have enjoyed the friendship and encouragement of an extraordinary man, Sergeant Danny Rhea, Texas Rangers Company "E," Ozona, Texas, since long before I wrote *Deadline*. Thanks, Danny, for everything.

Many thanks, too, to the Mystery Writers of America, Inc., for sending me much useful information on the anatomy of fire investigation and on the forensic pathology of thermal injuries. Their support for writers in the suspense field is invaluable.

As I sit out here writing in my solitary eighty-year-old ranch house, in the middle of the rolling plains of West Texas, I sometimes wonder if I could have made it without the cheerful telephone voice and enthusiastic assistance of my friend and former agent, Anita Diamant. I will always appreciate what she's done for me as she sends me on my way.

And I have been very fortunate indeed to have the privilege of working with one of the best editors in the business for three novels, Ginjer Buchanan. She's been a superb teacher.

Of course, I couldn't write a word without my husband, Kent, my love and my life, and my two precious children, Dustin and Jessica, who make each day of my life worth living.

Many Texan readers will recognize the geographical area described in *Deadline*: the Caprock and rolling plains of west-central Texas and the sandy desert area further west. However, I wouldn't think of patterning a town, ranch, any character, or even a crime after any existing person, place, or event. Though some scenes are set in the real cities of Midland, Lubbock, and Abilene, the other settings, crimes, and characters are wholly figments of the writer's imagination.

Great wits are sure to madness near allied,
  And thin partitions do their bounds divide.

        JOHN DRYDEN

CHAPTER ONE

"Is THIS A lucky break, or *what*?" David's familiar Yankee twang fairly sang over the telephone wire.

"Well, not for the people involved," murmured Tess, gripping the receiver in a palm suddenly sweaty.

He ignored her. "Y'got your former governor of Texas, one of the richest oilmen in the country, who missed by a hair's breadth being nominated as the Democratic candidate for President of the United States in the last election, your basic high-profile kinda guy, being indicted for murder and attempted murder of practically his entire family! This is great!"

"You're sick, David."

"And here we've got a best-selling true-crime author who happens to live right there in little ole Texas. I tell you, it's providential."

"I'm sure God was thinking the same thing when those people burned to death."

"Smoke inhalation. It was in the papers this morning. You gotta get down there, Tess."

"I'm already down here." She swallowed. Her mouth had gone dry.

"Right. So get there quick, wherever this podunk town is they've got him."

That West Texas podunk town was a day's drive from Tess's Hill Country home, one hundred miles, even, from the nearest airport. New Yorkers had no concept of *distance* when it came to Texas.

"Tess? You listening?"

"I'm sorry. What?" She struggled to concentrate, picturing her editor in front of her, with his balding hair fizzed out around his ears, round spectacles perched on a hawk nose, brown eyes fairly crackling with wit, intelligence, and an enthusiastic love for his work.

"You remember what happened when that Edwards guy, the one in Boston, claimed a black man shot him and his wife, then they found out he'd done it himself? Man, the media flocked to the case, trying to grab rights to the story. Movie people, publishers . . . They had a book out on it just a few months later."

"I don't write instant books, David. Don't ask me to. *Murder and Madness* took two years."

"I'm just saying. The quicker you get on it, the fresher the story, the less likely some Hollywood producer hasn't already paid them off for exclusivity."

"David, I'm tired. You know I just finished revisions on *Blood on Their Hands*."

"I know. You did a great job, by the way."

"Thanks. It's just . . . I really don't want to do this story."

"Why not? It could be the hottest of your career. And who better to write it than a fellow Texan? You're always griping about *damnyankee* authors portraying Texans like cartoon characters."

He had a point. Even a few Texan expatriates had made a fortune pandering to the national pastime of spoofing Texans, as though moving out of the state had somehow made them superior. She considered it, then shook her head. "I just . . . I'd rather not, David. You don't know the emotional toll it takes, interviewing families who've been victimized by violent crime. And this . . . the fire . . . It's just too awful."

He was silent a moment. "What's the matter with you, Tess? This is your business. And you're damn good at it. *Murder and Madness* has done even better than *I* thought it would. Your agent tells me she's been talking to some film producers."

David was right. Tess knew that David Feldman was one of the best editors in the business. He'd taken her rough first manuscript and helped her polish it until it shone. Then he'd guided it through the marketing labyrinth to the best-seller list. And he was right about other things. Crime reporting was her life. She'd been at it for twelve years, first for the

Deadline 3

Dallas Times Herald, then for the prestigious *Texas Monthly* magazine, then stringing for the Southwest Bureau of the *New York Times* and various national magazines. *Murder and Madness*, a serious study of the Matomoros cult killings, was critically acclaimed and a smash success. *Blood on Their Hands*, which examined several infamous serial killers, was well received by her publisher, and they were already talking about a promotional tour and a good-sized publicity budget.

And it *was* true that she'd been looking around for ideas for another project. She'd been following the Ross Chandler case ever since the tragic house fire which killed his wife, his daughter, and one grandchild, and which seriously maimed another grandchild. Years of studying crime and the criminal mind had left Tess just cynical enough that she'd been suspicious of the circumstances all along, although the fire department had never been able to prove arson. Consequently she hadn't been surprised when autopsy reports revealed what newspapers judiciously referred to as "foul play" in the deaths of the victims.

The surviving child, horrendously burned, had been mute for months. When she finally spoke, she pointed the finger of blame squarely at her grandfather.

Everything seemed fated for Tess Alexander to cover the trial and write the story, pulling away the carefully sculpted mask of a famous man who, if found guilty, could have cold-bloodedly burned his own family to death.

And yet . . . how could Tess explain to David the feeling of dread which immediately settled on her shoulders like a heavy cloak as soon as he brought up the subject, the quick pattering of her heart, the urge to run? Through the years, she'd trained herself not to get emotionally involved with the people whose stories she told. She'd held herself detached, much like the cops whose beats she'd covered. It was an important defense mechanism that protected one's sanity.

But with this . . . she was already involved, and she didn't know *why*.

"*Tess*! What, are you takin' a nap or something?"

"I'm sorry, David. It's just . . . I guess I'm tired."

His voice gentled. "I know you are. You've worked hard on *Blood on Their Hands*, and I know you deserve a rest.

But in your business, as you well know, you have to move with the events. You have no control over that."

"I know."

"I think this is the story that could make your career, Tess. You'd have a well-earned place beside Joe McGuiness, Ann Rule, and Joseph Wambaugh as a top true-crime author. It's a helluva story. And I don't think anybody could tell it better than you, like I said, because it's on your own home turf."

Home. That explained at least some of her apprehension. The fire which took the lives of Ross Chandler's family happened on his West Texas ranch, which happened to be located only thirty miles or so from the ranch where Tess had grown up. It would mean leaving her lakeside home near Austin and moving back in, at least for a while, with her mother and sister. And closer to the blank spaces, the gaps in her memory she was careful never to probe, the dark spots which hid things from her past she never wanted to face again.

She shivered.

"If you want me to beg, I will," David pleaded. "Be a lot more money in it for you, I can tell you that."

Biting her lip, Tess stood up to pace the floor. As she did so, she disturbed a pile of papers near the phone. A letter shook loose and floated softly to the floor. It was from her sister, Marah. She'd been avoiding that, too.

She watched the letter, written in her sister's loopy scrawl, skid across the hardwood floor. With a heavy sigh, she said, "No, David. I wouldn't want you to get your knees dirty. I'll go to West Texas. I'll do the book."

A loud whoop tickled her ear. "I *knew* I'd be able to talk you into it! Keep in touch, will you? I wanna know what's going on."

"Sure." A throbbing set in over her left eye.

"This'll be great," he said buoyantly. "Talk to you later."

"Okay." Little dark spots appeared in her vision. "Bye."

Slowly she picked up Marah's letter, wincing as a wave of dizziness washed over her when she straightened. Carrying it to the wraparound front porch of the two-story stone house overlooking a spangling blue lake, she attempted to read it again, but the brilliant light off the lake sent stabs of pain behind her eyes and she hurried into her bedroom, pulling the shades down behind gauzy white sheer draperies and stretching out on the ruffled white spread. Breathing deeply, trying to relax, she took another look at Marah's letter.

"Dear Tessie," Marah wrote, using the nickname she knew Tess despised, "I thought you needed to know that Mama is getting worse. I guess it's just as well Mack and I got divorced, because me and the kids would have probably been here all the time anyway. She thinks she's still running the ranch. I gave her a set of books from five years ago to piddle with and she doesn't even know the difference. Sometimes she stays up all night working on them and the next day you can't make any sense out of them at all. Then she starts all over again. It's like I got three kids instead of two. I have to watch her real close when she wants to cook.

"It just seems to me that if you gave a flying damn about her, you would want to come see her while she still knows who you are. MUST BE NICE to be able to fly up to New York whenever your little heart desires and make all this money and be a Big Shot writer. *I* wouldn't know. I'm too busy making sure Mama doesn't burn the house down.

"But just in case you want to get off your High Horse and rub shoulders with people who '*ain't*' so intellectual, this is the time to do it, and I'm not kidding. Anyway, the kids would like to see you. Write me back. Love, Marah.

"P.S. Thanx for the money you sent. It pretty much pays for Mama's medication."

Tess leaned her head back on a pillow. The whole left side of her face was screaming in pain. Her stomach churned. There was no point in trying to take anything. She knew it would come right back up again.

It had been a long time since she'd had a migraine.

She tried not to think about Marah's letter, tried not to think about anything. There were eight long years between the sisters, and there was so very much Marah did not know, would never know, about her big sister. She'd been too young, for example, to know how hard Tess had to struggle to get through college, working three jobs, sacrificing a social life, studying all night in hopes of winning a scholarship to ease some of the pressure. She couldn't know how hard Tess had fought to make her place in a male-dominated field, turning down opportunities to take the easy way out and write features for the society pages. She never knew how many articles Tess had done on spec, good articles that had been rejected just because she was an outsider. Not to mention some of the things she'd had to endure in order to be accepted by mostly male police officers.

And Daddy's Precious Girl had never, ever known just how differently he had treated her big sister from the way he'd treated her. Or how that house reeked of his presence, even after all these years since the night he left.

Her stomach revolted, and Tess barely made it to the bathroom in time. Yet, as with most of her migraines, emptying her stomach seemed to ease the pain somewhat. She crawled back onto the bed, succeeded in blanking her mind, and fell into the deep, unnatural sleep those blinding headaches always produced.

When she awoke, the house was filled with a strange murkiness. Thunder rumbled off the lake. The pain was gone, but she felt drained and heavy-limbed. She moved through the house, turning on soft-lit lamps as she went, leaving pools of light in the cool, high-ceilinged rooms. The furnishings were sparse because she was collecting antique pieces only as she was able to afford them, but she liked it that way. French doors, hardwood floors, and tall windows gave the house a feeling of openness. Like the white gauze sheers in her bedroom, it was clean.

The old house was drafty and creaky but it was located on prize lakefront land. Another buyer had wanted to raze the house and build something angled and modern, but Tess had outbid him, putting down almost the whole advance from *Blood on Their Hands* as a down payment. Between her twice-yearly royalty statements from *Murder and Madness*, Tess filled in the gaps with articles. She was just going over the galleys for one on a Vietnamese underworld crime ring in Houston. But not tonight. No way could she work tonight.

Humidity from the oncoming storm weighed on Tess, mixing and mingling with the depression brought on by Marah's letter and David's phone call. In the large, airy, plant-filled kitchen, she combined milk with a can of chicken noodle soup and placed it in the microwave. Lightning cracked someplace nearby and the lights flickered.

Marah was right. She needed to go see their mother; it was

Deadline 7

truly shameful that she'd neglected it this long. It wasn't that she didn't want to see her mother, it was just . . . that house. She could not bear being in that house. For years she'd been trying to get her mother to come to Austin for a visit, but her mother, still strong and healthy in her mid-fifties, had procrastinated, claiming she couldn't get away from the livestock.

They didn't know then. Couldn't have known.

But her mother . . . her mother *must* have known that, even in those early stages, she would be unable to drive herself hundreds of miles to Tess's for a visit. Could not, in fact, drive the hundred miles to an airport, park the car, and book a flight.

The microwave screeched and Tess jumped. She took out the soup, put it on the oak trestle table, and stared at it.

Alzheimer's was supposed to be for old people.

Her mother's hair was still soft and brown.

The soup blurred before her and she left it, wandering over to stare out the window between cheerful blue-sprigged curtains at the huge live oaks behind the house, tossing heavy manes in the stormy wind.

She was going to have to go back.

The book. The damned book. The thing was, this whole trip would be much less stressful if she weren't having to work on that awful book. That was it, then. She'd call David tomorrow, tell him she simply could not do this book, not with her mother sick and everything. He'd have to understand, that's all.

Feeling indescribably better, Tess sat down to the soup with a pad of paper and a pen, and began making a list of things she'd need to do to prepare for the trip.

The phone rang. *Let the machine get it.*

After three rings, it occurred to Tess that the lightning must have caused a power surge which temporarily disconnected the delicate answering machine device. She grabbed the receiver off the blue wall phone, stretching the extra-long cord over to the butcher-block cabinet to rinse out her bowl and spoon in the stainless-steel sink.

"Hello?"

"Tess Alexander?"

The deep, cultured male voice had a timbre to it that was

at once familiar and yet not. She hesitated, running through the memory files in her mind. She should know who this person was, and yet it was not a friend or relative. "Yes?"

"This is Ross Chandler."

The soup bowl clattered from Tess's hand. *Ross Chandler. The ex-governor.*

The accused.

CHAPTER TWO

FOR A MOMENT, Tess froze. Then she managed to say, "Governor. This is a surprise." She stumbled over to the trestle table and sat down, twisting the phone cord in her hand.

"I've just finished reading *Murder and Madness*. I want to commend you on a fine piece of journalism."

"Thank you, Governor." Her first thought was *His Texan accent isn't nearly as pronounced as it was when he was politicking*.

"I guess you've heard about the unfortunate trouble I've been in recently."

"Yes, I have."

"Now, I don't have to tell you that when you're in the public eye, like I am, things get published that have no relation to the truth whatsoever. Things quoted out of context, or misquoted altogether. And you don't have any way to defend yourself without coming off like a whiner."

"It can be a problem." *What was he getting at?*

"TV reporters and newspaper people are out to make a splash, move up the ladder. In a way, I can understand that. I know a little bit about ambition."

It was true. Ross Chandler had been born to sharecropper parents in the middle of the Panhandle Dust Bowl days, had built his fortune single-handedly on a wildcatting roller coaster in the early days of the West Texas oil industry, and had made his way to the governor's mansion on sheer iron will, money, and one of the nastiest campaigns in Texas history.

"But you don't have anything to prove," he went on. "You're already established as a reputable journalist, and

Murder and Madness has put you on the map as a talent to be reckoned with."

"Er, thank you, Governor."

"So I figured that you would be the perfect choice to tell my story. It's the only way the truth will ever get out."

"What?"

"Oh, I don't have any doubt that my lawyers will get me acquitted of all charges. That part doesn't bother me. But there's folks who believe that, once you're charged with something, you did it, period, whether the jury lets you off or not. This way, they could read my story the way it really happened. In a book, see, I can say everything I've ever wanted to say but didn't get the chance."

Tess's cheeks burned. "Governor, if you want to write the story of your life, do it yourself. Or hire a ghostwriter. What I tell is the *truth*, as my investigation reveals it. No way would I go into a book like this as your puppet."

There was a moment of stunned silence. Tess wondered if anybody had ever spoken to him this way. Power and money had a way of intimidating people.

Suddenly, loud laughter boomed over the receiver. "I like you, Miz Alexander. You got spunk."

Spunk? What a corny word.

"Now, I didn't mean to imply that I was going to tell you what to write. I just want to have the chance to have my say. I'm entitled, don't you think?"

"Certainly. And so is everyone else involved." *Except, of course, the dead people.*

"That's understood. I'd just like to be assured that the whole situation would be handled fairly, and with you, I think it would."

She wasn't sure what to say.

"Now, I'm prepared to offer your publisher exclusive rights to my story. I'd open up to you all my records and files—at least, those that didn't get burned. All article offers or film offers would be refused or channeled through your publisher. What do you think?"

I think David would faint dead away. Still, she had to think. She should be thrilled at such an opportunity, and yet . . . she could feel the cloak settling again on her shoulders. "I don't know, Governor . . ."

Deadline 11

"Miz Alexander . . . I'm innocent."

The words hovered. *I'm innocent.* What if he was? What if he really, truly was?

"But your granddaughter . . ."

"I can explain that. I've got enemies. It happens, when you live a tough political life. They've been working on her, in the hospital . . . They've got that poor baby so confused . . ." His voice broke.

"Okay." Tess could hear her voice speak, almost as if by itself. "I'll come to West Texas and do the book."

"Oh, thank you. You won't regret it."

"But Governor?"

"Yes?"

"You must understand, from the beginning, that this is not *your* story. It is *my* story, and I will write it as *I* see fit."

"Of course."

"You understand that? I'll sign an agreement to that effect—"

"That won't be necessary. I understand."

"Fine. I'll need a number where I can reach you."

He gave her several private listings, told her he was looking forward to meeting her, and hung up.

For a long time, Tess sat, listening to the ticking of the Austrian cuckoo clock she'd found at a flea market and had restored.

Try as she might, she couldn't get over the uncomfortable feeling that she had just been hustled.

Tess's little blue Ford Mustang groaned under the weight of all the computer equipment, files, reference books, tape recorders, and luggage she thought she'd need for an extended working trip away from home. If she was lucky with her interviews and the trial went speedily, she might be back to the Hill Country before summer heat withered the spectacular bluebonnet display that the heart of Texas seemed to reserve for her own each spring.

But for now, the almost constant rain of early March seemed to add to her gloom as she pulled away from the dark stone house by the moping lake, silver-gray now under the brooding clouds. There hadn't been time to find a housesitter, and she fretted about that. Vacant lake houses were prime targets for burglary and vandalism. A couple of her cop friends in the nearby community had offered to keep an eye on it for her, and she knew they would.

The wipers could barely keep up with the downpour, and Tess drove cautiously, more mindful of her expensive computer gear than of her own safety. She was between royalty statements, and having to come up with a couple of thousand dollars to replace it would be nearly impossible. It was doubtful her household insurance policy would cover damage from a car wreck.

The further she drove north and west, the worse the radio reception got, so she plugged a tape of some classical harp music into the tape deck to soothe her nerves. Other things changed with distance. The rain stopped and she left the clouds behind. Green rolling hills and crowds of trees gave way to rocky bluffs, dormant mesquites, and infinite horizons in earth tones of rust, sienna, tan, and brown.

The sun dropped down into her eyes and Tess was glad she'd remembered to toss a gimme cap into the front seat before leaving. It gave better shade than the skimpy car sun visor. Near the small city of San Angelo, Tess topped a bluff and the whole great countryside fell away before her, open and free, wild and majestic. She'd been driving for over an hour without a sign of habitation except an occasional isolated ranch house, wondering if she had enough gas to make it.

The scenery spelled h-o-m-e, reminded her of whence she came, comforted and disturbed her at the same time. It was rugged and lonely and you had to be tough to survive.

Outside San Angelo, which at a population of 85,000 was big by West Texas standards, Tess gassed up and ate an excellent Mexican dinner at a small, homey roadside café. She'd forgotten how warm and friendly the natives could be, a throwback, maybe, to the days when *any* company, short of Comanche raids, was welcome.

Out of San Angelo, she headed north. Warm sun scalded her through the driver's side window. About an hour later, just before the sun melted into the golden horizon, Tess could see, in the distance, a massive rust-colored cloud, like some science fiction fog, rolling inexorably toward her. The whole bottom half of the sky was rusty, in fact, and just before she drove into it, gale-force winds slammed into the little Mustang, almost shoving it off the road. She could taste grit in her teeth. Both hands on the wheel, Tess turned on useless headlights and struggled along, buffeted by the first full-scale dust storm she'd seen since childhood.

March in West Texas meant wind, brown skies, and rattlesnakes emerging from hibernation.

A Bible verse from the days when Tess's mother used to take her to Sunday school every week came to her now out of the raging brown storm. As Jesus prepared for the crucifixion, it said, "He set His face toward Jerusalem."

And so, pummeled and battered by the elements, Tess set her face toward home.

It was coal-dark as Tess turned off the paved farm-to-market road onto the rocky caleche lane leading to the ranch house. As a courtesy, she stopped to check the mailbox which perched at the turnoff. It was three more miles to the house and the busy ranchers didn't always make it to the mail every day. The nearest town to the ranch, the tiny village of Dryton, population 5,000, lay twenty miles to the north. Fifteen miles beyond that was the county seat of Windham County, Remington, population 18,000, which would host the trial of former governor Ross Chandler. Tess pulled a day-old Remington newspaper out of the mailbox and headed down the dusty road.

Without streetlights, her headlights bored yellow holes in the blackness. As a teenager, driving home from her after-school job in town, she'd often stopped midway and turned off the lights, just to marvel at the astonishing star-frosted sky. It was amazing how spectacular the night sky could be, when there were no city lights to blot out the stars, nor even buildings or tall trees to block the view.

It always reminded Tess of something she'd heard once: "You've never seen the sky until you've seen the plains." The space, the rugged beauty, and the unflinching elements of nature tended to put things in perspective. "It draws you into yourself," she thought.

Maybe that's what she was afraid of.

Clouds had moved in behind the dust storm, producing that strange phenomenon that could occur only in the Southwest:

little mud droplets, smeared across Tess's windshield by useless wipers.

An enormous jackrabbit bounded into the path of her lights, scissored his ridiculously long ears, then sprang down the road directly in front of her, confused into thinking he had to outrun her. She drove slowly, smiling. She'd forgotten what it was like to live surrounded by wildlife.

It wasn't all bad, she told herself.

She passed the turnoff to the house where Juan Garcia and his wife, Sophia, had lived for many years, helping to run the place. Juan and Sophia had raised a big happy family and had brought out many relatives from Mexico during their years on the Rocking A Ranch, since the days when Tess's mother was growing up. Nan had found Juan many years ago, half dead from thirst and hunger, walking cross-country to find work and send home for his young wife and family. He didn't speak a word of English then, but her daddy (Tess's grandfather, John Powell, whom they all called "Pa" or "Papa") had taken him in, given him work and food and a decent wage, not like some of the other "wetbacks" who were underpaid and overworked on other ranches. When Sophia joined him, Tess's grandfather had built them a home.

Eventually the entire Garcia family became American citizens. Sophia even passed a high school equivalency exam. Three of their hardworking five sons were college graduates, paid for, in part, by the cattle the old man had allowed Juan to run on the ranch along with his own. Juan and Sophia had repaid their employer's kindness with a lifetime of loyalty, love, and hard work.

When the old man was alive, times were better. More prosperous. But when Pa died—some said of a broken heart, after Rex Alexander wooed and married his only child—Rex had proceeded to squander Nan's inheritance. Recently discovered oil had promised riches beyond belief, but something happened, somewhere along the line—something Tess never understood and her mother was never willing to discuss—and the mineral rights were lost.

All they got in return for the destruction of the environment left behind by the oil companies as they pumped millions of dollars' worth of crude out of Rocking A ground was a few thousand dollars in "damages." Tess had long suspected that Rex signed away the rights in some kind of deal to save his neck from yet another gambling debt.

After that explosive night when Tess's father finally left, her mother had taken over the place and managed to keep them just one step ahead of the banks.

With a sharp pang in her heart, Tess suddenly faced the truth that her mother was no longer capable of managing the ranch, that it was up to Marah. Marah, thrice-divorced by the age of twenty-six, with only a few sporadic attempts at college behind her. Marah, who never seemed able to finish anything she started. Marah, who never slowed down for jackrabbits or stopped to look at the stars.

What would happen to the ranch? While there was no better cowhand or horseman than Juan, he was getting old now; besides, he had never handled the books. And none of his sons had stayed on the ranch. They'd all left, lured away by lucrative oil-field jobs or big-city sophistication.

She was still musing these depressing thoughts when two sleek cow dogs came charging into her headlights, baying a warning at the unfamiliar vehicle. She slowed to a crawl, topped a hill, and rounded a corner, and there it was: the hundred-year-old ranch house built by her great-grandfather with lumber hauled out from Dallas on oxcarts.

Gabled attic rooms added a third story to the white frame house. The lengthy front porch was screened in, but the smaller back porch was enclosed. Called the mud room, it was the place where dusty boots, sweaty hats, and faded Levi jackets were left behind before anyone dared set foot in Mama's kitchen. Most of the changes through the years had been made in the ground-floor rooms: walls knocked out and space opened up. Upstairs, cold hardwood floors had been carpeted, wallpaper painted over or paneled.

It was the attic floor that had been left basically the same, with its small, slant-ceilinged rooms, cubbyholes, and angled closets. Plenty of places for a terrified child to hide. For a while.

Unfolding herself from the car, Tess stretched and stood for a moment, mustering courage, fiddling with the dogs. The mud room light was on, and as she started for the house her sister stepped into it and held open the screen door, smiling broadly. "You came," she said.

They embraced awkwardly, still unsure of how to express love for one another. There was a mirrored hatrack by the door leading to the house. They both looked into it at the same moment and their eyes met.

This was where the differences between them were most apparent. Marah, at twenty-six, with their mother's curly brown hair and warm brown eyes, was pretty, petite, and spry, her olive skin tanned from working outdoors, laugh crinkles fanning out from the corners of her black-lashed eyes, a dimple in one corner of full red lips. She was wearing tight, sun-faded Levi's, moccasins, and a tee-shirt sporting a picture of country singer George Strait. When she wanted to be, Marah could be a real charmer, a flirt, a madcap; mostly around men.

Toward Tess and their mother she harbored bitterness for the night they'd faced down Rex Alexander with a shotgun and literally run him off the place when Marah was eight years old. Though he'd always lavished attention and affection on Marah when he was there, once he left, he'd never contacted her again. She blamed them for that; never him.

Tess, on the other hand, looked in this household almost as if she'd been placed here by an alien spaceship. At thirty-four, she was still tall and gangly, her long wavy hair a wild golden-red, her thick brows and lashes the color of sand, her creamy complexion freckle-scattered. Her eyes were so light as to startle someone unprepared for them, and they tended to change with her moods—the color of silver when she laughed; iron when she was angry; cloudy when she was confused or hurt. And she never tanned. Nor did she ever bother much with makeup; nothing other than her natural coloring ever looked quite right. "Pretty" was not a word used to describe Tess. "Striking" was.

She was wearing a man's brown and gold tweed suit coat, a gold silk blouse, brown creased trousers, and gold suede flats with a matching wide suede belt. Looking into Marah's critical eyes, she felt foolishly overdressed.

"It's good to have you home, Tess," said Marah, still watching her in the mirror. "I mean that. I've felt so . . .

alone, trying to take care of Mama and look after this place. I could use some support."

"I'm sorry it took me so long to come. It's not your fault. I know you're doing the best you can."

"Well, I appreciate that." Arm in arm, they entered the kitchen. "Cody! Molly! Aunt Tess is here!"

Squeals of delight erupted from the other room, and the two children came tumbling into the large square kitchen with its worn yellow linoleum, man-sized freezer, and big Formica table. Molly, at seven, was a mirror image of her mother except that her hair was almost black and her eyes a surprising bonny blue. She was destined to be a world-class beauty one day. Cody was more like his father, solid and square, with crisp brown hair cowboy-short, frank brown eyes, and healthy pink cheeks. Molly won the race with her five-year-old brother and flung herself into Tess's arms in a gale of giggles.

Cody jumped on Tess's back like a monkey and Tess gave herself up to the warm, squirming little bodies, wet kisses, and breathtaking hugs. Marah stood slightly apart, smiling indulgently.

No, it wasn't all bad, coming home.

The living room looked the same, with its real knotty-pine paneling, parquet floors, cowhide rugs, and hearth of hand-collected stones. The nail was still there which once held the head of a magnificent buck Rex had shot. Tess had never been able to bear staring into its sad brown eyes, and she'd taken it down and hauled it out to the barn the night he left. There were tears in the old brown leather couch now, with little tufts of fluff sticking out here and there. Her grandfather's collection of Indian arrowheads, mounted in velvet-backed frames, lined the wall over the solid pine rolltop desk. In one corner was the beautiful polished cradle he'd fashioned with his own hands out of a single mesquite stump.

She tried very hard to picture Pa in this room; not her father.

Tess had brought gifts for the kids and they finally settled down in front of the TV, Cody absorbed in his GI Joes and Molly immersed in Marguerite Henry's *Album of Horses*. Tess sank wearily onto the couch and gave Marah a curious look. "Where's Mama?"

Marah glanced at the kids. "Would you like a beer?"

"I'd love one."

She gave Tess a significant look and headed for the kitchen. Tess followed. They shared cold Lone Stars in long-neck bottles and sat in the yellow vinyl kitchen chairs. Marah picked at the label on her bottle. "Mama goes to bed really early now."

"But it's only eight o'clock!"

She sighed. "I know. She gets back up again in the middle of the night and roams the house until dawn."

"What do you mean, she roams the house?" Tess took a big swallow of beer. She thought she might have a couple more before the night was over.

Marah got up and rummaged in the cupboard for Doritos. "Just what I said. She wanders around."

"Don't you think that could be dangerous?"

Her sister crunched a chip. "She's harmless."

"How do you know?"

"I just *know*, that's all! I'm *here*, remember? You're not."

"Okay, okay. I'm sorry. It's just . . . never mind."

"Just what?" Marah's eyes narrowed in the way they always did when she was losing her temper.

"Just . . . can't you like, keep her up or something? Make her go to bed later so she'll sleep?"

Marah shook her head. "It doesn't work that way. You'll see." She tossed back a swig of beer and brown curls at the same time. After a moment, she said, "At least now I'll have some help around here. It's all I can do, keeping an eye on Mama, taking care of the kids, helping Juan. With you here I can go into town more often, do more work outside. It'll really help."

Tess shifted uncomfortably in her chair.

Marah shot her an accusing glance. *"What?"*

"I don't know that I'll be that much help to you." She faltered, ignoring those narrowed eyes, that high color in the cheeks that signified danger.

"What do you mean?" Marah spoke clearly, enunciating carefully. Another danger signal.

"It's just . . . I'm going to be working on a book. I'm covering the Ross Chandler trial."

"I knew it!" Marah sprang to her feet. "You selfish bitch! I should have known you didn't come here because you cared about Mama. You came so you'd have a free place to stay while you did your *big-deal writer* act."

"That's not true—"

"It *is* true. You haven't been here since Christmas a *year* ago. What is that, fifteen months? Do you realize what fifteen months means to Mama? *Do* you?"

"I'm sorry."

"Yeah, right. Tell it to Mama. Five minutes later, tell her *again*, because she won't remember." Marah whirled and headed for the door. She looked back, eyes blazing, cheeks flaming. "Thanks a helluva lot, Tess. Thanks for nothing."

Tess stared down at her beer. When she looked back up, Marah was gone.

"Welcome home," she muttered to herself.

Tess had forgotten what it was like to lie awake in the night, listening to the wind howl like a lonesome animal, pounding on doors and rattling windows as if, once it got into the house, it would calm down.

It brought other sounds with it, too. The dogs barked at phantoms. Unknown things clanked against the chain link fence that enclosed the front yard swing set. Ghosts rode the swings, tossing them high and tangling them together noisily. When she looked out, she could see tumbleweeds creeping along the fence line like hulking monsters looking for a way in.

The brass bed was unfamiliar and cold. She tossed and turned.

Suddenly the floor creaked outside her door. The china doorknob squeaked. Heart pounding, Tess turned on the bedside lamp and crept to the door.

She pulled it open.

"Mama."

There was much more gray in her mother's hair than she remembered from her last visit. At fifty-five, Nan Alexander was still trim, fully clothed in jeans and a flannel shirt, as if preparing to leave the house in the wee hours of the morning for a cattle working; yet her face had a pallor to it Tess had never noticed before. A big grin lit up her face and she threw her arms around her daughter.

"Tess, my darlin' girl! When did you get in?"

Tess hugged her mother tight, a bittersweet lump forming in her throat. "Not long ago," she said.

"It's so wonderful to see you," Nan said. Holding Tess's hand, she plunked down on the bed. "Tell me all about yourself. How's your love life?"

"Mama!"

Her mother laughed, a merry twinkle in her dark eyes, and Tess wondered fleetingly if maybe they'd made a mistake. Maybe she was all right after all. "I've been working on the books," Nan said. "Tax time is coming on, you know. I remember, Papa used to keep all those facts and figures in his head. Why, he knew every cow on the place by its markings. Can you imagine? Hereford cattle. They all look alike to most people, but not to Papa. Anyway, at tax time, he'd hand over this shoe box stuffed with receipts to this poor overworked accountant in town. What a mess!"

"Yeah, Pa was a character all right," Tess agreed, settling down beside her mother, holding her strong, calloused hand, hungry for the closeness. "So tell me, Mama, how have you been?"

"Oh, pretty good," her mother said, avoiding her eyes. "I've been a little forgetful. I'm surprised you came back so soon after Christmas, though." She smiled at Tess.

Tess stared at her. "Mama, I was home for Christmas *last* year, not this year."

"Oh." She glanced uncertainly away. "Time goes by, I guess," she said quietly. "Missy's been taking good care of us, though."

"Aunt Missy? She came down from Tennessee?"

Her mother waved her hands in front of her face in frustration. "No, no. Not Missy. Er . . ." she floundered, begging for help from Tess with her eyes but too proud to ask for it.

"You mean Marah?" she prodded gently.

"Of course. Of course I mean Marah. What an old coot I'm getting to be. Can't even think of my own daughter's name. I always get this way at tax time. It's tax time, you

Deadline

know. I remember, Papa used to keep all those facts and figures in his head. Did you know he could tell every cow apart by its markings?"

"Yes, Mama," said Tess, blinking back the tears. "I know."

CHAPTER THREE

"MOLLY! CODY! GET your rears in gear and come down to breakfast. The school bus will be here anytime now."

Tess opened her eyes to the sounds of Marah yelling at her kids outside the door and brilliant sunshine streaming through the curtains. She could no longer hear the wind.

A born night owl, she was used to working late into the night and sleeping equally late. Last night, she'd spent several hours with her mother, growing sadder with each passing minute. She glanced at her little bedside travel alarm: six-thirty. She was going to have to start getting used to country hours.

Tugging on a pair of jeans, Tess defiantly chose to wear a sweatshirt which was a personal favorite; it was white with enlarged black typescript across the chest which read: *I'd Rather Be Writing*. Adding a pair of white canvas Keds, she yanked a brush through her hair and scampered downstairs so she would be able to see the children before they left for school.

"Hi, Aunt Tess!" they chorused.

"Good afternoon," quipped Marah, shoveling pancakes onto their plates and cutting them into bite-sized pieces. She glanced at Tess and dimpled.

Although her barbed tongue and sarcastic wit could hurt, Marah had a flash-fire temper which faded quickly, unlike her older sister, whose temper worked on a slow boil and who tended to carry grudges for years. It was one more area of incompatibility between them.

"Can I do anything to help?" Tess asked coolly.

"Um, yes. You can get them some milk." Marah went back to the stove and poured more batter onto the grill.

Tess reached into the cabinet for some glasses.

"No—not those. Plastic mugs, bottom shelf," Marah said. "I can tell you don't have kids."

"Thanks for reminding me," snapped Tess. She collected the mugs and began pouring milk into them.

"Not all the way to the brim."

Tess stopped. "Do you want to do this?"

"I just don't want to have to clean up a spill, that's all. You're not used to being around kids. I'm just trying to help." She flipped a pancake.

Mouth pursed, Tess got herself some coffee. Marah placed a steaming stack of pancakes in front of her. "No thanks," Tess said. "I don't eat breakfast."

Marah snatched the pancakes away and plunked them down by an empty chair. "Thanks for mentioning it."

"Marah, you're twenty-six years old. I'm thirty-four. It's time you noticed that I do not now, nor have I ever, eaten breakfast."

"What are you going to write, Aunt Tess?" asked Molly.

The sisters stared at her, momentarily sidetracked by the interruption. "What?" asked Tess blankly.

"Your shirt. It says you'd rather be writing. What are you going to write?"

"Oh." She smiled. "I write books, honey."

Molly bounced excitedly in her chair. "Can I read them? Please?"

"I'm afraid not, sugar. They're R-rated."

"You can say that again," mumbled Marah, slathering butter on her pancakes.

"A lot you know," said Tess. "You haven't even read *Murder and Madness*."

"Couldn't get into it. It was so violent and depressing." Marah shuddered dramatically.

"I wish *I* could read it," pouted Molly.

"Someday, sugar." Tess patted her hand. She looked over at Marah as her sister soaked her pancakes with syrup. Yet one more point of contention. By completely ignoring Tess's work, by never asking about it or bothering to read it, she was, in effect, amputating a huge part of Tess's existence.

Which meant that she would never truly be able to understand her sister. *Not that she cares to,* thought Tess with the old resentment.

The dogs set up a clamor. "The bus is here!" cried Marah. "Quick! Get your book bags and your lunch boxes. I'll be in town today, so I'll just pick you up. They have such a long day when they ride the bus," Marah explained to Tess. "They don't get home until nearly five. That's hard on a little one like Cody. So I try to pick them up a couple of times a week." She planted kisses on each little face, both of which were presented then to Tess, while the bus pulled up outside with a wheezing rumble and a dog cacophony.

As the bus rattled on down the caleche road with the dogs in hot pursuit, Tess asked when their mother normally came downstairs.

"About ten," Marah said, gathering up syrupy plates. "When Sophia gets here."

"Sophia?"

"Yeah. She comes every day and helps out with Mama." She tossed leftover pancakes out the mud room door for the dogs, who were scampering importantly back. When she returned, Tess was standing by the table, hands on hips. "Let me get this straight. Sophia comes here every day to help out with Mama?"

"Yeah. Or the kids, if I need it."

"Uh-huh. What was all that business last night about how you needed all this help and support and how *alone* you'd been?"

Marah brushed past her, avoiding her eyes. "Well . . ." She faltered. "I can use all the help I can get."

Tess's slow boil erupted. "So that whole thing last night was just your typical dramatics! You exaggerated the situation just to make me feel bad!"

"Well, maybe you *needed* to feel bad!" shouted Marah. "You come waltzing in here once a year or so in your fancy clothes and try to tell *me* what to do!"

"I did not! I never said—"

"Girls!"

They both whirled toward the kitchen doorway.

"You stop that arguing," said Mama. "You'll wake up your father."

Deadline

• • •

From somewhere far away, Tess could hear Marah's voice. Her head was swimming and her left eye throbbed.

"I just cannot believe you said that," Marah was saying. "You can't be that brutal with Mama . . . Are you listening to me?"

Tess looked over at the door. Her mother was gone. She glanced at the clock. *Seven thirty.* The bus came at seven o'clock. She and Marah had been arguing as the bus was driving away.

Where had the half hour gone?

"Where's Mama?" she asked.

"A lot you care." Marah was pulling on her boots. "I'm going to see if Juan needs any help outside."

"Juan's here?"

"He just drove up. Didn't you hear the pickup?" Marah's eyes narrowed. "What's the matter with you?"

"Nothing. I just feel a migraine coming on."

"Oh. Well, there's aspirin in the upstairs bathroom." Marah never got migraines and had little sympathy for those who did. She hesitated a moment. "Look, Tess . . . you have to be gentle with Mama. She knows what's happening to her and it's breaking her heart. You can't lose your cool. I mean, I want to scream at her sometimes but you just can't. And when she gets mixed up about time, just bring her carefully back into the present."

Heart pounding, Tess nodded dumbly. *What had she said?* Somewhere, somehow . . . Tess had lost a half hour of her life. Just like that. She didn't know *what* she had said to her mother.

Marah left. Lowering herself numbly into a kitchen chair, Tess buried her head in her hands. Her stomach churned. *What had she done?* Tess had always been closer to their mother than Marah. She would never do anything to hurt her.

Sharp needles of pain set in over her left eye. Could Tess's greatest fear be happening to her?

Words. Words were Tess's life. Language. The assimilation, processing, and organizing of ideas. Ever since Mama's diagnosis, Tess had lived with a deep-seated fear that she would one day become a statistic: the children of Alzheimer's patients were fifty percent more likely to develop the disease themselves.

But I'm only thirty-four.

And her mother had only been fifty when she first started forgetting, becoming disoriented, losing blocks of time, and getting lost while driving.

Tess had never heard of Alzheimer's slowly entwining its deadly tentacles into the brain of someone still in her thirties, but research into the disease was still new. Perhaps the illness sometimes manifested itself much earlier in some people, but they merely passed it off as absentmindedness or preoccupation. Tess had suffered memory lapses before, but nothing so frightening as this.

Slowly she got to her feet and made her careful way to her mother's bedroom. She knocked and entered. Her mother was making notations with a pencil in a heavy ledger with the date "1985" on it.

"Mama?"

Nan looked up and smiled at her daughter. "Hi, darlin' girl." She went back to work.

"Mama . . . I'm so sorry if I hurt your feelings earlier."

Her mother frowned, looked up. "Earlier?"

"Marah said I . . . was mean to you."

"Oh, Marah." Nan waved her hand with the pencil back and forth. "She takes herself too seriously."

It occurred to Tess that Mama might not even remember the exchange itself. If it hadn't been so sad, she might have laughed. Her eyes stung. "I love you." Her voice broke.

Nan smiled tenderly. "I know. You're my darlin' girl. And you always will be. Now, I have to get back to work. It's tax time, you know."

Tess nodded and stepped back, closing the door softly behind her as she went.

What was she going to do? *I'll be like Scarlett,* she thought. *I won't think about that now.*

What she *did* have to think about was setting up an interview with Ross Chandler. And getting old Doc Perkins to fill her migraine prescription.

But for now, all she could do was lie down, pray for relief, and try not to think.

• • •

Sophia Garcia was of the old school of ranchers' wives: she was in the habit of preparing a huge midday "dinner," then saving the leftovers for a light supper. It was the smell of sizzling chicken fried steak, buttery mashed potatoes, savory red beans, and delectable peach cobbler that drew Tess downstairs after her migraine-grogged sleep.

Sophia spotted her at the door, and with a deep-chested laugh of delight, enfolded Tess in her huge arms against her ample bosom. Nobody ever dared ask Sophia her weight, but the wiry Juan joked out of earshot that she had to weigh herself on the cattle scale.

Tess adored her.

"You skinny girl!" shouted Sophia. "You gonna sit down and eat my cookin' and you gonna fatten up." She waved a beany spoon around in her plump hand. Her hair, which she had styled once a week at a beauty shop in town, fluffed around her broad face in gray curls, and glasses in heavy plastic old-fashioned frames kept slipping down her sweaty nose as she worked; her black eyes twinkled over them at Tess.

Tess grinned broadly. "Yes, Sophia." She accepted a large tumbler of sweetened tea (though she preferred unsweetened), and spent a pleasurable half hour hearing all the local gossip while Sophia cooked. She knew better than to offer to help.

"Marah's gone to town already," Sophia harrumphed, clearly offended that Marah hadn't eaten first. "I gave her a list but I know what she's gonna do. She's gonna buy a *ham*." Sophia tsk-tsked. To her, buying pork was wasteful, since they lived on a cattle ranch and had their beef provided. Eating anything other than beef was almost sacrilegious to Sophia.

Nan came into the kitchen. "I wanted to cook dinner, but you-know-who gets so *bossy* sometimes." She grinned at Tess.

"Yeah, and you gonna burn the house down someday."

"Well, I can remember how to read a cookbook, you know," remarked Nan.

"Yeah, and you forget which ingredients you already put in."

Tess worried that Sophia was hurting her mother's feelings,

but she needn't have. There was a loving understanding between the two women that allowed them to say to each other things that no one else would say to either one.

Juan joined them, sinewy and dark as a pecan from years of outside work, his hair only lightly streaked with gray as he took off his hat and hung it up. (A true gentleman, they all knew, never wore his hat indoors.) Juan never said much around his wife, allowing her to monopolize the conversation, but Tess had observed through the years that he always laughed at her wisecracks and never seemed bored. They were as comfortable together as matching old slippers.

"Tess is working on a book," announced Nan.

"Oh, another one," enthused Sophia. "I loved *Murder and Madness*."

"Why, thank you, Sophia. I appreciate that."

"I'm just ashamed those Matamoros killings had to happen in Mexico," she said, shaking her head sadly. (She pronounced the "x" like an "h.") "It makes all Mexicanos look like fools."

"I don't think so, Sophia." Tess shook her head. "Did Charles Manson make all Americans look like fools?"

Sophia raised her eyebrows and cocked her head. She liked that idea.

"Tess's new book is about . . ." Nan stopped and pursed her lips. "Wait a minute. Don't tell me. It's that guy. He used to be governor. Aw, hell, I *know* the guy. We go way back. Rex and I knew him before he even *thought* about being governor. Um . . ."

Tess, Sophia, and Juan all glanced away awkwardly. It was painful to watch the deterioration of a quick, accomplished mind.

"Don't worry about it, Mama."

"I *have* to worry about it!" Nan shouted, pounding the table with her fist, sending a fork clattering to the floor. *"I'm losing my mind and I have to worry about it! I hate this! I hate this!"*

"Mama—" Tess reached out and stroked her mother's sleeve.

Her mother jerked away her arm, knocking over her tea, and sprang to her feet. "You don't know what it's like. You *can't* know what it's like! I'm a *prisoner*, trapped in my own *body!*"

"It's okay." Tess felt helpless. Seldom in her life had she ever seen her mother in a rage, and never, never like this. Nan's face was contorted as she screamed and railed at her life.

"It's *not* okay! I don't have the attention span of *Cody*! How would *you* like to lose . . . little . . . *pieces* of your mind, like an incomplete jigsaw puzzle. Someday I won't be able to see the picture at all. Oh God, how I wish someone would just take me out to a pasture with a shotgun and put me out of my misery." She whirled to face Tess. "We did it with Shep. Remember Shep?"

Tess nodded mutely.

"He got so crippled up with arthritis and he was in such pain. We loved him so much that we couldn't stand to see him suffer anymore." She was crying now, pitiful tears that fell in droplets onto the tablecloth. She grabbed Tess's shoulders. "If you really loved me, you'd do the same thing for me."

For a long moment her eyes probed the depths of Tess's soul, then she ran from the room and slammed her bedroom door.

While Tess sat in shock, Sophia silently mopped up the spilled tea and retrieved the lost fork. Then she reached over and patted Tess's hand. "Honey, she gets like this sometimes. Just goes *loco* angry. It's not your fault. It's not anybody's fault. She's just frustrated is all. Don't worry. She gets over it real quick."

Sophia's good meal congealed in Tess's stomach like cold clay. She would never, as long as she lived, forget that look in her mother's eyes.

It wasn't so much what she saw in her mother's eyes that she wouldn't forget, but what her mother's eyes had uncovered in her own.

Fear.

Raw. Exposed. Powerless.

And it wasn't just the fear of lost words, though that was ragged enough.

It had something to do, she knew, with the man whose name her mother couldn't remember.

CHAPTER FOUR

TESS HAD BEEN driving in her dusty Mustang for an hour before she faced the fact that she was lost. Once she'd left the state highway and turned west on a farm-to-market road, then north on another farm-to-market road, she began to remember just how difficult landmarks were to find on a rolling landscape which stretched out as far as the eye could see in basically the same formation.

Juan, she knew, could have found the governor's ranch easily and quickly. He could read the land like a newspaper and besides, he already knew most of the back roads. But it had been a long time since Tess had traveled them. The governor's ranch sprawled out over six thousand rig-spotted acres, so she could have been driving through his country for miles without even realizing it.

And of course, there wasn't a handy phone booth.

She stopped in the middle of the road without bothering to pull over and got out, shading her eyes and looking around to get her bearings. Warm, dry wind whipped her hair around her face, which stung her eyes and got caught in her mouth. Bending down into the car, she pulled a pair of dark sunglasses out of her bag and put them on. It helped.

She'd already left rich, flat, winter-barren cotton fields behind and was now in "surenuff" cattle country. The hated prickly pear cactus—which cattle liked to eat but which proliferated so rapidly that it crowded out valuable grazing—dotted the rocky pastures. Flat-top blue mesas and miniature craggy mountains crowded with wind-stunted, hardy cedar trees swept up in the distance toward a vast sky so blue it hurt to look at it. Sleek red, white-faced Hereford cattle freckled the tawny landscape.

The silence, except for the persistent wind, was total.

Insistent doubts nagged at Tess. *Why had she gotten lost?* Was this the way, in the beginning, her mother had felt? Frustrated and frightened at the same time?

Looking up and down the road, she prayed for a car to flag down, but there was no one. Finally she climbed back in, pulled a U-turn in the middle of the road, and headed back south, watching for the caleche road the governor had said she'd find after so many miles. Finding roads in West Texas meant paying close attention to your odometer.

It occurred to her, as she searched for the road, that she'd been gradually climbing as she drove north. She remembered that the governor's ranch was perched on the edge of the magnificent Caprock formation, a geological wonder which literally divided the Texas Panhandle from the rest of the state. As if on a jagged dotted line, the ironing-board-flat high plains of the midwestern United States and the Texas Panhandle literally dropped off a series of cliffs, giving way to the beginnings of the rolling hills of west-central Texas. The governor had told her that his new house had been built right on the edge of the Caprock.

She passed a turnoff and hit the brakes with a screech, backing up and slowly heading down the caleche road, kicking up a powdery cloud of dust behind. Another winding caleche road connected to this one, marked by a stone archway over a broad cattle guard, upholding the famous Chandler Bar-C brand. Whew. She'd made it.

Her heart began to pound and Tess slowed a bit, wrapping her fingers around the steering wheel. Every fiber in her being wanted to turn around. She did not want to do this book; might not have, actually, if David hadn't been so wildly ecstatic about Chandler's offer. He was sure they were onto a smash best-seller, with book club and movie rights sold before the book was out of galleys. All Tess had to do was write the thing.

Minor details.

And what was she supposed to tell David, anyway? *Hey, I don't want to do this book because I've got this miserable feeling of dread in my gut that won't go away, even though I've never even met the man.*

Maybe she was just tired. There'd been no recupe time after *Blood on Their Hands*.

Tess topped a rise and caught her breath. Less than half a mile ahead, the world seemed to take a leap into space, undulating far below and away in artist's colors of sage and taupe and russet and, in the far distance, hazy soft violet and blue.

At the end of this drop-off squatted the house, cantilevered in flat-topped adobe and rustic wood. She slowed as she pulled into the semicircle gravel drive in front and parked next to a clean, navy-blue Jeep and matching new Cadillac Eldorado. The yard was naturally landscaped with cactus and desert flowers. The view behind was the perfect backdrop to the house, almost like a movie set.

For a few moments, Tess procrastinated going in, using the opportunity to collect her briefcase and her thoughts. She flipped down the visor and used the mirror to quick-check her hair and face, which had been roughed up somewhat in the wind. Fortunately her tousled hairstyle had weathered the beating with no great loss. She'd selected her clothing with care, an all-business charcoal-gray suit with white silk blouse and conservative silver earrings, brooch, and bracelet. Armor, perhaps, against Ross Chandler's invasive charm.

After a moment's indecision, she withdrew a gray, velvet-covered headband and used it to pull back her somewhat wild hair from her face, fretting that she should have put her hair up in the first place. Then she took the headband off. Then she put on her dark shades. Then she took them off. With a final, infuriated sigh, she left headband and glasses in the car and braced herself for Ross Chandler.

Crossing a shady patio of cool Mexican Saltillo tile, Tess came to a huge, heavy, hand-carved Spanish Peñasco door set deep in the adobe wall. To the left was a stoneware lighting fixture. To the right was a black wrought-iron bell and rope. She pulled the rope. The bell gonged.

After a few excruciating moments, Ross Chandler himself opened the door. Tess's first thought was that he was much better looking than he appeared on television. A distinguished mane of silver hair (a little too long to blend in with

Deadline 33

the local farmers and ranchers) set off a craggy suntanned face and sharp blue eyes. He was wearing a rich-rancher outfit of a snowy-white cotton western shirt with pearl snaps, pressed Levi's, soft deerskin western jacket, and expensive hand-tooled snakeskin boots and matching belt with a heavy silver buckle. His wristwatch was a wide, hammered silver band, studded with turquoise. *Thank God,* thought Tess, *he's not wearing a bolo tie.*

He broke into a broad politician's grin and grasped Tess's hand firmly. "Miz Alexander. It's good to see you. Did you have any trouble finding the place?" All the while, he never stopped smiling.

Tess shook her head. "None at all."

"Ah, you're an old country girl, I see. If the streets don't have names, city folk get lost, don't they?"

She smiled.

"Well, come on in." He gave her a size-up glance. "You're even more attractive than your book-jacket photo," he said. Before she could respond, he smacked his hands together. "Let me show you around the place. We just got finished with it a couple of months ago."

Tess followed the governor into a long, two-story, white room with a rough-hewn, beamed ceiling. Brilliantly hued, handwoven Navaho rugs were scattered over the Saltillo-tile floor. The governor pointed at a stunning painting which hung over a white sofa along one wall. "An original Georgia O'Keeffe," he beamed. On another wall hung an R. C. Gorman in shades of turquoise and purple.

Most of the furnishings, explained the governor, were handcrafted in Mexico, carved intricately and stained or painted white or turquoise or coral. A fireplace was built into the opposite wall, and the governor showed off some of his Indian art collections which surrounded it: a squat Mogallan storage jar, Pueblo pottery, individually designed Apache baskets, black jet Zuni medicine bears, and an authentic Apache storyteller doll, mouth open, gesturing with one hand while a lapful of fat babies listened with painted smiles. Hanging above the mantel on the white wall were three colorful Navaho pottery snakes, squiggling along as if alive.

On either side of the fireplace, glass doors and ceiling-high windows showed off the spectacular view.

After showing her the dining room and kitchen (more wooden furniture, pottery, and baskets), the governor asked her what she thought.

"It's beautiful," said Tess. "Very Santa Fe. But not what I would have expected of a former governor of Texas."

For the fleetest moment he registered surprise, then said, "Very astute observation, Miz Alexander. Actually, most of these furnishings came from my ski lodge at Angel Fire. I lost so many personal mementos of my years at the Capitol when my home burned."

Tess felt a hot flush spreading from her neck up. What an inexcusable gaffe. How could she have forgotten her reason for coming? Ducking her head, she mumbled, "I'm sorry."

"Don't worry about it. To tell you the truth, the house that burned, that was my wife's thing. She liked all this fancy stuff, you know, marble and pile carpeting and glass-topped tables. Things a man feels uncomfortable around. There's no place where he can put up his feet, see. This"—he held one arm out—"is mine. Well, mine and Bunni's. She helped me a lot with the decorating."

"Bunni?"

"My secretary. You'll meet her in just a minute. She's a great girl." He grinned, flashing his famous teeth.

I'm sure she is, thought Tess.

As if on cue, in swished the subject of their conversation, in a turquoise calf-length trail skirt over high-heeled black boots, a wide red sash cinched tightly around a tiny waist, and a white, Spanish-style blouse, open to reveal tempting swells. Both wrists were laden with silver and turquoise. A heavy squash-blossom turquoise necklace hung around her slender neck. Her filmy, shoulder-length hair was saffron, her eyes contact-turquoise, her smile practiced and flawless. She had probably not seen her twenty-second birthday. She gave Tess a limp handshake over the governor's buoyant introductions, and settled down next to him in a magazine-cover pose.

"Okay," said the governor. "Where shall we start?"

By killing David Feldman, thought Tess.

"At the beginning," she said.

"It was the most terrible night of my life," said the governor, his eyes misting. "I didn't even want to go to that stupid rubber-chicken fund-raiser in the first place, but Sam Dickens had been my lieutenant governor and I owed him my support for the next gubernatorial race, even if I *did* think he was a jerk." He shook his head with a low chuckle. "Texas politics is like nothing else in the world. The lieutenant governor, you know, is like a Vice President, only he runs on a completely separate ticket than the governor. In this state, you can have a governor and a lieutenant governor from two different parties. Anyway, Sam was a member of my party and I had no choice but to back him in the race. So I went to the damn dinner in Odessa that night."

"And your wife?"

"Libby hated those things. She hated politics, as a matter of fact. When we got married, I was just another oil-field redneck, going to school nights and trying to get ahead." He gazed out the windows and his voice grew quiet. "We had lots of dreams then, and none of them included politics." He shrugged. "Things change." For a long moment, he was silent.

"So Mrs. Chandler stayed home?" Tess gently prodded.

He nodded. "She wasn't feeling too good that night. Had a bad headache, one of those migraine things."

Tess gave a sympathetic nod.

Chandler sighed. "I think Libby thought that once I retired from politics we'd settle down, spend more time together. She didn't realize that your obligations never end. Anyway, she didn't really want me to go that night, but like I said, I didn't have any choice."

We all have choices, mused Tess.

"I was going to duck out early, but people buttonhole you, want to visit and whatnot, so I was later getting back than I intended. Sometimes I wonder what might have happened if I *had* gotten away early." He shuddered. Bunni, still as a mannikin up until now, reached over and patted his arm.

For a long pause, he stared at his hands, then he said, "Miz Alexander, have you ever seen a fire at night across the prairie? The glow, I mean. You can see it for miles."

Her mouth went dry. She swallowed.

His voice slipped into a hypnotic tone. "You drive like a bat out of hell, *praying* it's somewhere else, something else, anything but *your home*. And the closer you get, the more you despair, the more futile your prayers get. Then you think, *It'll be all right, as long as everyone's okay.*"

Tess broke into the mesmerizing monotone. "By 'everyone,' you mean your daughter and grandkids as well, right?"

"No!" The word echoed off the high beams. "I didn't know they were there! My daughter, Amanda, came by later for a visit, *after* I left. She decided to stay the night, and I didn't even know they were there!" The urgency in his tone was almost frantic. His eyes searched her own, looking for assurance that she understood.

Tess kept her face neutral, a trick she'd learned from hanging around cops. "So what happened then?"

"When I got home I ran all around the house, looking for a way in, but it was engulfed in flames. I mean, I got in partway through the back door. My hands got burned and I had smoke damage to my lungs. I can't imagine what happened because we had several smoke detectors in that house. They should have been warned." His hands were shaking. He clasped them together. Tears glimmered at the edges of his lashes.

Tess glanced at the tape recorder on the table between them to see that it was functioning properly. It seemed to be. "Tell me about Annie," she said softly.

He swallowed. "Bunni dear, would you please fetch us something to drink? Scotch rocks for me. Miz Alexander?"

"Ice water will be fine."

"Perrier?"

"No. Plain will do."

Bunni nodded and sashayed out of the room with a click of heels on the polished clay-tile floors.

"Annie." The governor got up and wandered over to the windows, looking out with his hands clasped behind his back. Tess moved the recorder to the other end of the table and prepared to take furious notes in case his voice didn't carry. Indeed, it seemed to drop. Bunni returned with the drinks in record time and the governor took a healthy swig before going on. "Annie is our miracle child. You know"—he turned back to face her, his face shadowed by the backlighting—"there are no fire hydrants in the country. They have to call in oil-field water tankers and pray there are some nearby. Plus it takes fire departments a while just to get to the place. But

Deadline 37

it was like . . . fate . . . that everything seemed to work together." He took another swallow of Scotch. "Do you believe in serendipity, Miz Alexander?"

"I'm not sure."

"Well, that's all it could be. See, if I hadn't had a car phone, I couldn't even have called the fire department without driving a number of miles to the nearest ranch house.

"For some miraculous reason, it all worked together to save that child's life. A real blessing." He drained the glass and held it out to Bunni, who went wordlessly for a refill.

Tess strained to read his face. "But now she says you set the fire, Governor."

He lifted his hands, palms up. "I can't imagine why she would say such a thing. She's only nine years old. Why would she tell such a lie to hurt me? I mean, maybe I haven't been the most attentive grandfather in the world, but I can't believe she would hate me this much. I tell you, someone is putting her up to it."

With sudden, rapid movements, he crossed the room and sat down so close to Tess their knees almost touched. "You've got to find out who put her up to this. You've *got* to. It could be my life."

"Wherever the truth is, Governor," Tess said, not flinching from his piercing gaze, "I'll find it."

Before leaving the ranch, Tess decided to inspect the site of the fire, which was located about a mile from the new house and not visible from it. Fortunately she did not get lost this time, and it was easy to spot the seared fireplace rubble, the scorched earth and burned ruins. From here, there was no dramatic view of the Caprock. Only winter-stark mesquites, spiked cactus, and a split-rail fence surrounding black destruction.

As soon as Tess got out of the car, she could smell that unmistakable charred odor, even after so many months of lying exposed to the elements. Walking slowly closer, the smell assailed her nostrils. A wave of dizziness swept over her. Her stomach began to churn.

Trembling now, she reached the blackened shell of a home and began to pick her way through it. Something incongruous caught her eye, something carnival-red in the middle of death.

Pushing aside an ashy board, Tess pulled out the remains of a melted doll, still clothed in some sort of fireproof red fabric.

"Tessie! Tessie! Tessie!"

Haunted screams echoed in her ears. Tess whirled around, looking to see who had called, but there was no one but the wind and, far above, a dangling red-tailed hawk.

The hawk. That was it. They made a piercing cry.

"Tessie! Tessie! Tessie!"

Tess buckled over, her hands clasped over her ears. *Fire.* She could smell fire. *Oh God, oh God, she could smell it.* Oh God, it was everywhere, in her nose and mouth and lungs, *it was everywhere*, but . . . *Why was Jonathan calling her? What was Jonathan doing here?*

"Jonathan!" she cried, leaping to her feet, but the dizziness caught her from behind and all she saw was blackness.

CHAPTER FIVE

SHE WAS DRIVING down a caleche road in the flat middle of dry ranchland. An occasional oil rig seesawed after its lonely fashion, pumping up money from under the ground. She did not know where she was. She did not know how she had gotten there.

She did not know who "Jonathan" was.

A two-lane paved road ran adjacent to the road she was on and Tess turned south. Nothing looked familiar. Loud country and western music twanged from the radio and she punched the button to her favorite classical station—then remembered that the station was in Austin, not West Texas. She turned the radio off.

She could still taste smoke in her mouth.

Panic bubbled into her throat. *How could someone get into a car and drive without even knowing it?* Her heart thumpety-thumped in rapid, irregular rhythms high in her chest.

Breathe deeply.

She had to get herself under control. There had to be a logical explanation.

Jonathan.

Grief sliced through her chest with such force that Tess sucked in her breath.

It hurt. God, it hurt.

How could you grieve for someone you didn't know?

The paved road emptied into a four-lane highway Tess recognized. With relief, she joined the highway and kicked the little Mustang up to seventy. All she wanted was to get home.

"*Not your home. You don't belong there and you never did.*"

Where had *that* come from? She'd heard it somewhere. Sometime. From someone.

Towering cumulus clouds up ahead warned of an approaching storm. It was tornado season, and Texas country thunderstorms could be terrifying experiences.

She headed toward a slate-blue wall of cloud and watched as white-hot snakes of lightning struck the earth.

By the time Tess pulled into the yard, Juan was busy at the barn, feeding the horses their evening oats. Spectacular mountains of clouds continued to put on a strobe-light show to the east, but mellow golden sunlight from the western sun lay over the ranch like melted butter on toast, softening its harsh angles and gilding the cloud-mountains.

Tess got out of the car and filled her jittery lungs with rain-scented air. Juan waved at her from the corral gate. "Too far to the east of us," he said with a sad shake of his head. "It's gonna miss us altogether."

Tess was grateful for that but knew better than to say so to a West Texas cowman. "Maybe next time," she called, then after a brief, hesitant look at her leather pumps, Tess decided to stroll toward the barn anyway and let herself in through the gate. She needn't have worried. The ground in the lots was hard as cement. They really did need rain.

The horses moved soft, busy lips over their troughs and munched the oats with satisfied sighs. She knew they could eat several quarts of oats and leave an unwanted nail or rock lying in the bottom of their feed troughs.

She ran her hand over the back of the big black who had worked more cattle in his day and allowed more children to clamber over his body than any horse she could imagine. Gray hairs were scattered now among the black. Tess inhaled the reassuring, horsey scent of him and was calmed.

"How ya doin', Jet?" she murmured. "Still keeping these young whippersnappers in line?"

His gray-tipped ears swiveled back at her touch and voice and he relaxed one hind foot, his way of letting her know he was comfortable in her presence. She leaned her head into his neck.

"You better watch out in them fancy shoes," fretted Juan

over her shoulder. "That ole boy steps on you, you gonna know it for a long time."

She turned to go, smiling at Juan. "You've been taking care of us all our lives, haven't you?"

"Well, somebody has to. Look at you. You're a mess. Where you been, anyway?"

For the first time, Tess surveyed charcoal-blackened hands, torn stockings, and grubby knees. "I've been to see the governor." She cocked her head at him.

He shook his head. "You always was a strange one." He smiled to take the sting out of his words and headed back into the barn.

"Juan?"

He looked back.

"Do we know anybody named *Jonathan*?"

Shock blanched his face. "I got work to do," he said abruptly, and ducked into the barn.

For a moment, she stared after him. He had to know something he wasn't telling her. But why in the world not?

Weariness set in. Tension tugged at her shoulders. One could only do so much furious thinking in a day. Still lost in a mind fog, Tess walked slowly toward the house and pulled open the screen door leading to the mud room. The sounds of shouting slammed against her.

"You hardheaded old Mexican. What's the matter with you, anyway?"

"Don't you talk to me like that. And there ain't nothin' the matter with me. It's you who ought to know better."

Tess stood next to the mirror-hatrack, uncertain as to what to do. Obviously they hadn't heard her come in, and she didn't want to barge in on their argument.

"Aw, c'mon, Sophia. Be reasonable. If I had to hire a nurse or a companion to look after Mama all day, it would cost us a fortune. The least you could do is let me compensate you for all the time you have to spend here with her."

"You don't understand *nothin'*."

"Well, explain it to me, then." Marah's voice raised to a whine of exasperation.

"The Garcias look after their own. Your mama . . . she's like our *own*, you understand? She's family. And you don't owe us *nothin'*. The *patrón*, he saved my Juan's life. He built our home. He gave our sons work. He helped us bring our family out of Mexico. The *patrón* took care of us, and now we take care of his daughter. You understand? You *insult* me with your money!"

The floor creaked as Sophia stomped toward the door. Tess shrank back against the wall behind the hatrack. Sophia brushed past with a *thwack* of the screen door. Tess could hear pots and pans clattering with loud emphasis in the kitchen and she went in.

Marah was talking to herself. "Fat old ornery bitch. Try to do something nice. Try to help her out. Do I get a thank-you? No. She's too busy being *insulted*." She looked up as Tess walked in.

Tess said, "I heard."

Marah appealed to her, waving a skillet in the air. "Tess— why don't *you* talk to Sophia? She'd listen to you. I mean, I feel *guilty* asking her to do so much around here. She hardly gets to see her grandkids anymore. She *earns* the money."

Tess shook her head. "No, Marah. Sophia has a right to her dignity. We're *family* to her and Juan. I mean, nobody's paying *you* to take care of Mama, are they?"

Marah's cheeks flamed. "Free room and board for me and my kids, if you want to get technical." She slammed the skillet down onto the stove. "Thanks, Tess," she hurled over her shoulder. "I knew I could count on you for support."

Tess lacked the energy for a fight with her sister and dragged herself past Marah without responding to the bait. At the hallway door she hesitated.

"Marah?"

"What?" Marah lit a flame over the gas burner with a match. The pilots no longer worked on the old stove.

Tess stared at the flame.

"What?"

"Do . . . do we know anybody . . . or have we ever known anybody named . . . *Jonathan*?"

Without looking over her shoulder, Marah said, "Nope. Never heard of him." She took a package of chicken breasts out of the sink. "Why?"

Lonely despair wrapped itself around Tess. There was no way she could tell her sister, or anybody, for that matter, what had happened to her this afternoon at the burned ruins of the governor's house. "I just . . . heard the name somewhere, that's all." She turned to go, thought better of it, and said, "Marah, when Mama first got sick, did she ever . . . lose time? I mean like in chunks?"

"Oh, yeah. And it's getting worse. Have you noticed she's been wearing the same clothes now for several days? She just doesn't seem to realize that the time has gone by."

Tess's heart constricted. "I don't guess she . . . drives anymore, huh?"

Flashes of light gleamed off the sharp knife in Marah's hand as she sliced off sections of chicken. "No way. It got to the point that she'd like, wake up someplace, like she'd been sleepwalking or something, and she wouldn't know where she was. It happened once when the kids were in the car with her and I said, *Never again.*" A smooth piece of meat fell away. "She still can't understand why we won't let her drive." She glanced over her shoulder at Tess and lifted one greasy hand to her face to push the hair back, using her wrist. "Remember how we've always left the keys in the vehicles so that if anybody needed to move one for any reason he could? Well, we can't do that anymore, not with Mama wandering around at all hours."

"I'm not used to leaving my keys in the car, anyway," said Tess woodenly. The loneliness and despair fit over her arms like a straitjacket. How much time did she have left before someone would have to hide *her* car keys? She implored her sister's back with her eyes. *Look at me. Help me.*

"I've got a date tomorrow night," said Marah, washing her hands. "You wouldn't mind looking after the kids, would you?"

Friday morning sunshine helped to push back a few of the dank, dark cobwebs of fear that had crowded Tess's sleep. She applied a little makeup to the ravages the night had left on her face and selected with care her clothes for an interview with the prosecutor. Blanking yesterday's visit to the governor's from her mind, she dressed in a silver-tone silk blouse with black slacks, belt, and flats. Artfully she arranged a silk scarf in a brilliant design of black, silver, and red over her shoulders and wore simple pearl studs in her ears. The colors showcased her tawny hair and large gray eyes, and the clothes were dressy without being overdressed for a small-town Texas courthouse.

With a last approving glance into the mirror she gathered up her things and headed for the Windham County Courthouse, thirty-five miles away.

Rather than follow the examples of some surrounding counties, which had torn down or covered up their courthouses with modern, impersonal structures that served as monuments to oil money, the county commissioners had chosen to refurbish the old building, restoring its original dignity with grace and charm. Placed imposingly in the middle of the town square, its deep-red sandstone exterior glowed in the morning sun as Tess parked the Mustang beside a granite monument to the county's war dead.

She got out and looked around the square with interest. The city of Remington, Texas, had recently revamped its town square, restoring many of the buildings to their Old West ambiance in an attempt to draw business and tourists to the area. Tess didn't know if it was working, but she liked the effect. She glanced up past Romanesque corner towers on the courthouse to a high central dome clock, which announced the standard time of nine A.M.

Inside, the central foyer was paneled in dark, cool mahogany. Polished hardwood floors creaked as she walked over to a glassed-in listing of the various offices. The office of the district attorney was located on the third floor, and Tess bypassed the modern elevator to take a sweeping spiral staircase, admiring along the way the intricate floral patterns local artisans had carved into the handrail a century before.

Tess was shown into the prosecutor's office by an iron-haired, no-nonsense secretary. Frank Baxter was a solidly built, square-jawed man with a high forehead, receding blond hair, and piercing blue eyes. He crushed Tess's hand with his own and gestured her into a chair opposite his heavy, cluttered desk.

His office, which smelled of leather and furniture polish, was lined with lawbooks and mementos, including many from his children. He gave Tess a long look commensurate with his name and asked how he could help.

"As I told you over the phone, I'm researching a book about the Ross Chandler case."

He steepled his hands beneath his chin and nodded. "Yes. I read *Murder and Madness*, by the way. Impressive work."

"Thank you. I hope you could tell by my work that I am meticulous in research and try to present the case in an impartial light." He didn't say anything and she went on. "I was hoping that I could count on your cooperation as I research and write this story."

Tess could tell already that she as not going to get much out of this man. Years of working with law enforcement officers had taught her to sense guardedness and suspicion. She suppressed a sigh. She'd hoped that she would not be forced to prove herself trustworthy to yet another officer of the court, but she could see in Baxter's eyes that she was going to have to.

He lowered his hands. "I'd like to help you, Tess, but surely you must know that my hands are tied before the trial. I can't give you any information that might threaten disclosure or taint confidentiality of witness statements."

She leaned forward. "In Dallas, they have an open-book policy with defense lawyers. They're allowed to preview all the material the prosecution has before it's presented in court."

He nodded. "That's Dallas. We don't work that way here. We make available only that information which we are bound by law to give. Offense reports and witness statements are kept confidential." He shrugged. "If I let *you* see that stuff—"

"I guarantee my trustworthiness, Mr. Baxter. I'd be happy to produce letters of recommendation from other law enforcement agencies."

"Please, call me Frank. And don't misunderstand me. It's not that I don't trust you to keep quiet. It's just that if the defense attorneys found out somehow that I was making this material available to you, then they could go to the judge and have the whole issue of confidentiality thrown out of court. We'd have to open it all up to *them*, see, without you ever having said a word. I'm sorry."

Understanding the man's point made it no less frustrating.

"I was hoping to be allowed to sit in on witness interviews, as I did for *Murder and Madness*."

He nodded. "I know. But that's Mexican law. It's different. It's even different here, in various cities, to some extent. But I can't take that risk. I *can* tell you that I believe wholeheartedly that Ross Chandler is guilty as hell of setting fire to his own home and deliberately murdering his entire family, and I know why he did it. We'll prove it in court."

"What about after the trial?"

He relaxed. "After the trial I'd be happy to turn over to you every notepad and smidgeon of documentation we have. I'll give you lengthy interviews as to what was going through our minds at the time. I'd be happy to cooperate to the fullest extent, *after* the trial."

"Well, I appreciate that, Frank. Under the circumstances, I don't see how I can ask for more." Tess got to her feet. "Who's handling the investigation?"

"The Windham County sheriff's department handled the original investigation along with the state fire marshal's office. The district Texas Ranger, Ethan Samuels, is assisting in the investigation. He's handling it now, for the most part."

"A Texas Ranger?" A mental image flashed across her mind: handlebar mustache, ten-gallon hat, and long-barreled six-shooter.

"Ethan's a good guy. Go pay him a visit, if you can track him down. He's pretty busy these days. Just got back from helicopter flight school."

CHAPTER SIX

FOLLOWING FRANK BAXTER'S directions, Tess found the offices of the Department of Public Safety building located a couple of miles outside the Remington city limits in a red, institution-brick building. A flagpole clanked in the wind; it was a melancholy sound.

Inside, a fresh-faced dispatcher directed her down the hall to Samuels's office. "He's not here right now but just have a seat, ma'am. He should be here anytime now."

The office was small and cluttered with paperwork. Tess looked around with interest. There was no secretary, only a battered wooden desk piled with forms, files, and copies of the *Texas Penal Code* and the *Texas Code of Criminal Procedure*. Metal bookshelves lined the walls, and a couple of hard wooden chairs faced the desk.

On the wall over the desk hung a red-velvet-covered shadow box containing an antique Colt .45 revolver. A Texas map, divided into the six Ranger districts, adorned another wall, along with an eight-by-ten-inch photograph of the fifteen Rangers in Samuels's company. Samuels, like most rural Rangers, worked alone and was himself responsible for assisting law enforcement investigations in five sprawling, sparsely populated West Texas counties covering thousands of square miles.

The shelves contained various texts on criminal pathology, forensic medicine, criminal investigation, legal procedures, constitutional law, historical studies of the Texas Rangers . . . and a copy, she was pleased to see, of *Murder and Madness*. Leaning against the wall on the top shelf were a framed degree in criminology from the University of Texas and a plaque which read, "No man in the wrong can stand up against a fellow that's in the right and keeps on acomin'." The quote was attributed to Captain Bill McDonald, a turn-of-the-century Ranger.

On the desk was a framed portrait of a handsome dark-haired man in a pearl-gray Stetson, a smiling blonde, and a little boy.

Tess sat down in one of the wooden chairs and leafed through a pamphlet called "Silver Stars and Sixguns: the Texas Rangers." Originally formed by Stephen F. Austin in 1823 to patrol the perimeters of his settlement, the Rangers had enjoyed a colorful Old West history of fighting Indians, Mexican bandits, bootleggers, bank robbers, and renegade feuding ranchers. The elite agency now employed only ninety-four Rangers statewide, whose job was to assist local law enforcement in felony crime investigations by making available, particularly in remote rural areas, sophisticated technology and criminal expertise.

The famous and distinctive silver badge was still fashioned out of a Mexican peso.

"Feldman's going to *love* this," mused Tess aloud.

"Love what? And who's Feldman?" came a deep voice from behind her.

Tess dropped the pamphlet and scrambled to her feet, furious at the blush which stung her cheeks. After all, she hadn't been doing anything wrong, just thinking amusing thoughts about the jubilant reaction she was bound to get from her Woody Allenish New York editor when he learned that a real-life Texas Ranger was going to be a major player in the Ross Chandler drama.

And now here he was, almost larger than life. Ethan Samuels stood well over six feet tall and was an impressive figure in a gray felt Stetson, white western shirt, brown tie, brown leather vest proudly sporting the silver badge, dark slacks, and cowboy boots. He had the craggy Marlboro ad look about him, chiseled features and dark eyes and brows. Deep lines ran from his nose to the corners of his generous mouth. There was even a cleft in his chin.

Tess's first thought was, *Why are the best ones always married?* She extended her hand.

He took off his hat in a courtly gesture and shook her hand.

His handshake was warm and firm and his gaze so direct it made her feel as if he could read her mind. "I'm Tess Alexander," she said, cursing her hot cheeks.

He blinked and pointed toward the bookshelf. "*That* Tess Alexander?"

She nodded and he pulled *Murder and Madness* from the shelf. "It's a real honor to meet you, Ms. Alexander. I really enjoyed this book. I thought you handled the whole Matamoros situation with taste and dignity."

"Why, thank you." She sat down on her purse, jumped up, moved the purse, bit her lip.

Ethan hung his hat on a tall spindly hatrack near the door and sat down behind his desk. His presence seemed to fill the small room. "What I liked most about it was that you never patronized the Mexican police. You really seemed to get into their obsession to track this guy down and break up the cult."

"Well, I was practically raised by a Mexican family on our ranch. They taught me fluent Spanish. I went into the project with a little better understanding than most Anglo writers, I think."

"Oh? Where'd you grow up?"

"The Rocking A Ranch out near Dryton."

"I know the place. Are you talking about the Garcia family?"

"Yes . . . why?"

"I know Juan Garcia. He helped us on an investigation once—some illegal aliens who were smuggling drugs into this area for distribution. He's a good man."

She nodded. For a moment they stared at one another. Tess felt like a silly high school girl. "Uh, I see you went to UT Austin." She gestured toward the diploma.

"Yeah. As a matter of fact, I'm a city boy. Grew up in Austin."

"Really? I went to UT, too. I live by Lake Travis now."

"Beautiful lake. When were you on campus?"

"I graduated in eighty."

"Then I was finishing up just as you were starting. I attended on the GI Bill after the service."

"Well, there are only sixty thousand people on campus. I can't believe we don't remember each other." She grinned.

"Oh, I'd remember you, all right." He smiled at her, and her mouth went dry.

Stop it, she thought. *Grow up.*

He leaned back in his squeaky swivel chair. "What can I do for you, Ms. Alexander?"

"Please, call me Tess."

"Be my pleasure."

His charm, she discovered, was completely genuine. Maybe that's what flustered her. "I'm working on another book now . . . the Ross Chandler case. I was wondering what you could tell me which might help."

The chair squawked as Ethan leaned forward. A transparent curtain seemed to fall over his face. There wasn't as much suspicion in his expression as she might have expected, but there was a great deal of reluctance. Tess suppressed a sigh.

"I'm afraid I can't tell you much of anything. The investigation is ongoing, even with the trial so near."

"Sergeant Samuels, surely you know that all I seek here is the truth. I have no intention of whitewashing anything in this story."

"It's 'Ethan.' Look, I know you've got a job to do, and I respect that. But so do I. Chandler's got lawyers so slippery even *he* can't hold on to them. All I'd have to do is make one statement out of turn and the whole thing could be blown." He raised his hands. "I'm sorry."

"What if I agreed to keep all my notes and tapes strictly confidential until after the trial? It'll take me months to organize and write the story, anyway, and months more for it to work through the publication process." She leaned forward earnestly. "I'm not a newspaper reporter. I'm not going to go running off and publish something right in the middle of the trial."

"You write for *Texas Monthly*."

She sat back. "How did you know that?"

"I subscribe to the magazine. I've read your stuff. It's the reason I bought your book in the first place."

Tess nodded slowly. "Okay. Fair enough. But even if I did a piece for *Texas Monthly*, it would still be months before it was printed."

He regarded her thoughtfully. "Have you met Ross Chandler?"

"Yes."

"What did you think of him?"

She shrugged. "He's a politician. I don't take anything at face value. I'll probably interview dozens of people who know him well before I put together a composite picture of his character."

He smiled. "Sounds like what we do in an investigation."

"Exactly." She waited, giving him time to think.

To her great frustration, he shook his head. "I'm sorry, Tess. I'd love to help you, but it's just too risky. Come to me—"

"I know," she said wearily. "After the trial." She gathered her things together.

Ethan got to his feet and came around from behind his desk, standing close enough to her to bring on more of that silly high school feeling. "Say." He looked down into her eyes. "If you learned something in all those interviews that you thought could help us, would you come and tell us?"

She cocked her head up at him and gave him a flirtatious smile. "Let me put it this way. Maybe we could work out some sort of trade. My info for yours."

He smiled back. "You drive a hard bargain, lady."

"Well?"

He pursed his lips. "I'll think about it."

As she turned to go, he touched her arm. A sexual tingle shot through her body. Struck shy, she fiddled with her purse and notebook. He held out *Murder and Madness* to her. "Would you mind terribly signing this for me?" he asked.

"Of course not," she said. Sitting back down, she balanced the book on her lap and wrote in the flyleaf, "To Sgt. Ethan Samuels . . ." Tess hesitated, her mind awhirl. She wanted to say something like, "The sexiest, best-looking man I've ever met. See you in bed."

But of course, that would never do.

Instead, she wrote, "To Sgt. Ethan Samuels, a law enforcement officer who embodies the true spirit of Texas. With best wishes and hopes for a long friendship. Tess Alexandr."

She had to go back and add the "e."

It had not been a good day. It angered and frustrated Tess that, even with all her credentials with other law enforcement agencies around the state and her impeccable reputation as a crime author, she still had to prove herself, still had to earn the trust of those involved in a case. She'd been told by other officers in the past that they'd been burned so many times by the media, misquoted or represented in a brutal, unfair light, that there was a natural, built-in suspicion toward all writers.

Tess considered it an honor that she could count as her friends many fine officers from different branches of law enforcement in different cities, but the exasperating truth was that anytime she walked into a new situation, she had to start all over again. And, she had to admit, she wasn't certain yet where her sympathies rested in this case. The governor swore he was innocent. *What if he was?*

By aligning herself squarely in the camp of the prosecution, she would be alienating those witnesses who were supporting the governor's story. They might not even be willing to grant her interviews. On the other hand, if she gave her full support to the governor before a verdict was delivered, she would be blinding herself to any information which could incriminate him.

The truth, she knew, lay somewhere in the middle.

There was a week remaining before the trial began. During that week she would be very busy, interviewing defense attorneys, witnesses who'd seen the governor at the fund-raiser, family members and political acquaintances, and the therapist who'd been working with Annie, the surviving grandchild.

By the time Tess pulled up behind the old ranch house, long shadows nearly hid Molly, who came scampering out to the car before Tess had opened the door.

"Aunt Tess, would you go riding with me? Mommy's getting ready to go out. Juan said he'd saddle the horses for us. *Plee-e-e-ze?*" She hopped up and down, her whole body begging Tess for a *yes*.

Tired, aggravated by the day's events, and distracted, Tess nearly refused the child, but one look into those big blue eyes hooked her. She put her hand against Molly's soft cheek. "All right, sweetie. I have to change clothes. Ask Juan if he would mind saddling Jet with the children's saddle and Maverick for me."

With an ecstatic leap of triumph, Molly bolted for the barn, and Tess shook her head at herself. She couldn't remember when she'd last been horseback riding. She left her slacks, knee-high stockings, and blouse in a heap and changed into worn jeans, a soft old UT Longhorns sweatshirt, and a borrowed pair of Marah's boots.

Out in the barn, she found Juan gently scolding Molly for walking directly behind the horses. "They can't see you back there. You could get kicked. You don't need to be afraid of them but you do need to respect them."

"But I don't think Jet would hurt me," pouted Molly.

"Not on purpose. But what if he got mad at Maverick and tried to kick him and there you were? Huh?"

Tess smiled. He'd said exactly the same words to her once upon a time. Juan had been the only kind male figure Tess had known after Pa died. Rex never dared mistreat her around Juan. Instead, he'd sneak around and catch her when no one was looking. She swallowed the bitter memory and turned her attention to Molly.

They headed east, across rolling, mesquite-studded pastures, past a solitary windmill creaking in the evening breeze, through a barbed-wire gate, and down a craggy arroyo. The dogs trailed along behind. Occasionally a bobwhite quail pierced the air with its mournful call. Peace blanketed the land. Tess could feel the tension drain from her shoulders.

Jet, the boss horse, took the lead, following winding cattle trails. Maverick, the younger sorrel, followed closely behind. For a while, Molly chattered over her shoulder, her tales of playground intrigue and brotherly plagues washing over Tess like a warm bath, then, as the sky turned pink and violet, she too grew quiet. They stood their horses side by side on a canyon rim while purple shadows crept up red-orange rock and the land grew hushed.

For a brief, breathless moment, Tess felt a oneness with all that surrounded her, and she drew on that for strength, because she knew, somehow, that calm always comes before the storm . . . and the clouds, she could see, were just over the horizon.

CHAPTER SEVEN

"WHAT ARE YOU doing, dear?" Tess's mother leaned over her shoulder where she labored at the dining room table later that evening. It was the best place she could find to set up her computer equipment, files, and paperwork. Since the family ate most of their meals in the kitchen, anyway, it seemed a fair arrangement.

"I'm checking the galleys of an article, Mama."

"Oh, may I read it?"

"Well . . ." Tess wasn't sure how much of what her mother read she was able to comprehend. It couldn't hurt, she decided, and handed her mother the galleys, where she had made a few changes by red pen.

"What is this, more blood and guts?" Marah swept into the room on a wave of sweet Chantilly perfume, wearing skintight jeans and a flattering, well-molded scarlet satin western blouse.

"Where are *you* going?" asked Tess, wiggling her nose in an effort not to sneeze.

"Dancing with Jimmy Baker."

"I don't know him."

"He drives a truck for Wexton Pipeline."

"Oh."

"Don't *oh* me, you snob. At least I can *get* a man."

"More than one, apparently."

Her sister took the insult as a compliment, dimpling at Tess, then picked up some of the papers by Tess's computer and read a little bit. "A Vietnamese crime ring in Houston?"

"Yeah. The underworld of crime is changing its complexion these days. You got your Cubans, your Haitians, your skinheads, and your Vietnamese underworld, all vying for the drug trade, prostitution, whatever."

Marah rolled her eyes. "Where do you *get* this stuff?"

"Well, in this case, a lot of my information came from an informant named Bic Tran. Of course, I'm using an alias in the article."

"Why?"

"They might kill him if they found out, that's why."

"Oh, I can't really believe that." Marah put down the papers and dismissed the subject with a shrug. "I think you just say that to make yourself sound more important."

"Well, granted, it's not as important as going dancing with Jimmy Baker."

Marah narrowed her eyes at Tess. "I'll remember that tonight when I'm in his arms and you're stuck here with your old computer." With a toss of her glossy dark hair, she headed for the door. "You better find Mama before she loses your story."

After Marah left, Tess turned back to the computer screen where she was finishing up another article, but she couldn't concentrate. As usual, her sister's words had struck closer to the truth than she liked. She *was* lonely, and it *did* hurt. And here was Marah, with two terrific kids and her choice of any truck driver she wanted.

Ethan Samuels's handsome face flashed across her mind. Tess heaved a mighty sigh. Married men, in her book, were strictly off limits. The trouble was, the older she got, the more married men there were around. Still, it was an inner code she would not break. Not even for Ethan Samuels, dammit.

With great effort, she shoved his face out of her mind and went back to work.

After a few minutes, Mama came back into the room, holding the galleys of Tess's article limply in her hand, her face bewildered. "What am I doing with this?" she asked plaintively. "I've got it here in my hand and I can't remember what it's for."

Gently Tess removed the pages from her mother's hand. "Don't worry about it, Mama. You were holding it for me."

Her mother nodded and, for a long moment, stared into

Tess's eyes with a blank, helpless, hopeless look. Then she wandered from the room.

Tess sat down and stared at the cursor, blinking, blinking on the computer screen. Then, with mechanical movements, she exited the document, withdrew the disc, and shut off the machine.

She didn't feel much like working anymore.

"Tessie! Tessie!"

Tess sat bolt upright in bed. Chill bumps swarmed over her body.

It was Jonathan. She knew it was.

Flinging back the covers, Tess sprang out of bed and flew down the hall, clutching the corner post of the stairway banister and peering down below.

"Tessie! Tessie!"

No. It was coming from up the steps. She bolted upstairs. She had to get to him. Had to find him. Had to hurry.

"Tessie! Tessie!"

Through the door. A passageway. He was on the other side of that passageway!

Oh God. Hurry!

She squeezed through the narrow passageway and crawled along a rough surface, groping, groping . . . It was cold, so very cold. Drafty and cold.

She slipped.

Sliding. She was *sliding*. Scrambling for handholds. Rough. Cold. Windy. Falling. *Falling!*

With a wrench of her arms, Tess snapped awake.

Her mind swirling up from the fog of sleep, she glanced around and cried out in shock.

She was out on the roof.

Grappling for a fresh handhold, Tess craned her neck. Barely she could see her own open second-floor window below.

She'd been sleepwalking.

Not since childhood had Tess had an episode of somnambulism. A cold wind whipped through her hair. Rough shingles dug into her knees and elbows. Her hands ached from clinging to the pitched siding. Only her cramped toes, digging into the small decorative ledge, kept her from dropping three floors down.

How had she gotten onto the roof, for God's sake?

"Help!" she cried weakly, but the wind and dark snatched away her voice.

Think. *Think.*

She could try to inch her way back up to the window, or she could let go and drop to the ground and pray she'd land on a soft place. Gingerly she lifted one foot and tried to gain a hold. The shingle loosened and Tess slipped. With a desperate cry she managed to catch herself on the ledge again.

Or she could wait for dawn.

She tried calling for help again, but it was useless. For a long time she clung to her position, tempted to laugh aloud at the spectacle she would make down below by dawn's early light. When the muscles in her calves began to cramp, it wasn't so funny anymore.

Tess was deathly afraid of heights. She knew it had something to do with Rex and the barn but she didn't want to know what. All she knew was that if something didn't happen *soon*, her own panic, not the fall, would kill her.

Her hands began to go numb. A sob caught in her throat. *Jump*, said a voice from somewhere deep inside. *Just do it.* She moved her hands over the shingles. Another one came loose and fell to the ground below with a rattle. *The walkway.* There was a cement walkway directly below her.

The dogs set up a sudden baying. Tess jerked and flailed away for a moment before regaining her precarious hold. It was the middle of the night. What were they barking at? She could hear a whooshing sound over the lonely whining of the wind, and carefully turned her head to see.

Patchy moonlight revealed the ground below. Dizziness assailed Tess and she pressed her forehead into the rugged shingles.

The dogs were barking furiously. A car door slammed. Voices. Laughter.

"Help," she whispered. "*Help!*" she screamed.

The voices stopped.

"*Up here! Help me!*"

Footsteps crunching on gravel. "*What in the world?*" Marah's voice.

Marah's blessed, slightly drunken voice.

"What the hell is going on?" A male voice.

"The ladder," called Tess shakily.

"Oh, right. Jimmy—it's right inside the barn door. *Wait!* Do you need a flashlight?"

"Does the barn have lights?"

"There's a switch inside the door."

"Okay." Running steps.

"Tess, what the hell are you doing up there?"

"I . . . I was trying to help a cat."

"Of all the stupid things. You know those cats can get themselves up and down and all around that roof."

Tess pressed her face into the shingles. One set of toes gave way. She cried out, scrambling for another handhold.

"Don't worry, Tess. I'll catch you!"

This time she couldn't help but laugh.

Running footsteps *(thank you God oh thank you dear God)* clanking and banging just below . . . "Okay, Tess. The ladder's right below you. Just step down." Her sister's voice was reassuring.

"I . . . I can't."

"Sure you can. It's right there. Jimmy's holding it."

Tess's whole body was trembling. She didn't move.

"Hold the ladder, Marah," said the male voice. "That's it. I'll go up and get her."

Creaking steps . . . and a warm hand on the small of her back, firm through her gown. "I'm right here. I won't let you fall. Just step down. That's it. Kinda cold up here, isn't it?"

Her legs were so cramped she could barely move them, but step by painstaking step, she and Jimmy made it down to the blessed earth.

"Thank you," she said. Her knees buckled. She leaned hard against the ladder.

"Jimmy's a volunteer fireman," bragged Marah. Tess could see neither of their faces in the dark shadow of the house.

"Nice to meet you," she said, wondering if her legs would carry her into the house.

"You say you went out there to help a cat?" he said, his darkened face lifted upward. "I don't see how even a cat could get up there."

"I guess I was sleepy," she hedged. "Not thinking too clearly."

"You can say that again. That woulda been a nasty fall, though. Might've busted both your legs."

"Or she could have landed on her head and not got hurt at all," put in Marah. When Tess didn't respond, Marah reached out and took her arm. "Hey, sis . . . You all right?"

No! Tess wanted to shout. *No, I'm not all right! Things are happening to me that I don't understand, and I'm terrified!*

"Sure," she said instead. "Let's go inside. I don't know about you, but I could use a cup of coffee."

Tess's midnight adventure was the subject of much weekend discussion. Everyone wanted to know why she had done something so stupid as crawl out on the roof in the middle of the night for a nimble-footed cat. They all wanted details.

She made up a few.

Jimmy, who turned out to be short, pleasant-faced, and a bit of an expert on most everything, explained about the bone structure and sense of balance that enabled cats to land on their feet and walk almost anywhere without falling.

Tess just wanted to drop the whole thing.

Eager to finish the article she was working on before plunging wholesale into research for the book, which she had tentatively titled *Firestorm*, Tess burrowed into the dining room whenever she could.

Her life had taken on a sense of unreality, as if everything she was doing was one step removed from her. The somnambulism episode had shaken her badly, fragmenting her sense of concentration. Once, when she walked into her room for something and then couldn't remember what it was, she thought of her mother and almost suffocated from panic.

Every day, it seemed, she was confronting her own destiny.

The fear of it sometimes took her breath away.

Late Sunday evening, Tess pulled the finished article from the printer, checked it over, and placed it beside the computer for mailing the next day along with the galleys on the Houston crime ring story. She had a busy week ahead of her. In a way, she looked forward to it. Interviewing witnesses and other people involved in this case would take her out of herself.

She was a good interviewer. Maybe that would help to restore her battered self-confidence.

Around eleven P.M., the phone rang, and Tess could hear Marah in the next room, speaking quietly. A while later, she came into the dining room. "That Chandler trial doesn't start for a week, right?"

Preoccupied with addressing a large brown envelope, Tess nodded.

"Well, good. That was Sophia. She has a new grandbaby, and she's going to help Miguel and Maria out for a few days."

"Oh? Miguel has a new baby? Boy or girl?"

"A girl."

"I'm so glad. They've got three sons already. I'll have to pick out a gift."

"Yes, well, Sophia won't be here, so I was counting on you to help out."

Tess stopped what she was doing and looked at her sister. "I'm sorry, Marah. I can't."

"But you said the trial isn't for a week!"

"I know that, but I'm doing a lot more than just sitting in on the trial. I've got interviews lined up all this week, all over West Texas."

"Can't you change them? Do them later?"

Tess sighed. "Marah, it's not that easy. Some of these people are professional working people. They've made time in their schedules for me. And they'll give me valuable background information to take into the trial."

Marah flung her hands up in the air. "Why can't you interview them in the evenings, or after the trial or something? I need you to help me with Mama and the kids."

"I *can* help you. Every single evening I'll come home and take care of everything. You can go out with Jimmy or whatever you want to do."

"But I need you during the *day*, Tess. When I go buy groceries. You don't know what it's like, buying groceries with Mama."

Tess bit her lip. It had taken her days on the phone to line up those interviews. Some of the people had been reluctant to talk to her at all. If she canceled now . . . they might never talk to her.

"In the evenings, Marah. I'll be here in the evenings."

Deadline

Marah's eyes narrowed. She placed her hands on her hips and her voice grew deadly quiet. "You are the most selfish, self-centered, self-absorbed, hateful bitch I ever knew. All I ask you for is one week, *one miserable week* of your time, and you can't even manage that. We're *supposed* to be sisters, but I can count on those damn dogs outside more than I can count on you."

"Look, Marah, I have to work! Is that so hard to understand? I'll be here *every night*. I'll cook supper, put the kids to bed, look after Mama, whatever you want!" Throbbing set in over Tess's left eye. She hadn't been sleeping well. Stresses were adding up. Her sister was incapable of even considering a compromise of any kind. No wonder she'd been divorced three times.

"You don't *have* to work," spat Marah. "I don't see any time clocks around here. You could help me if you wanted to."

"I *will* help you!" shouted Tess. Spots danced before her eyes and nausea gripped her stomach. "Do you think this is *easy* for me? Do you think this is some kind of vacation?"

"I don't give a shit what it is," snapped Marah.

"You're *home* all day, Marah. The kids are in school. Surely you can handle Mama for one week with me at home nights. I'm doing the best I can."

"Oh, yeah, the best *you* can, as *you* see it . . ." Marah's voice seemed to be coming to Tess from a long tunnel. Needles of pain stabbed her face and her head swam.

The next thing she knew, Marah was gone. The air crackled with tension. Tess could almost feel the blood rushing through her veins. Her headache was blinding her. Slowly she groped her way up the stairs. The hallway clock struck twelve slow gongs.

Somewhere, Tess had lost another hour of her life.

CHAPTER EIGHT

MONDAY MORNING CAME howling down from the north with subfreezing temperatures, X-ray force winds, and brooding, murky skies. The old house, never sufficiently well heated, was icy in the bedrooms. Tess stood shivering in front of her closet, dismayed that she could have forgotten the flip-flop springtime weather of West Texas. Accustomed to mild, rainy, flowery Austin springs, she had packed no sweaters and had not even thought to bring a winter coat, only a light trench coat for rain. She'd forgotten, too, how little rain there was, even in spring.

And here she stood, nearly a head taller than her sister and her mother, like a goose among ducklings. She couldn't even borrow a coat; her arms would stick out like Popsicle sticks.

Finally she settled on the outfit she'd driven up in from Austin, the man's tweed jacket, brown slacks, and gold blouse. Hopeless against the wind, but better than bare arms.

Downstairs, she all but dove for the coffee maker. The kids were bundled into snuggy winter sweaters, chattering happily about the possibility of snow. Tess wrapped her hands around her coffee mug. "Marah, have you heard anything on the radio about the roads between here and Midland?"

Her sister calmly stirred oatmeal at the stove.

"Marah?"

She doled it into bowls.

"Okay, look. I'm sorry we fought last night. And I'm sorry I can't stay here all day, but I promise that I'll get back as soon as possible every day to help out. I'll do whatever you need."

Marah added sugar and butter and placed the bowls in front of the children. "You guys want hot chocolate or juice?"

"Hot chocolate!" they chorused.

"This is ridiculous," fumed Tess.

"Molly, would you please inform your Aunt Tess that I have nothing to say to her. Not now. Not ever. I will never forgive her for the things she said to me last night and I would appreciate it if she just leaves me alone from now on. Oh, and I don't want or need her lousy two-bit help, either."

Molly blinked. "Aunt Tess, Mommy said—"

"Forget it. I heard." Tess took a fresh look at Marah. Her face was hardened and set; bitterness in stone. She ran through the mental tape of what had transpired the night before and could remember saying nothing to her sister that would cause this violent a reaction from her.

The twelve gongs of the clock flashed into her mind. *Had she said something during that time that she couldn't remember? Something awful?*

She touched her sister's arm. "Hey. I had a horrible migraine headache last night. I say things sometimes when I'm like that . . . things I don't mean. If I hurt you, I'm truly sorry."

Marah jerked away her arm and turned a smoldering gaze on Tess. "Why don't you just leave? Just go back to your little life and leave us alone? All you've done since you got here is upset things. We don't need it, and we don't need *you*." She turned her back to Tess.

A physical slap wouldn't have hurt Tess more. For a brief moment, she considered pouring out to her sister all that had been happening to her, the memory lapses and migraines and sleepwalking; her terror that she was already displaying symptoms of Alzheimer's. She so desperately needed reassurance. Maybe, by confiding in her sister, it would help to smooth things over. Maybe Marah would even help her. At the very least, she might understand.

"Marah . . . there's something you don't understand—"

"Oh, I understand perfectly well, Tess. You're a user. You came here just to use us so that you could pack another bestseller under your belt. You don't even care about us. All you care about is your work. Fine, then. Go back to your work.

And don't worry about Mama. She won't even notice you're gone." She stalked out of the room.

For a long, numb moment, Tess sat, clenching her teeth and blinking hard, trying to think what to do next, where to go. A little hand crept over her arm and she clutched at it. "Aunt Tess," whispered Molly. "Please don't go. If you were gone, *I* would notice."

A sob caught in Tess's throat and she hugged the child tight. She looked up to see Mama standing in the doorway. She didn't say anything; she just stared deeply into Tess's soul, as if by doing so she could recapture her own lost wisdom. After a long moment, Tess nodded.

"I won't go," she said over Molly's shoulder, looking into her mother's eyes. "I won't leave you."

The law offices of Thornton and Douglas were located in a suite owned by Ross Chandler on the top floor of a skyscraping Midland bank. Window walls overviewed the depressed city, the bleak landscape. Gone were the rolling hills, canyons, and cedar breaks of Tess's home; here was flat and more flat surrounding a city that contained only a skeleton of the once-bustling oil industry that had made its fortune. Like most oil towns, Midland was having to scramble to find a new tax base and attract new businesses. So far, the small city's only claim to fame had been a little girl who'd fallen down a well.

The law offices were still opulent, however. Perhaps business from the now-defunct savings and loan industry was keeping them prosperous. Tess was shown into a plush-carpeted room with deep leather wing-back chairs facing an enormous glossy desk made of teak. Cameron Thornton, seated at the desk, was Chandler's age, almost completely bald, with a bland, easygoing way. Charles Douglas, who stood just to the side of Thornton, was fortyish and attractive in an intense yuppie way. Both men welcomed her warmly and displayed none of the reticence she'd seen from the prosecution.

"Ross told us you were coming," said Thornton. "He thinks very highly of you, which makes you all right in my book."

"*Murder and Madness* is due out soon in paperback, isn't

it?" asked Douglas. "I understand your publisher is eager to get the real story behind Ross Chandler's tragedy as well."

"Well, we all are," said Tess evasively.

"It's a terrible thing when a man has to suffer such a terrible loss and then gets blamed for it," said Thornton. "You can't imagine what that man has had to endure."

Not as much as Annie, thought Tess.

"This whole case should never have gone to trial," said Douglas, pushing his preppie-frame glasses up on his nose. "The prosecution hasn't got a damned thing but circumstantial stuff and they know it."

"Well, there's Annie's testimony."

"Let's talk about that," said Thornton, wrinkling together bushy white brows. "There's been this therapist working with that kid for months, trying to get her to talk."

"Trying to get her to blame Ross," interjected Douglas.

"The thing is, she just said whatever that therapist wanted to hear—to please her, you know," said Thornton sadly.

"There's no way Ross could have even been there," added Douglas. "We've got twenty witnesses who saw him at that fund-raiser."

"But when did he leave? That's the question," said Tess.

"We have a witness who visited with him until well past ten. It takes an hour to drive from Odessa to Ross's ranch. The house was already burning when he got there."

"He tried to save them, poor man. It was terrible," said Thornton. His eyes misted over. "I knew Libby. Knew his daughter, Amanda, and that poor child Jenny who died. Terrible tragedy. Just terrible."

"So you don't think the prosecution has a case?"

"The whole thing's ridiculous," said Douglas. "They don't even have a solid case proving arson. They're hanging everything on that child, and I think the jury will see that, under the circumstances, her testimony could be prejudiced."

"But there *was* foul play."

"Well, now, that depends," said Thornton, his eyes keen, "on which forensic expert you believe."

"But what about the life insurance?"

There was a moment of silence, then both men tried to speak at once. Douglas demurred to the older partner. "I know that looks bad, no doubt about it."

"Three million dollars . . ." Tess raised her brows.

"I know. I know. But Ross Chandler is a wealthy man. It's not all that unusual for a wealthy man to have a million-dollar policy on his wife and a half million on his daughter."

Tess wasn't so sure about that, especially since they were double indemnity policies, but she didn't say anything. Finally she hazarded, "What about Bunni?"

"What about her?" asked Douglas in a somewhat testy voice.

"Well, it just doesn't look very good, that's all."

"Why not? Everybody needs a secretary. Bunni's been very helpful to Ross."

"You're sure that's all she is? A secretary?"

Thornton gave her a shrewd, assessing look. "Honey, whose side are you on?"

Tess looked from one to the other. "I thought I made it clear to the governor that I'm not here to write his biography. I'm here to write the story of this trial and this case. I guess you could say I'm on the side of the truth."

He leaned back and spread apart his palms. "Well, then, that's what you're getting. The truth." His eyes narrowed, and Tess was treated to the wiliness she was sure he usually reserved for the courtroom. "Just remember one thing, honey. Things are not always what they seem."

"There's no way Ross Chandler could have ever done anything to hurt his family," said Susannah Chandler-Forghum, sniffling delicately into a lace handkerchief clutched in exquisitely manicured fingers. Mrs. Thadeus Forghum III was a handsome older woman with hair in the blond bouffant favored by many Texas society grandes dames.

"I just can't believe they're putting my poor brother through this. If you could have seen him at the hospital that night—he was positively *hysterical*. They had to *restrain* him! It's a wonder he didn't burn up himself, trying to get to them. His hands were all burned." She dabbed delicately at her nose.

Tess took a sip of tea from a Wedgwood china cup and placed it on the glass-topped coffee table. "What about Annie, Mrs. Forghum?"

"That's just the saddest thing of all. Don't you see? Annie

described a man who *looked* like her granddaddy in the house that night, setting fire to it. But Ross wasn't *there*. He was in Odessa. I mean, hasn't it occurred to *anyone* that someone *else* could have set that fire? Someone who was trying to frame Ross?"

Tess cocked her head at the woman.

Mrs. Forghum leaned forward. "Ross Chandler was a tough, tough politician. A street fighter. They say that, in a campaign he, well, he went right for his opponent's testicles."

Even if his opponent was a woman, mused Tess.

"He made a lot of enemies. You do, in Texas politics. It's been so since the days of Sam Houston." Mrs. Forghum was regaining her composure. "I'm telling you. I think somebody else did this horrible thing and made it look like it was Ross. I just don't know why nobody has thought to investigate that angle of it."

Tess stared at her notes and wondered, *Why, indeed?*

"Thank you for seeing me on such short notice, Lieutenant Governor Dickens. Mrs. Forghum told me you were only in town for a day or two and I know how busy you must be." Tess glanced around the well-appointed hotel suite. Two assistants worked quietly over in one corner, one on the phone, one at a lap-top computer.

Sam Dickens was a bush-browed, stern-faced redhead with a barrel chest and huge freckled hands. "Well, as you know, this has been one helluva runoff for the Democratic primary. I been on such a fast track I can take a whiz in one county and pull up my britches in another."

Tess smiled, remembering Ross Chandler's assessment of the lieutenant governor.

"But Mrs. Chandler-Forghum has been a solid supporter of mine, and anything I can do for her I'm glad to do. I understand you're working on a book about the governor."

"Well, not exactly about the governor, but more about this tragedy in his life now."

"Yes. Awful thing. Happened the night of one of my fundraisers in Odessa last October. I already spoke to the investigating officers about it. They can tell you whatever you need to know."

Don't count on it, thought Tess. "To tell you the truth, Lieutenant Governor, I'm not here to talk about that night. What I need to know is more of a personal nature concerning the governor. I was wondering . . . who you might consider to be enemies of Ross Chandler."

"Enemies?" Dickens got up and crossed over to a wet bar. "Drink?"

"No, thanks." She watched as he sloshed straight Bourbon into a glass, took a swig, then added more. The man who'd been talking on the phone hung up and watched them closely.

"Miz Alexander, you gotta understand. I'm in the middle of a political campaign here. I cain't tell you anything that would turn my ass to grass."

"I assure you your identity would be protected. I have no intention of quoting you on this subject."

He took a thoughtful drink, then gestured toward the tape recorder. "That thing on?"

She reached over, cut it off, and held it up for his inspection. "It's off." The phone man got to his feet and approached them.

"You tell me something. Why do you want to know?" Dickens appraised her over his glass.

"Let's just say that the governor is innocent until proven guilty. I'm examining all the possibilities."

"You mean a setup." The younger man, clean-cut and wearing a tie and a worried expression, murmured something in the lieutenant governor's ear. He nodded. "I know. I know." He gave Tess a sharp-eyed look. "Ross Chandler's been in the oil business a long time. He fought and scratched his way into a fortune, and he didn't care much who got stepped on along the way. And he's been in politics a long time. I mean, he'd *bury* his opponents in mud." His assistant whispered again in his ear, more urgently this time.

Tess said, "You're saying, Ross Chandler made a lot of enemies through the years."

He shrugged his massive shoulders. "I'm sayin', take your pick." Then he gave her a TV smile. "And that's *all* I'm sayin'."

• • •

Deadline

Tess's mind swirled through the labyrinth of her day's interviews as she drove home on icy roads. It was later than she'd expected. By the time she finally got home, the family had eaten and the kids were sprawled in front of the TV in the den, watching sitcoms. Marah was talking on the phone; from the sounds of her lilting, laughing voice, Tess suspected it was a man, probably Jimmy.

She dragged her weary body up the cold stairs, longing for a hot bath and bed. She had another full day tomorrow. She'd stopped at the mall in Midland and bought a few winter things on sale; she balanced the sack along with her briefcase. Just as she reached the door to her room, she heard a creak from above.

Tess froze.

For a long time, she heard nothing else. Then another creak. Her heart banged painfully against her rib cage. Someone was moving around on the third floor. Nobody *ever* went up to the unheated third floor, especially not in cold weather.

Carefully she set down her bags and briefcase and headed for the shadowy, narrow stairs which branched off the upstairs hallway and reached into the darkness of the third floor. One step at a time, Tess fit each foot on the stairs. One step groaned, and Tess bit her dry bottom lip.

When she reached the top step, she waited a moment for her eyes to adjust to the darkness. Where was that light switch? There. She clicked it. Nothing happened. Someone must have removed the bulb.

A shadow, darker than the others, hulked near a small cubby door beneath an overhang. She heard a grunt. Swallowing cotton, she said, her voice quavering, "Who's there?"

There was a loud *thump*, then a soft chuckle.

Tess sighed. "Mama? What are you doing up here? It's freezing."

"I'm just trying to get this door open," said her mother. "I've been looking for Jonathan. I think he might be hiding there."

CHAPTER NINE

LIKE FROZEN BREATH crystals, the name hung suspended between them.

Jonathan.

"Mama? Did you say 'Jonathan'?"

"Of course I did. Who else would be hiding in here?" Shifting her weight with a creak of floorboards, her mother tugged on the little door again.

Tess stumbled to her mother's side. "Mama . . . who *is* Jonathan?"

"Well, if I can't get the door open, then he must not be in here," Nan mumbled.

"Mama!"

Tess could feel her mother looking at her in the darkness. "Tell me, please. Who is Jonathan?"

There was a soft chuckle; she could feel her mother's gentle pat on her arm. "What a silly question," Mama said, getting to her feet with a soft crackle of anklebones. She receded from Tess, heading for the stairway. At the doorway she paused, rubbing her arms with her hands. "Sure is cold up here."

Tess scrambled after her. "Mama—"

Her mother took a couple of steps down.

Tess reached the doorway.

Nan had reached a landing, and as she turned toward the next stairway, Tess could hear her muttering, "Now what was I looking for?"

Then she was gone, and Tess was alone. The day's accumulated fatigue seemed to grasp her with cold fingers; attic

Deadline 71

shadows pressed her from all around. And she, like her mother, was wandering the darkness, looking for Jonathan.

West Texas could look pretty barren indeed in the cold cloudy glare of midday, when spring still lay buried beneath fallow fields, and all colors seemed brown. Even the wind-whipped sky was dusted with its dullness as Tess turned wearily down the governor's drive in her brownish blue Mustang.

Ever since the sleepwalking episode Tess slept on guard, not trusting herself to relax too deeply; that is, when she was able to sleep. Mostly she stared at the high ceiling above, listened to the wind, and tried to remember Jonathan.

Memories, she'd found, were something she couldn't force. The closer she got, the further they eluded her.

It was getting tougher and tougher to drag herself out of bed each morning and face Marah's frozen face. Harder and harder to come home in the evenings to the vague smile which had once been her mother.

And the book. *Damn* the book. The deeper she got into it, the less she wanted to do it. She just wanted to run back to her old life on the edge of the lake, where she didn't walk in her sleep, forget what she said to people, or torment herself over somebody named Jonathan.

Every day she awoke to some unnamed fear, a vague dread that she didn't understand. It wasn't exactly a premonition, but she couldn't shake the feeling that something awful was going to happen to her.

"Something awful *is* happening to me," she mumbled as she pulled up next to the spotless dark blue Cadillac.

Struggling to tame her scattered thoughts and concentrate on the interview at hand, Tess dragged herself and her briefcase up to the beautifully carved door and pulled the bell rope. Bunni herself answered the door, dressed this time in black tights, leopard-print leotards, and black leg warmers. She showed Tess into the main room and vanished into a back room, presumably to continue her workout.

After a few minutes the governor joined her, wearing stylish warm-ups and the everlasting smile.

"Thanks for seeing me on such short notice, Governor," said Tess, mustering up an answering smile. "I came to ask you something personal that I didn't wish to discuss over the phone."

Carefully arranging a look of concern on his face, Chandler offered to help any way he could.

"I need to know if there is anyone in your life whom you would be willing to classify as a real enemy."

Chandler's brows shot up and his eyes grew shrewd. "Why are you asking?"

"I think it might prove significant," said Tess guardedly.

"Significant in what way?" He leaned forward, elbows on knees.

Tess hesitated. She did not want to come right out and say that she was investigating the possibility that the governor had been framed for the murder of his family. If she did that, it would taint everything he told her from that point on, as if he were preparing a case for her to present to the readers of the book which would exonerate him regardless of the trial results. And that, as she had patiently explained, was not her purpose for writing the story.

On the other hand, if he *was* innocent, truly innocent, and she could in some way unearth some important evidence which would reveal the true killers, wasn't she morally bound to pursue it?

He was watching her, and Tess had a feeling that he knew everything going on in her mind as his keen blue eyes scavenged her face. Finally she said, "You are accused of a very serious crime. I think justice demands that every alternative be examined."

He gave her a hard smile with just the faintest trace of triumph in it. "Why don't you just come right out and admit that you think I was set up by someone?"

"I'm not sure yet what I think, Governor," she said honestly. "It's just like I said. I'm examining possibilities."

He shook his head. "Possibilities don't count in court. You got to have evidence."

"I'm not a representative of the court. I'm a writer."

"What are you saying?"

"I'm saying that I'm examining possibilities. If some evidence should come to light, naturally I'd make that available to your attorneys."

He held her gaze with his own. For the first time since

meeting him, Tess felt the full impact of the man's power. He was one of the wealthiest, most influential men in the state. He had enemies, and he also had friends. Powerful friends.

She was careful not to blink.

He said quietly, "And what if you found evidence to the contrary?"

Without hesitation, she said, "Then I'd turn that over to the prosecution."

After a long, frightening moment, he nodded slowly. "Fair enough. Of course, you won't find any evidence like that because, as I told you, I'm innocent."

"Then you shouldn't mind cooperating with me."

He leaned back, still locking gazes. "I don't want to get sued for anything I say in this book."

She shrugged. "Then have your lawyers check over your statements before they are included. Or make some of your statements off the record."

"You would respect that?"

"I'm a journalist."

He smiled and Tess relaxed slightly. "I like you," Chandler said finally. "You don't scare easily."

She almost laughed at that one.

He got up and fixed himself a drink at the wet bar, bringing back Tess some ice water without asking. "Okay. Off the record."

She nodded.

"You remember my gubernatorial campaign back in eighty-six?"

"It made the national news every night of election week as being the nastiest campaign in gubernatorial history. To tell you the truth, I found it embarrassing to be a Texan then."

He grinned and settled back onto the couch. "If you can't take the heat, get out of the kitchen."

She shrugged.

"I crucified Chuck Gibson in that election."

"Yeah. After destroying Susan Sanders in the primaries."

"Those were the good ole days," he said wistfully.

Tess shook her head and took a sip of water.

"We had spies swarming all over Gibson's campaign, pretending to be supporters, digging out dirt, reporting back to us. It was great." He swirled the ice around in his drink. "That blond model who seduced him during the campaign and claimed they smoked pot together in bed—she was working for us." He threw back his head and laughed. "We knew that idiot was a womanizer. Everybody in Austin knew it, too. It was just a matter of timing. You know, not too early in the campaign, not too late."

"It wrecked his marriage!"

Chandler slammed his drink down on the coffee table, sending a shard of ice flying. Tess jumped. He fixed her with another intent gaze. "*He* wrecked his marriage, little girl, and don't you forget it! If he'd kept his pants zipped in the first place, none of it would've ever happened. All we had to do, see, was find out the man's own weakness, and exploit it. That's all. Then all we had to do was sit back and watch him drag himself down into the mud."

Goose bumps popped up on Tess's arms. "But . . . didn't his wife commit suicide after the election?"

His face grew fierce. "The woman was unstable! Don't blame *me* for her problems. I'm telling you, Chuck Gibson would have destroyed his own self, and his family, in his own time anyway. *We* didn't have to do anything."

It was an argument that could go on all day, and Tess had no intention of being drawn into it. She remained silent.

His voice grew calmer. "Look. All I'm saying is that, if you want to find an enemy of mine, go knock on Chuck Gibson's door. The man's hatred of me is public knowledge. If anybody had a reason to destroy my life, it would be him."

Two days of cold weather got pushed out of West Texas by a hot dry wind from the west, which reared its sandy head the day after Tess's interview with the governor. She'd been trying to track down Chuck Gibson's address but the man seemed to disappear after his wife's death. In 1988 he'd filed for bankruptcy in a Dallas court and Tess could find no current address on him.

In the library she'd gone through stacks of newspapers and periodicals from the gubernatorial campaign in question and was struck by a remarkable similarity between the two men in height and build.

It was disturbing, but it was not proof.

Deadline   75

Marah was still behaving stoically as if Tess did not exist, insisting on cooking supper even when Tess offered, and refusing help with the cleanup, so Tess settled down with the kids in front of the TV, hoping their energy and restlessness would perk up her own sluggish bones. Hoping, maybe, to forget about Ross Chandler for a while.

The phone which sat on a corner table rang and Tess lazily picked it up. "Hello?"

"Is this Tess Alexander?"

She recognized the voice instantly and sat up straight. "Speaking."

"This is Ethan Samuels."

"Yes. How are you?"

"Perplexed, if you really want to know."

"Oh? By what?"

"I thought we kind of had a deal. If you found out anything while doing your book, you'd talk to me about it."

"What are you talking about?"

"You haven't seen today's paper?"

"No, not yet. We get our paper in the mail, the next day."

"Oh. I forgot." He paused.

"Ethan? What's going on?" Tess knew, even as she asked, that she would not like the answer.

"There's an AP wire report which talks about you being here, researching your book, and it says that you may be investigating the possibility that Ross Chandler was framed for the deaths of his family."

Tess leaped to her feet. *"What?"*

"You mean, you didn't even know about the article?"

"Of course I didn't know, Ethan. I never even talked to an AP reporter."

"It says you were, let's see . . . *unavailable for comment.*"

Tess began pacing the floor. The kids were staring at her but she hardly noticed them. "I can't believe this. I can't *believe* it!"

"Well? Is it true?"

"That son of a bitch!" Tess shouted. "He *leaked* it to the press!"

"Who did? Chandler?"

Tess groaned. "I've been an *idiot*! I should have known he

would use me like this!" Over the turmoil in her mind, she could hear Ethan's voice.

"Hey. *Hey.* Calm down."

She stopped pacing, but started twisting the cord in her hand.

"Why don't we get together and talk this over?" said Ethan. "There's a fairly decent club out on the highway east of Dryton. I can meet you there for a drink."

"When?"

"Right now."

"But it's late!"

"So? You're upset. And I think we need to talk about this, don't you?"

"Yes . . . but not *now*. Not at a *bar*."

"Why not?"

Tess's cheeks burned. "I should think that would be obvious."

There was a brief silence on the other end of the line. "Well, it's not obvious to me."

On top of the shock of Ethan's announcement, Tess was angry at him. The man was *married*. He had no business traipsing out long after dark to meet a woman at a bar to supposedly talk about something that *could* be discussed the next day in his office. "Why can't we talk about this later?" she asked.

"Because I'd like to see you again, if you want to know the truth," he said.

"That's just what I thought!" she snapped, her anger spilling over.

"Is that such a great sin?" There was genuine bewilderment in his voice. Typically male, she thought.

"To *me* it is! And anyway, I don't have anything to say to you about this."

"Okay." His tone was cool. "I just don't want you to fall into any traps here."

"I can take care of myself," she said. *And Ross Chandler, the bastard.*

Tess said good-bye, hung up, then stormed into the kitchen where Marah was finishing up. "Did an Associated Press reporter call here for me?" she demanded.

"Maybe." Marah placed a plate in the cabinet.

Tess grabbed her wrist. "What do you mean, *maybe*?"

Marah jerked away her wrist. "A few times."

"Then why in *hell* didn't you tell me?" Tess wanted to strangle her, wipe that cool, complacent expression off her face. She was so furious she couldn't even get her thoughts in order.

Marah looked at her and smiled sweetly. "Because," she said, her voice smooth as butter, "I'm not your goddamned secretary."

Tess clenched her hands, digging the fingernails into her palms.

"Who was that on the phone?" Nan stood in the doorway, looking surprisingly normal. She was holding a kitchen-sized matchbox in her hand.

"Ethan Samuels," said Tess mechanically.

"Oh? The Texas Ranger?"

Tess whirled to face her mother. "You know him?"

"Oh, yes. Such a nice man. And such a pity about his wife."

Tess swallowed. "His wife?"

Nan pulled open the matchbox and Tess glanced inside. It was stuffed with pennies. "Remember, Marah? What was her name?"

"Linda, I think." Marah's tone was surly.

Tess struggled to keep her patience. "What happened to Linda?"

Nan began sorting through the pennies. "She died. Couple of years ago, I think. Breast cancer, wasn't it, Marah?"

CHAPTER TEN

TESS HAD MANAGED to push her humiliating encounter of the night before with Ethan Samuels far out of her mind by the time she pulled up next to the navy Cadillac with a screech of tires and a cloud of dust. She took scarce notice of the black BMW parked in the drive as she sprinted up the steps and yanked on the bell rope.

The long, sleepless night had not dissipated her rage.

Bunni answered the door, dressed in a pink cashmere sweater cinched tightly around her small waist with a wide black belt, and a tight black miniskirt. Tess brushed past her into the large main room. Ross Chandler was huddled in serious conference with Cameron Thornton and Charles Douglas. They blinked at her as she swept into the room and took a stance directly in front of the governor.

"How dare you," she said.

He pulled off a pair of reading glasses and gave her an innocent look. "I'm sure I don't understand."

"And *I'm* sure you do. How dare you use me to manipulate prospective jurors."

"What are you talking about?" demanded Thornton, his bald head gleaming beneath artfully arranged track lighting.

"I'm talking about this." Tess tossed the newspaper with the AP story onto the hand-carved coffee table. "You deliberately leaked private information about my project to the press in order to make yourself look better at my expense."

Douglas shot a look at the governor. Chandler smiled patronizingly. "Tess, I've been forbidden by my attorneys to talk to the press. I didn't leak anything to them."

"You're lying."

Deadline

There was a sharp intake of breath in the room from Bunni's general direction. Chandler's face hardened and his eyes took on a sharp brilliance. "If I were you, I'd check my facts before making any accusations."

Tess lifted her chin and looked him directly in the eye. "Governor, I'm not doing this book for you, and I'm not doing it because you called me. I'm doing it for my publisher, and I'm doing it for my readers, and I'm doing it for the sake of truth. I will not, and I repeat, *will not* tolerate being manipulated by you"—she glanced at the lawyers—"or anybody else. You pull another stunt like this and I'm dropping the whole project. You can find yourself another ghostwriter."

With that, Tess turned on her heel, crossed the long room with a clickety-click of heels on hard cold tile, and let herself out.

It wasn't until she tried to fit the key into the ignition of her car that she realized just how hard she was shaking.

Lubbock, Texas, was a college town of about 100,000 people, located on the high dry plains of the Panhandle about seventy-five miles north of Remington, surrounded by miles of monotonous flatness that had only recently been discovered to be ideal grape-growing and wine-making country. Perhaps because of the terrain, or maybe because of the big university (Texas Tech), the people reflected a warm openness that Tess had always found attractive. The city was also laid out in an ingenious and convenient grid, with broad, multilaned streets arranged in vertical numbers and horizontal letters, surrounded overall by a gigantic encircling freeway. She managed to find Dr. Ellyn Frazier's office with no trouble at all.

The reception area was decorated in soothing earth tones and filled with antique toys, dolls, and stuffed animals which, according to a sign, children were encouraged to play with. The room was bustling and busy as the therapist's waiting clients did just that. They all appeared comfortable as they waited. The only individuals Tess could spot sitting silently in corners biting nails were the accompanying parents.

A cheerful receptionist showed Tess into a room built like a child-sized turn-of-the-century town, complete with a general store and post office just waiting to invite a child's curious exploration. She sat in a small chair and watched one little girl busy at play before being escorted, finally, into the therapist's comfortable, homey, and plant-filled private office. After a few moments of perusing several attractively framed Normal Rockwell prints, Tess heard the door behind her open with a soft swish and Ellyn Frazier bustled into the room, long gray hair flying loose from various pins which held it in a chignon at the nape of her neck. She was just plump enough to be nonthreatening, and her smile was genuine as she took Tess's hand.

Speaking with a British accent, she said, "So sorry you had to wait, my dear. I seem to be running perennially behind, but then, when one works with children, one can't always interrupt a tear-filled session with an abrupt 'Sorry, luv, your time's up.' " She dropped an armful of files on the desk and turned to a hot plate which sat behind the desk. "Tea?"

"Please."

She poured a cup for Tess, added honey without asking, and handed her a delicate cup and saucer. Tess took a sip. It was strong and delicious. Dr. Frazier took a satisfying sip of her own and said, "So revivifying, don't you think?" Her eyes over the cup were intelligent blue.

"I love your offices," said Tess with a nod.

"Yes. No need for the youngsters sitting out there agonizing, is there?"

"I saw a few anxiety-ridden parents," Tess said, smiling.

"Yes, well, if it weren't for the parents, I probably wouldn't have any patients."

"But I thought most mental illness is now believed to be a simple problem of chemical imbalance," Tess teased.

"I'll let those theorists stick to their lab rats. I deal with people. Children, to be specific."

Tess sipped her tea.

"To tell the truth, most of my patients are not seriously ill and do not require hospitalization or medication. If they did, I'd have to turn them over to a psychiatrist. I'm a psychologist. I deal with emotional problems which can usually be worked through over a reasonably brief period of time. A few months, at most."

"How did you come to work with Annie Mitchell, Ross Chandler's granddaughter?"

Dr. Frazier shook her head sadly. "The doctor who was treating her burns phoned me. He's a friend of mine. When she'd been thoroughly examined and was being treated for her physical injuries, he made the decision that there was no medical reason why she was not speaking."

"There was some smoke inhalation."

"Yes. Lung damage. First-degree burns over forty percent of her body. Second-degree burns over ten percent, mostly the face, arms, and hands, I'm sorry to say. But her vocal cords were not seriously damaged. She should have been able to speak to the doctors and police officers and tell them what happened. When she refused to speak for three days after regaining consciousness, her doctor called me."

"I understand she was close to death for some time."

"Oh, yes. First they had to treat her for severe shock, then toxemia poisoning and then bronchopneumonia. I didn't work with her at all until they'd stabilized her from the pneumonia. At that point they hadn't even told her about her mother and sister. Even then she showed little reaction. It's my belief that the news came as no surprise to her."

"You mean—"

"I mean she witnessed their deaths."

Tess's mouth went dry and her heart began to race. She wasn't sure why. She tried not to give the appearance of nervousness. "From the fire?"

Dr. Frazier pulled off wire-rimmed glasses and rubbed her eyes. "No. Her mother, sister, and grandmother did not die from the fire. They were murdered."

Tess let pent-up breath out slowly. "Is this what she told you?"

"More tea?" Dr. Frazier reached for the pot.

"No."

She poured herself another cup. "What do you know about hypnosis, Ms. Alexander?"

"Please call me Tess. I know there is still some lingering debate about its usefulness. But I know that most law enforcement agencies consider it a viable tool in, say, putting together composite drawings of suspects or in obtaining complete statements from witnesses."

"What do you think?"

"I think it depends on the hypnotist. I believe there are charlatans out there."

"Exactly." Dr. Frazier sipped her tea. "It took three months of working with Annie in the hospital just to get her to talk again. Like a baby, we had to draw her along, one word at a time. She couldn't discuss her mother and sister and grandmother at all. Every time we tried, she would get hysterical."

Tess nodded, surprised at her own immediate understanding.

"Finally we obtained permission from the courts to hypnotize her." Dr. Frazier shook her head. "It gave me goose bumps." Drumming her fingertips on the desk, she eyed Tess. "I tell you what. Normally I wouldn't consider doing anything like this, but in another few weeks, it will all be public knowledge, anyway, because of the trial." She got up and crossed to a cabinet, where she opened it and withdrew a videocassette. For a long moment, she stared at it in her hand.

Tess waited. She dreaded what the doctor was going to say next, and yet, in a curious way, she yearned for it. There was something in that tape, she knew, that she needed to see. Something that had nothing to do with the book.

"I've given a copy of this tape to the prosecution to help in preparing their case. It will be shown in court and quoted at large in the media, so patient confidentiality no longer applies." She gave Tess a frank look. "I read some of your work before this interview. I believe you are a writer of integrity."

"Why, thank you."

"Can I trust you not to release contents of this tape before the trial?"

"Absolutely."

Dr. Frazier chuckled. "I could get into serious trouble with all those lawyers, I tell you."

"I won't even take notes or use my tape recorder. I'll wait and get a full transcription from trial records." She paused. "Why are you taking this risk with me, Dr. Frazier? I'm curious."

The woman shrugged. "I'm not sure. When you've been in the business of studying people as long as I have, you learn to size them up pretty fast, though, I admit, maybe too fast sometimes. It's an occupational hazard among therapists to make snap judgments about people." She smiled at Tess over her glasses. "There's something about you . . . not just a desire for truth, but a compassion for this child."

Tess nodded. "Am I that transparent?"

"Probably not to anybody else." She tapped her fingers on the tape. "Tell you what. I'm going to plug in this tape for you to watch. I'd like to watch it with you, but I'm late for another appointment. You watch it. Write down any questions you may have. I'll be back after an hour, if you don't mind waiting—or you can leave and return in the next hour and we can discuss it. I'd like to get your impressions." She sighed. "Those prosecuting attorneys just descended upon it like vultures." With a wry smile, she added, "I think they believe they are in possession of the only copy."

"I am so grateful, Dr. Frazier." Tess watched as the therapist plugged the tape into a television which also hid behind those same cabinet doors. She wanted to leave. She wanted to stay.

Dr. Frazier paused long enough to check that the tape was properly set, then slipped quietly out the door.

The image that came to life on the screen took Tess's breath away. The child was propped on soft egg-carton-looking foam rubber—not sheets as another patient might be—in a hospital room. She had no hair or eyebrows, though her lashes were long and luxuriant. Her lips and nose had not been burned away as had another famous child burning victim Tess remembered, but the scarring was nonetheless disfiguring. There were obviously numerous plastic surgery operations yet to come.

There was a sadness in the little girl's eyes so deep it plumbed the depths of Tess's soul. She knew from her research that the father had abandoned the family some years before, and though he'd been tracked down since the fire, he had no interest in taking over the demanding job of pulling this child through such a trauma. With the exception of a great-aunt (her grandmother's sister), she seemed completely alone in the world. According to hospital nurses, her grandfather had been to see her only once before she regained consciousness.

Dr. Frazier was seated on a chair, pulled up close to the bed. The back of her head was visible to the camera. She was telling the child to relax in a velvety, singsong voice, so calming and syrupy that even Tess had a little trouble keeping alert. Annie closed her eyes.

"We're going to watch a movie, Annie. It's going to be a scary movie, but it can't hurt you. You are not in this movie, sweetheart. You are sitting in the theater, and in your hand, you have a remote control. You can speed up the movie, or slow it down, or run it backward. You can even bring it closer. You are going to watch the movie, Annie, but it can't hurt you.

"Now. In the movie, we are back at your grandma and granddad's house. Annie and Jenny are getting ready for bed. What do you see?"

Annie smiled, an otherworldly smile that brought goose bumps to Tess. "I see Jenny taking Kermit to her bed and I have Miss Piggy in my bed. Grandma told Jenny we can ride horses tomorrow. Mommy is coming into our room and she gives us big hugs and kisses. She says, 'Sleep tight and have sweet dreams.' She says that every night when she kisses us."

Annie's voice droned on in an odd monotone. Tess couldn't keep her eyes off the pitiful, maimed little face.

"Do Jenny and Annie go to sleep?" asked Dr. Frazier.

"Yes, but I . . . I mean Annie . . . wakes up and has to go to the bathroom. It's dark." Annie choked suddenly and starts to cry. "*No!* I don't want to watch this movie anymore. I want to run the movie backward now and see my mommy again!" She began to sob, strange, sleepwalking sobs through her closed lids.

"The movie can't hurt you, sweetheart. Just stay with me, okay? Let's not run the movie back just yet. What does Annie see when she gets up to go to the bathroom?"

The pathetic sobs grew louder. "Somebody in Mommy's room. Somebody with a big stick. I see him *hit* Mommy!"

"What does Annie do? In the movie, what does she do? It's all right, sweetheart. The man can't hurt you."

"Annie runs to get Jenny. She pulls on Jenny's arm but Jenny won't wake up. She says, 'Leave me alone. Go away.' " The sobs grew louder.

Deadline 85

Tess's heart began a wild hammering in her chest, painful jerks she could feel in her throat. *Stop it,* she wanted to say. *Leave her alone. Let her turn back the movie.*

"It's all right, sweetheart. The movie is almost over. What happens to Annie?"

"I can't! I want to stop the movie!"

"Just a little longer. What happens to Annie?"

"Annie . . . hears the man coming . . . Jenny won't get up! She's mad at Annie and she won't get up oh no oh no I'm so s-s-scared!"

"It's all right. I'm right here, sweetheart. You're watching a movie. You can make it go faster and it will be over sooner."

The sobs turn to soul-wrenching cries. "Annie hides in the closet because the *man* is coming! And she sees, she sees . . ."

"What, sweetheart?"

"It's Granddad! And Annie wants to run to him but just then he raises up a big stick and . . . and . . ."

The sobs tore at Tess's heart. Tears began streaming down her face. Clutching her arms across her chest, she began to rock back and forth.

"What, sweetheart? It's all right. It's only a movie. It can't hurt you. What does Annie see?"

"Annie sees Granddad hit Jenny with a stick." A howl filled the sound track.

Nausea crowded Tess's mouth with a bitter taste. Her head swam and she squeezed shut her eyes.

"It's almost over, sweetheart. What's happening now?"

"Granddad looks around for something. He's looking for something and he comes toward the closet oh no oh no . . . but he's in a big hurry and he leaves and Annie wants to go help Jenny but she's so scared! She's so scared she just hides there. And then, and now, *no no no no no* . . ."

"Just a little more, sweetheart."

"Smoke!"

"Does Annie smell smoke?"

"Yes. And she wants to keep hiding in the closet, but she has to help Jenny and Mommy and Grandma, because they're asleep and they don't know about the smoke."

"Does she help them?"

Tortured, high-pitched animal cries filled Tess's ears and eyes and brain.

"They won't wake up! They won't wake up and then the fire comes! Oh no oh no oh no oh no . . . *Help! Help! Mommy! Mommy! It's burning! It's burning! Mommy! Jenny! Jenny!*"

Tess doubled over, pressing her hands hard over her ears.

"Jenny! Jenny!"

"Tessie! Tessie!"

Pinpricks swarmed over Tess's body. Her brain was swelling with the child's cries, swelling until she thought it would explode, and no matter how hard she pressed her hands against her ears she could not shut out the cries, could not block them out because they were inside her and all around her, swimming against the blackness that was rapidly drowning her.

CHAPTER ELEVEN

COUNTRY AND WESTERN music so loud it shook the walls thumped against Tess's eardrums. It was coming from a band who performed enthusiastically from a small stage in the corner of a club so crowded people bumped elbows on the dance floor. Dark shadows and cigarette smoke masked facial flaws, age lines, and other identifying marks of boozy patrons as they flirted and seduced their way past the other inadequacies of their lives.

Tess was perched on a barstool next to a huge bearded man who leered at her over the foam of his beer as he pressed his sweaty body hard against her side.

She had no idea who he was, where she was, or how she had gotten there. She counted five empty beer bottles ringed around her frosted mug and did not remember drinking them. Nor did she feel drunk.

"Well, Alexandra, shall we have another little toast? Then how about you and me quit this joint and go someplace where we can get better acquainted?" The bearded man pushed his face close to hers. He smelled of cheap strong after-shave and beer.

"My name is not Alexandra," she shouted over the pounding, twanging music. "It's *Alexander*. Tess Alexander."

He nodded, grinned a toothy grin through his beard, and took a huge swig. "That's just what I said." He patted her leg with hammy fingers and let them linger.

Tess got to her feet and pushed away from him. "I have to go now." She looked around for her purse.

"Good idea." He shoved a few bills across the bar and got up with her.

"No. I'm going alone." She could scarcely think over the music, much less make herself heard. Retrieving her purse from the sawdusted hardwood floor, she elbowed her way through the throng toward a door marked "Exit."

He-Man followed along behind.

"No." She pushed against his massive chest. "Go away."

"Aw, now, is that any way to act after I bought you all those beers?" He draped a heavy arm across her shoulders.

"Stop it!" Tess writhed to get out from under him and headed toward the door. She felt a big hand tighten around her arm.

"What's the matter with you?" he boomed. "You some kinda tease or what?"

"Let me go!" she cried, struggling against his grip.

"Is there some kind of problem here?" A muscled, clean-cut young man stood before them in a tightly fitting tee-shirt with the word *Sonny's* emblazoned across the chest. Tess assumed *Sonny's* was the name of the club and that this was a bouncer.

"I'm trying to leave and this man won't let me go," she said gratefully.

The two men squared off and the bearded man blinked first. After a long moment, he let her go with a slight shove. "Fuck off, then, bitch," he mumbled, and turned back to the bar.

"Thank you," she said to the young man, blinking back tears of fear, frustration, and humiliation.

"You need an escort to your car?" he asked.

"If you'll just keep an eye on me from the door, I'll be all right," she said, groping in her bag for her keys. Of course, she had no idea where she was parked. She could only hope she was still in Lubbock. At least then she could get herself home without getting lost. Maybe.

The young man was true to his word, clearing a path through the crowd for her to the door, and standing guard just outside it as she spotted her car and fairly ran toward it. A cold wind helped to clear her senses. After driving around awhile she discovered that she was indeed still in Lubbock.

An hour and a half from home. According to her watch it was ten-thirty.

This time she'd managed to lose a whole afternoon and evening.

Trembling overtook Tess and she gripped the wheel as she hurried the little car out of town. She'd never been to that bar before in her life. In fact, she hated country and western music and couldn't imagine what had drawn her to that club in the first place. And why would she have ever let that baboon buy her those beers?

Tess could remember nothing after viewing the tape in the therapist's office.

Nothing.

The trembling grew worse and Tess clenched her teeth in a futile effort to stop it.

What if the next time she lost a block of time, she had Molly and Cody with her? It had happened to her mother. Where might she take them? What risks might she put them in? Tess resolved never to take the children anywhere in her car again.

A sob caught in her throat.

Had her mother been this terrified?

Tess had never felt more out of control in her life.

Please, she prayed, *just let me finish this book. Maybe it will earn enough that I won't have to be a burden on my family.*

Family. Marah was just about the only family she had left who was capable of helping her. And Marah hated her.

Maybe, she thought, when she started getting really bad, she could check herself into a hospital of some kind. In the meantime, she would have to work twice as hard on this book, see if she could finish it sooner than her other projects, before . . . before she found herself unable to work at all.

The irony of it all was that the book itself seemed to be making her worse.

A catch-22. Like, knowing that you don't have enough gasoline in the car to make it to the next gas station, so you drive twice as fast in order to cover more ground, only you burn up twice as much gas in the process.

In the end, you still wind up empty, Tess thought.

Black dread clutched at her heart. *It's too soon,* she despaired. *Too soon.*

Little Annie Mitchell, she figured, must surely have felt the same way.

As Tess's headlights bored holes in the blackness of the long road from the mailbox to the house, she blinked to stay awake. Exhaustion deeper than any she'd ever known had possessed her on the hypnotic drive home. It was the fatigue of hopelessness.

A human figure flashed into the glare of her lights and Tess slammed on the brakes, fishtailing over the narrow caleche road. Heart pounding, Tess peered ahead as the figure reentered the pool of light.

It was Mama.

Steadily onward she wandered ghostlike, ignoring the automobile in front of her as though she alone traveled the lane. Tess sprang from the car and ran to her mother. "Mama. *Mama!*"

Nan finally stopped and acknowledged Tess's presence with a misty smile.

"Mama, what are you doing out here? It's the middle of the night."

To her shock, her mother pulled free of her grasp and continued walking down the road, as if Tess and her car weren't even there. Tess hurried after her and forcefully, if gently, pushed her into the car. "You sit right there," she commanded, locking the door. All the way back to the house, she fretted that her mother would jump out of the car, but Nan sat quietly where she'd been placed, humming softly to herself.

Tess pulled her mother into the house and, as an afterthought, went around locking all the doors, something they'd never done before in this remote country home.

"Mama," she said, staring into her mother's vacant eyes. "You can't go wandering outdoors. Stay in the house, do you hear?"

Nan smiled, patted her daughter's arm, and drifted out of the room. With a heavy sigh, Tess crumpled into a kitchen chair, folded her arms on the table and pressed her face

Deadline

against them, wondering desperately just how much time she really had.

"Mama can't be trusted alone at night anymore," said Tess to her sister's stiff back the next morning. Marah stirred eggs at a skillet while Tess sipped black coffee so hot it scalded her tongue. She'd already told Marah about finding Nan wandering the road at midnight.

To her surprise, Marah nodded. "I've wondered when it would come to this," she said, her voice filled with weary sadness.

"I thought maybe we'd take turns," said Tess. "When the trial starts, I'll need to be alert. I can't stay up with her every night, but I'm willing to do it every other night."

"Like a new baby," said Marah with a bitter chuckle. "Okay. I think that's fair enough." She scraped eggs onto plates for the children, who sat silently behind them at the kitchen table. "When Sophia gets back, maybe I can take night duty full-time. I mean, I can take naps during the day when she's here to help."

Tess's eyebrows went up. "Why, Marah, that would help a great deal. I'd appreciate that." She couldn't say anything to her sister, but Tess was deeply worried about blacking out while caring for her mother. What if she "woke up" in some strange place and her mother had vanished? She took another steaming sip of coffee. "You know we're going to have to think about—"

"I know. Just not yet, is all," said her sister, doling out plates to the kids and avoiding Tess's eyes.

Tess nodded. On this rare point, anyway, they were in agreement. She wondered what her sister would think if she knew that Tess, too, suffered from Alzheimer's? Would she grieve for her sister, or would she fear for her *own* future?

With an awkward pat on Marah's drooping shoulder, Tess left the kitchen and dragged herself up the stairs. There was so very much work left to be done and so little time left to do it in.

"Ross Chandler is a monster. I hope they put him to death for what he has done. It wouldn't be punishment enough," said Hilda Simpson to Tess in her modest older home in Abilene. While much the same size as Lubbock, Abilene, located one hundred miles southeast of Remington, had a whole different personality. The small city managed to support three church-affiliated universities and a powerful fundamentalist community. Tangled neighborhood streets seemed to send a message to bewildered outsiders of ingrown suspiciousness. Tess had never felt particularly welcome there.

"My sister did everything possible to make that man happy over thirty-five years of marriage and all he ever did was belittle her and make her feel worthless."

"He seems charming enough to me," commented Tess wryly.

"Oh, sure. To people who don't know him very well. People he can use. If he can't use you or he doesn't need you for anything, he'd cut you in half soon as look at you." Hilda Simpson had the salt-of-the-earth appearance of a middle-class, white, devout churchgoer who had never in her life known poverty or prejudice or violence. The world was black or white to such a woman, and obviously, Ross Chandler wore a decidedly black hat.

"Did Mrs. Chandler love her husband?"

Hilda dabbed at her eyes with a soggy Kleenex tissue. "That's just the thing. Libby adored that man from the minute she laid eyes on him. She'd've done anything in the world for him. Not that he noticed. He was too busy entertaining bimbos in his little love nest."

Tess leaned forward. "What love nest?"

"Oh, he thought Libby didn't know, the old fool, but she did. She just didn't know what to do about it, poor thing."

"Are you saying he had an apartment where he took women?"

"That's exactly what I'm saying." Hilda blew her nose. "He always kept another place in Midland, then he leased it out when he got elected governor. When he got out of office, she thought those days were behind him, but she was telling me just a few days before the fire that she found that randy goat was at it again. Some little blond cutie."

Bunni. Tess regarded the woman seriously. "Did you tell the investigating officers about this?"

Hilda shook her head. "I really didn't think it was necessary. My sister was dead and there was no point in this . . . smut coming out and embarrassing the family name."

"Then why are you telling me now?"

The good woman shrugged. "I think it's time people found out just what kind of person Ross Chandler is. I've been reading things in the paper." She cut a sharp accusing glance at Tess. "Like, about how he might have been set up or framed or whatever. Let me tell you something. That monster did this, pure and simple." Her fair smooth face burned beneath a hot blush. "I just wanted you to know that, Miss Alexander."

Tess tapped her notebook with a pen. "Mrs. Simpson, do you have any idea how I could check this out for myself?"

Hilda sniffed and shuddered. "I hope God has a special place in hell reserved for the torments a man like that deserves."

"Mrs. Simpson? The apartment?"

"Yes. Well, let me see . . ." Hilda patted her iron-clad hairdo and pondered the question awhile. "I can't remember the name of the apartments, but Libby said he rented the place under another name."

Tess stifled her impatience. "Do you remember the name?"

The woman wrinkled her brow and chewed the inside of one cheek. "Let me see . . ." She pursed her lips and shook her head.

Tess looked down at her notebook.

"Yes!"

She looked up.

"It was . . . um . . . Tex . . . no . . . Rex. Yes, that's it. Rex Anderson, or Alexson, or . . . It might even be Alexander. But that couldn't be right. That's your name, isn't it? Must be confusing me."

Tess could see the woman's mouth moving after that, but she couldn't hear a sound.

CHAPTER TWELVE

"WINDRIDGE APARTMENTS."

"Good afternoon. I'm calling from the On-time Bill Collecting Service. We're trying to track down someone who listed these apartments as his last address. Would you be so kind as to check that out for me?"

"I'm sorry. We don't give out that information."

"I understand. Okay, well, I guess I'll just have to go the subpoena route, then."

"Subpoena?"

"Well, this man is in a great deal of debt. I've no doubt he's even behind in his rent."

"Hm-m-m-m. Good point. All right. Wait just a moment and I'll check. What did you say his name was?"

"Rex Alexander." Tess waited, chewing the inside of her cheek. This was the tenth apartment complex she'd called so far.

"Ma-am? Uh, we had a Rex Alexander residing here about six months ago. And he wasn't behind on his rent. In fact, according to the records here, he usually paid up his rent six months in advance. Tell the truth, he had a little lease time left, but he moved out without a word to anybody."

"Did he leave a forwarding address?"

"No."

Tess drew a red circle around *Windridge Apartments* on her list, then said, "One more thing. Could you describe Rex Alexander? I want to be sure it's the same man we're after."

"Sorry. I've only been here two weeks, and we're under new management. I don't know if anybody could tell you what he looked like."

"All right. Thanks anyway."

"You bet. Hey—would you not tell the manager that you got this information from me? I don't want to get into any trouble."

"Don't worry," said Tess. "I won't tell anybody."

In the next phone call, Bunni revealed that the governor was spending the day at his offices in Midland. After hanging up, Tess sighed and rubbed her burning eyes. How could she have forgotten the frustration of living in far-flung West Texas? If she wanted to meet with the governor's granddaughter's therapist, she had to drive almost a hundred miles to the north to Lubbock. The governor and his attorneys had offices in Midland, about the same distance to the west, and several important family members lived in Abilene, seventy miles to the south. Her own Austin-area home, and several important contacts in state government, lay a day's drive away. She already had a pile of gasoline credit card slips stuffed away for her accountant come tax time.

The town of Remington had a small airport with a landing strip long enough for the governor's Learjet, at least, back in the days when he had one. On the night of the fire, he'd driven himself to Odessa for the fund-raiser.

Was that like him? Was it the kind of thing he might do, in these slower-paced retirement days? A weekend trip to Austin might be in order, she reflected, so that she could talk to some of the people who knew him best in government. She could leave her car parked at the Midland airport and fly, then rent a car there to take her home.

There you go, like Scarlett again. Running home to Tara.

It was true. More than anything she longed to lean back on her porch rocker and gaze out over the sparkling lake, watching the colorful triangles of distant sailboats glide over the water. Away from hateful sisters. Away from zoned-out mothers. Away from tormented screaming children on videos. Away from her own memories.

Away. Away.

Instead, she called the governor's Midland office to make sure he was in and to let him know she was on her way. Then, assuming a battle stance in front of the closet door,

Tess selected clothes for the trip as if they were a suit of armor.

The governor's office was western-opulent, with several expensive bronze sculptures depicting cowboys or Native Americans, as well as paintings from several well-known western artists who continued to supply many rich Texans with the decor for ranch homes and hunting lodges. (Urban Texas rich leaned toward the "let's copy New York so we'll look sophisticated" ambiance.) The carpet was plush and the paneled walls filled with framed photographs of the governor standing next to various celebrities, politicians, and athletes. Tess wondered just how many of his mementos had actually been lost in the fire. It looked to her as if most of them remained untouched, right here in his office.

Was his smile just a shade less welcoming, his handshake just a little less firm?

It seemed so to Tess, but maybe her heightened sensitivity was merely fatigue. "Thank you for seeing me, Governor," she said politely.

"You're not going to bite my head off again, are you?" He grinned at her.

"I was just establishing our boundaries," she said, but not without an answering smile.

"Like I said, you got spunk. I admire that in a woman."

"And I admire honesty in a man," she answered. "I can't work with you on this book if you hold back information from me."

He spread wide his palms. "Whatever you want to know."

"All right." She leaned forward and fixed him with a no-nonsense gaze. "I want to know why you rented an apartment in Midland under my father's name. I want to know what my father's connection is to you. And I want to know why you never told me you knew him."

He blinked, but he was too savvy to let her see full-fledged surprise register on his face. For a long moment he measured her with his eyes, then said, "Who you been talking to?"

"I checked it out for myself, Governor. The Windridge Apartments."

Finally he nodded slowly. "Okay. I got tired of living in

a fishbowl. I rented myself a little escape valve. Someplace to get away from it all. You can understand that."

"Maybe I can, but could your wife?"

His face flushed and his eyes narrowed. "That's personal."

"Governor, when you go to trial, nothing about your life is going to be personal anymore."

Chandler sighed, then rubbed his eyes with his hands. "You got that right." After a moment, he said, "Do the police know about this?"

Tess answered truthfully, "I don't know." *Just because Hilda Simpson didn't tell them doesn't mean they don't know.*

He leaned back and stared into space.

"Governor, I have to know. What is your connection to my father?" Her heart began to pound with the question and the palms of her hands broke out in a sudden sweat. The pen slipped in her hand.

He glanced at her and shrugged. "I knew Rex and your mother years ago, back when I was just starting out in the oil business. I don't know if you ever knew, but your old man was a ring-tailed tooter." He chuckled.

Yeah, he was a real barrel of laughs, all right. She laid down the pen and rubbed her hands on her slacks.

"Anyway, since he took off years ago and nobody'd heard from him in all this time, and I needed a name where I wouldn't be recognized, I picked 'Rex Alexander.'"

She let out pent-up breath slowly. "You haven't seen him? You don't know where he is?"

"Why would I?"

Tess doodled for a moment on her notebook, trying to collect fragmented thoughts under the onslaught of remembered emotions which buffeted them. She looked up. Chandler was watching her shrewdly. "You knew I was Rex Alexander's daughter when you first called me up, didn't you?"

He nodded.

"Why didn't you tell me?"

"Because it had nothing to do with the project. I didn't think it made any difference."

Something about that didn't sound right. Politicians were in the habit of calling on old friends and acquaintances for favors, in return for other favors. Like, "You tell my story the way I want it told and I'll give you exclusive rights to a best-seller. It's the least you could do for an old family friend."

Yet, he'd never mentioned it. Suddenly Tess remembered her mother saying, *"Rex and I knew him years ago. We go way back, long before he even thought about being governor."* She should have paid closer attention.

Tess began to tremble. "You know where my father is, don't you?" she blurted, shocking them both.

He began shaking his head.

"How do I know my father wasn't living in that apartment all along, and you just used it whenever you wanted it?"

"What?"

She rose on shaky knees and said, "This whole thing is probably his idea, just to torment me, just to make me remember the fire." Then Tess stopped stock-still. *What fire?*

The governor was staring at her, but she wasn't looking at him. She was looking inward, someplace so deep inside, the blackness seemed impenetrable. Her own words had surprised her.

What fire?

Dizziness swarmed behind her eyes and Tess leaned against the governor's massive desk for support. She was dimly aware that he had gotten to his feet and come around to where she was. He was saying something to her from a distance so far away she could barely hear over the clamor in her brain.

"Tessie! Tessie!"

Strong hands gripped her arms and she was guided back into the chair. The scrunch of leather snapped her into the present moment like the crack of a whip, and suddenly there was the governor, leaning over her, asking, "Are you all right? Can I get you something?"

She tried to swallow and said yes, she could use a drink. What she'd *meant* to ask for was water, but she heard herself ask for a drink instead, and when the governor brought her a glass of Weller and water, she gulped it with a gasp. The whiskey burned her throat and warmed her freezing hands and she thanked Chandler for it.

He perched on the edge of his desk and leaned over her.

Deadline

"Tess, how could you remember the fire that burned *my* house?"

Yes. That would be true Ross Chandler. Ever self-preoccupied, it never occurred to him that she meant anything other than what applied to his own situation.

She shook her head. "Please forgive me, Governor. My mother is very ill"—her voice broke, in spite of herself, and she struggled not to break down—"and I've been very tired. Memories of my father are not, well, pleasant . . . and I guess I was just . . . overcome."

He patted her arm. "I understand. We've all been under a great deal of strain lately. Do you feel well enough to drive yourself home?"

She nodded, but continued sitting for a long moment, dreading the endless monotonous drive, battling exhaustion so pervasive she wondered if she really *could* get herself home.

Secrets.

Ever since she'd begun the book, she'd been plagued by secrets. Secrets which the governor kept from her. Secrets buried in her mother's withering brain. Secrets her own heart hid from her. Secrets that were eating away at her like erosion on a coastline. And her carefully structured life, battered by the waves from within, was threatening to collapse into the sea.

She didn't know how much more she could take.

And the long trial was just beginning.

CHAPTER THIRTEEN

JUDGE TAYLOR MCKENZIE fit the stereotype of a judge up to a point. He cut an imposing figure in his black robe, with his hawk eyes, bushy brows, regal nose, silver hair, and deep booming voice. However, a sun-leathered face and calloused hands gave away his true love, after law: showing fine cutting horses in weekend competitions around the state.

A well-trained cutting horse could pick a wily calf out of a herd of range-wild cattle, separate it from the group, and drive it down the arena and into a narrow chute. The rider was supposed to give the horse no commands by rein or foot. The best horses would zigzag in a delicate ballet with their four-legged charges, buckling down to their knees if necessary to keep the calf from breaking loose and dashing back to lose itself in the nervous herd.

Like his quarter horses, Judge McKenzie was known for his ability to focus his full powers of concentration on the task at hand, and dog an issue until getting his way. He had run without opponents for years in his district because he had a strong reputation for fairness and integrity.

He had already denied a defense motion for change of venue, on the grounds that the governor was well known all over the state, not just in his home county, and could get just as fair a trial there as in any other county. Indeed, Chandler had not been actively involved in the community for years and did not spend all his time at his ranch home.

McKenzie's courtroom contained the same beautiful paneling and wood carving as the rest of the old courthouse, including a three-dimensional depiction of the battle of the Alamo directly over the judge's bench. Tall narrow windows along one wall let in golden slants of sunlight and overlooked huge pecan trees that shaded the courthouse grounds. Its peacefulness contrasted with the sharp argument in progress between defense attorneys and the prosecution over a motion to suppress the videotape of Annie Mitchell that Tess had viewed.

Tess sat on a hard contoured bench in the spectators' area and strained to hear. Other than the lawyers and the judge and a few reporters, she was the only one present this Monday morning of pretrial hearings and jury selection.

The past three days after her meeting with the governor had passed in a blur of work, plowing through documents, letters, photographs, and other materials which had been given to her by Susannah Chandler-Forghum, Hilda Simpson, and the governor himself. Her mind had been split, it seemed: part of it busy reconstructing Ross Chandler's life, career, and marriage; part of it striving in vain to remember her own past.

What fire?

Again, she'd asked Marah if she knew anyone named Jonathan, or if there had been any fire in their childhood. Marah, still cool toward Tess, had insisted that there was no Jonathan in their lives and no fire.

But there *had* been a Jonathan, and there *had* been a fire.

Tess was sure of that now. She'd even tried asking her mother once, but Nan's mental state seemed to be getting worse all the time. She was having enough difficulty answering simple questions; conjuring up painful memories seemed impossible at this point. Tess had sat up with her all Saturday night. While she worked through stacks and boxes of scrapbooks and letters and legal documents detailing Ross Chandler's life, her mother wandered the house, hiding more matchboxes stuffed full of pennies, murmuring softly to herself, setting food out in the kitchen and then walking away from it, reaching out to give Tess's shoulder a vague pat as she passed by.

Tess didn't know which kind of exhaustion was worse: physical or emotional, but she had discovered that emotional fatigue often prevented physical rest.

And the more tired she got, the more often she found herself forgetting things, misplacing things, and repeating herself.

Which made her even more scared.

"Your Honor, the recent Supreme Court decision does not apply to hypnosis." Charles Douglas's voice rapped sharply into Tess's wandering thoughts.

She snapped to attention.

"If the prosecution's case rests solely on this child's testimony against our client," added Cameron Thornton softly, "then he has a right to face his accuser and to subject her to cross-examination. *Without* her therapist," he added pointedly.

"Your Honor, the child is still in the hospital recovering from the burns she received in the fire. She can hardly be expected to appear in court." Frank Baxter's fair complexion was flushed.

Tough break for a prosecutor, thought Tess. It wasn't wise to show any emotion in court. Chandler's team now had a perfect barometer as to when their opponent was flustered.

The judge gave a thoughtful tilt to his head. "Mr. Baxter, you know it's been six months now. What do you think are the chances that the child could be brought here, say, by ambulance, and testify from a wheelchair?"

Tess almost leaped to her feet. Such testimony would be high drama and could make a striking impression on the jury. It could make or break the case for either team. She was stunned that the judge had even suggested it.

Thornton and Douglas exchanged glances. They'd been safe in the knowledge that the child was hospitalized, confident that they could get the highly incriminating videotape thrown out of the court, and thus break the prosecution's case. If that pitifully wounded and maimed little girl came to court and pointed her finger at her grandfather, the burden would be on *them* to discredit her testimony—an act which could, in itself, inflame the jurors against them.

Baxter had a hasty whispered conference with his assistant, a sloe-eyed, dark-haired young woman with an intense expression and quick mannerisms, named Kristen Palmer, who was not long out of law school. This was Palmer's first big case, which gave her a real advantage over young big-city prosecutors, who often had to start out in misdemeanors and work their way up through a seniority system to the high-profile cases.

After a moment, Baxter turned back to the judge. "Your Honor, the final decision will have to rest with Annie's doctors, of course, but we think she may be sufficiently recovered for a brief, supervised visit to the trial to testify."

The three reporters who'd sat scattered throughout the spectators' area without speaking to one another now rose together as if on cue and hurried out of the room.

Tess closed her eyes and slowly shook her head. Poor little Annie Mitchell had already had one trial by fire.

Now she was going to have another one.

"We need twelve good and fair people who decide a case, not based on sympathy or emotion, but on the facts."

Kristen Palmer was handling the jury selection of the trial with surprising skill. Her sleek dark hair was pulled back in a smart clasp at the nape of her neck, and it swept gracefully back and forth across her shoulders as she moved her head. Dressed in a navy skirt and a wool-blend blazer of navy, gray, and brown with padded shoulders, navy hose, navy heels, a white blouse with a brooch at the throat, and attractive preppie glasses, she gave an impression that belied her youth and experience, or for that matter, her sex. In rural West Texas, it was still very much a man's world.

"It is not up to the state to prove *why* a crime was committed, but it does have to prove *how*. This isn't like TV. The law doesn't even require hard physical evidence. On the other hand, the jury can't speculate. Your job is simply to be fact finders. The judge will judge on rules of evidence and points of law. But *you* are the power. It's a big responsibility."

Tess scanned the group of people from whom the jurors would be selected. Solid, hardworking, law-abiding citizens. Voters. People like Hilda Simpson. Middle-aged, mostly. A few blacks and Hispanics, but mostly white. Churchgoers. Members of the Rotary and Ladies Auxiliary. Middle-class and working-class people who lived lives of good common sense and had no concept whatsoever of the high-powered world Ross Chandler had inhabited for most of his life.

In his instructions to the prospective jurors, Judge Mc-

Kenzie had asked them to consider whether a witness could be lying.

Was Ross Chandler lying?

Even Tess couldn't tell. Would these people be able to? Would anyone?

Charles Douglas had explained to the prospective jurors that the defense did not have to *prove* anything, did not, in fact, even have to present evidence of the defendant's innocence. The burden of proof, he said, rested solely on the prosecution.

Through it all, Ross Chandler sat impassive in an impeccable dark gray suit and red silk tie, looking less like a criminal than any defendant Tess had ever seen in a criminal court. The horrendous nature of the crime with which he was charged seemed so far removed from him that it almost made a macabre joke of the proceedings. Tess knew the prosecution would take every care to seat a jury who would not likely be deceived by appearances.

And the defense would make every effort to seat one who was.

She wondered if Chandler's well-paid defense team had hired a jury specialist for this trial; someone who'd spend the entire proceedings watching the jury's every bodily move, matching them with background profiles, and reporting each day on the closest probable state of mind of the jury as it viewed evidence, so that the defense could assemble the best possible rebuttal.

She'd even heard of "ghost juries," spectators hired because they so closely resembled the jurors in background that they could present even a closer estimation of the progress of the trial to the defense, so that even cross-examination methods could be tailored to the jury's preferences. (Too tough on the witness? The jury's getting annoyed at the defense attorney. Lighten up to regain their sympathy.)

Tess believed Chandler and his cronies capable of most anything in order to win his freedom. She also believed he had enemies powerful enough to frame him for a terrible crime and destroy his life.

The selection of the jury droned on all week. By Friday, twelve people good and true had been selected: seven women, five men; eight whites, two blacks, and two Hispanics. There were two retired citizens, one legal secretary, two farmers, a shopkeeper, two oil-field workers, two housewives, a teacher, and a Baptist minister.

Judge McKenzie gave instructions for the jury to be sequestered as soon as the trial began the following Monday, and ordered them not to discuss the case or read anything about it over the weekend.

Tess looked at the serious-faced men and women as they listened closely to the judge.

Not one of them could be considered a true peer to former governor and rich oilman Ross Chandler.

Juggling notebook, pens, and tape recorder, Tess staggered out the courtroom doors and crashed headlong into Ethan Samuels.

He grabbed her shoulders to steady her and laughed. "Well, I was hoping to bump into you again."

Her stomach flip-flopped. She'd almost forgotten how good-looking he was. Or how *single*.

"Sorry," she said with a smile, stooping to retrieve a scattered pen. "I had my mind on the trial."

"So how's it going? I'll probably testify Monday or Tuesday." He joined in step beside her as she headed down the corridor.

"I was just thinking about Claus Von Bulow and Oliver North."

He arched an eyebrow. "What have they got to do with Ross Chandler?"

"It's just a little silly to think that individuals of such wealth or influence can actually be tried by a jury of their *peers*. It's like two universes colliding."

"Are you saying Chandler won't get a fair trial?"

They stopped at a door and Ethan held it open for her. "Oh, no." She grinned. "I think he'll get as fair a trial as money can buy."

He stopped and she turned back to face him. "Are you saying you think he's guilty?" he asked.

"Not at all." She pressed an elevator button. The door opened and they stepped in together. It was a tiny elevator, and Tess was very aware of Ethan's closeness as they descended. "Do we still have a deal?" she asked.

"I don't know. Do you have some useful information?"

"Maybe."

The door opened and they walked into the old-fashioned lobby of the courthouse. As they crossed the floor and exited into blinding late afternoon sunlight, Ethan put his cowboy hat (which he'd been carrying in his hand) back on his head and gave her a grin from beneath its brim that Tess found terribly sexy. He said, "I'd ask you out for dinner to discuss it, but I'm afraid you might assault me."

She felt a hot flush in her cheeks. "Ethan . . ." She reached out and touched his sleeve. "When you called me the other night, I thought . . . I mean, I didn't know . . . I mean, well . . . I saw the picture of your family on your desk, and I just assumed . . . *Help* me here!"

"You thought I was married."

"Right." She looked away.

He shrugged. "Honest mistake. Anyway, it shows you have principles."

"Ethan, I'm very sorry about your wife."

This time he glanced away. "It hasn't been easy, especially for Josh, my little boy. But we're about to get a handle on things, I think." Looking back at Tess, he said, "I probably ought to put that picture away anyhow. Linda's been gone over two years. Time to accept it, I guess."

There was an awkward silence between them. Tess didn't know what to say. He probably did need to put the picture away, but she didn't feel it was her place to tell him so. They stood together underneath a budding pecan tree which rustled in the incessant wind. The courthouse had virtually emptied.

"Josh is spending the night away with a friend," Ethan said suddenly. "Would you like to come over for dinner, or don't you trust me?"

"Well, if you can't trust the Texas Rangers . . ."

"Who *can* you trust, right?"

He was smiling. She smiled back. "Right." Behind her smile, she was thinking, *Nyah, nyah, Marah. I've got a date tonight!*

CHAPTER FOURTEEN

ETHAN SAMUELS LIVED on a little five-acre plot of land just on the outskirts of Remington, which sported straight rows of fruit trees and a ravaged remnant of what must have once been a thriving vegetable garden. Tangled rosebushes ran amok in a shaggy yard against the modest red brick home.

Linda, then, must have been the gardener, thought Tess as she swerved around a bicycle and parked in a wide cement driveway underneath a basketball hoop. The thought saddened her, but she dismissed it firmly. She was feeling festive and flirtatious and didn't want anything to ruin her mood.

Though she didn't intend to admit it to Ethan, this was Tess's first date in over a year. A serious relationship had come to a bumpy halt then, just as her career was taking off. Tess blamed the time her career took away from the relationship, but the truth was that her history with men was rocky at best. There seemed to be almost an automatic-destruct mechanism within her—as soon as a man got too close, the relationship would automatically begin to fall apart, sometimes against her will.

The breakup with Jack was particularly painful, but Tess had characteristically immersed herself in her work: writing and revising *Blood on Their Hands*, promoting and publicizing *Murder and Madness*, fulfilling various magazine article assignments, and now plunging into *Firestorm*.

It wasn't until she'd settled into the emotional turmoil of living in her parents' home again that she'd realized just how lonely she really was.

And each day it got worse.

But Ethan Samuels was handsome and sexy and easy to talk to. She liked him. Besides, she needed a break.

He answered the door dressed in a pinstripe western shirt with pearl snaps and well-molded Levi's. His smile lifted her spirits all over again.

The house was comfortably cluttered but basically clean. There were numerous framed photographs of a dark-haired little boy with a dimple in his chin and a snaggle-toothed grin that reminded Tess of Ethan. Judging from the matching print curtains and sofa cushions, Tess figured his wife must have decorated the living room, but the big leather recliner had to be Ethan's. She was drawn to bookshelves which lined the walls on both sides and examined titles of all sorts, from bestsellers to classics.

"Impressive," she mused to Ethan, who was standing next to her.

"What did you expect?"

"I don't know. Maybe Louis L'Amour?"

He laughed and indicated to her a copy of *Sackett*.

They made their way into the kitchen. Two fat sirloins lay on the counter. Ethan washed off a couple of potatoes, punched them with a fork, wrapped them in paper towels, and popped them into the microwave. He opened the refrigerator. "Beer?"

She nodded.

He handed her a cold can of Budweiser and she followed him out to the backyard, where he stooped over a hole in the ground which was a couple of feet wide and a couple of feet deep. Into the hole he made a small pyramid of mesquite twigs, added some newspaper, lit the fire, then added some larger mesquite branches. As the pungent smoke rose into the air, Tess asked, "Wouldn't it be easier just to throw some charcoal into a barbecue grill and squirt on a little lighter fluid?"

He gave her a withering glare, but she could see a twinkle in his eyes. "This is much better," he said. "More natural. Meat tastes better, and it's better for the environment."

"Besides, it's just the kind of thing a Texas Ranger would do."

"Oh, no. I was doing this long before I became a Ranger."

Deadline 109

They made a salad together while keeping an eye on the fire through the kitchen window. Because they both knew Austin and had both attended the University of Texas, conversation flowed easily and smoothly. While Ethan tended the steaks over the fire, Tess helped herself to another beer and sat on a lawn chair in the cool evening calm.

While they ate, they shared mutual adventures in the law enforcement field. Unlike many men, who tended to monopolize the conversation and center it mostly on themselves and their own work, Ethan seemed fascinated with Tess's work and respectful of what she had accomplished.

When she asked him what being a rural Ranger was like, he answered truthfully that the long hours and travel kept him away from his son far more than he liked. "I've put in a transfer to Austin for that reason," he said. "I'd still be busy down there, but Josh would have grandparents and cousins to be with. He wouldn't feel so, well, *abandoned*." He tapped the side of his beer. "But Austin is one of the most highly requested duties, and you have to wait for someone to retire, usually, to get an opening, so it could be a while yet. Maybe several more years."

Through the glow of Tess's third beer, she thought, *Austin? He's transferring to Austin?* She looked at him with even stronger interest than she had before. *Austin.*

He seemed reluctant to mention his wife and Tess didn't ask. Neither of them seemed to want to sadden the sweetness of the evening.

They shared another beer in the living room while Ethan stoked up a comfortable fire in the fireplace. Tess began to wonder if she would be able to drive herself home. And then, when Ethan joined her on the couch, they looked into each other's eyes and Tess knew she wouldn't have to worry about it. He took her in his arms and she responded with a surprising passion.

They didn't even make it into the bedroom.

Their lovemaking had a soft fury to it that left Tess breathless. Ethan had a powerful, demanding masculinity that swept Tess away and set her free to devour him with a lonely hunger that seemed, sometimes, as if it would never be satisfied.

Afterward they both apologized.

"You must think I'm an animal," said Ethan, groping around under the couch for his underwear.

"And you must think I'm a—I mean, I've never made love to anyone on the first date before." She pulled her blouse on over her nakedness and then noticed she'd grabbed his shirt instead.

"I don't mean to rush you or anything, but you're the first woman . . . well, since Linda."

"And you're the first man I've been with since Jack. We broke up over a year ago."

They stared at one another and then both broke out laughing.

"We been workin' too hard," drawled Ethan.

She smiled.

"God, you're sexy." He stroked her hair. "Tall and rangy and wild." His voice grew husky.

"And *you* are a very passionate man." She rubbed the hairs on his forearm.

"Let's do it right this time," he whispered, and led her into the bedroom.

"She didn't tell anyone about the lump in her breast for several weeks. She was just too scared. Linda was like that. We met in high school and she never lost that little-girl quality."

Ethan was holding Tess beneath the covers of his big warm bed, and in the darkness, he told her about the death of his wife. "I felt the lump one night when we were making love. God, it gave me chills."

He trembled, and Tess drew closer to him.

"By the time I dragged her in for a mammogram it had spread all over the place. We watched her die for one whole year."

Tess hugged him and waited.

"It was hardest on Josh. I had my work. I wasn't doing it very well, but at least I had it to occupy my mind. Josh saw it all, the vomiting and weight loss and baldness. He's never been the same."

"Maybe it helped him to prepare for her loss," said Tess.

He was silent a moment. "I never thought of it that way."

"Does he talk about her much?"

"Some. Like I said, we're getting used to it a little more day by day." He squeezed her shoulders. "Hey, I'm sorry. I didn't mean to make you feel bad."

"No. I wanted to know what happened. I'm glad you told me. I'm looking forward to meeting Josh."

"He's a great kid."

"With a father like you, I don't doubt it."

"I don't know," Ethan said guiltily. "I'm gone so much. I worry about him all the time."

"But he *knows* you love him. As long as a child knows that, he can adapt to most anything."

"You think so?"

"I know so. My dad hated me. You can't imagine what that's like."

He shook his head against her hair. "Surely he didn't *hate* you. He just couldn't express his lo—"

"No. He hated me."

Ethan was silent for a long time. Finally he said, "What makes you think that?"

"Because he tortured me."

Tess had never said those words aloud before to a single soul. She began to tremble.

"Hey." He rubbed her arms. "You're not kidding, are you?"

"I c-can't remember all of it," Tess stammered. "Just bits and pieces. There are these big gaps."

"Where was your mother?"

"She didn't know. He did it behind her back."

"She must have noticed something."

"If she did, she never said a word."

He didn't say any more for a while, just held her until she stopped shaking.

Now I've really blown it, she thought, her heart sinking. *He's going to think I'm all screwed up and he's going to bail out before we even get started. I can't believe I could have been so stupid.*

Finally he asked, "Where is your father now?"

"I don't know. He took off when I was sixteen. My mother caught him trying to rape me one night when I got home from a date. She turned a shotgun on him. It's the last time we ever saw the bastard." Trembling overtook her again.

"Jesus." He held her tight, as if the power of his will could erase the evil from her life.

Tess squeezed shut her eyes, feeling a nakedness more profound than just the absence of clothes. It was the absence of her *guard*, and she wondered why she'd let it down so quickly to this man. She wondered if he could handle it.

"You've been on your own all your life, then, haven't you?"

It was a simple question, but it contained a gentle wisdom that both relieved and comforted her. To be understood was a powerful thing. Not trusting herself to speak, she nodded.

Putting his big hand on the side of her face, he tilted it toward him. She could see the gleam of his eyes in the dark room. "My brave girl," he said, and kissed her twice, once on each eyelid.

A tiny sob escaped her then but she didn't cry. Instead, she rolled over until she was straddling his body, lowered her face until her long hair curtained his head, and kissed him with all the tenderness and passion she could muster.

There was no more need for tears.

Tessie! Tessie!

Tess sat straight up in bed. Ignoring the figure beside her, she flung back the covers, lowered her feet to the floor, and waited.

Tessie! Tes-sie!

She could smell it then. The smoke. It filled her nostrils and choked her lungs.

"Jonathan! Jonathan, where are you?" she cried, stumbling toward the door. Rushing headlong through the doorway, she reached for the doorknob she knew was there, but instead, heard a mind-splitting crash, lost her balance, and fell, flailing her arms and cracking her knee painfully on something cold and hard.

She woke up.

"*What the hell is going on here?*" Blinding light pierced her eyes and threw into bas-relief the bathroom and her body draped half in, half out of a bathtub, surrounded by shattered shards of Plexiglas shower stalling; and Ethan, standing bewildered and naked in the doorway.

"Tess, are you all right? What happened? Are you hurt?" He helped her to her feet and examined her knee, which was bleeding.

I can't tell him I sleepwalk, she thought, *or he'll dump me for sure.* "I had to go to the bathroom. I guess I got confused in the dark and ran into the shower stall. I'm so sorry I broke it." She looked in dazed disbelief at the mangled shower.

"I don't care about that. The shower can be fixed. It's you I'm worried about." He poked at her knee and she winced. "I don't think it needs stitches," he said. "I think I've got some antibiotic ointment in here." He rooted around in the medicine chest.

Tess ducked her head to hide the despair which was bound to show in her eyes. It was miserable enough that she had lied to him.

Even worse was the truth.

This man had already watched one loved one die. She couldn't let him and his little boy watch her turn slowly into her mother.

"I . . . I have to go anyway, Ethan," she said, turning away before he could see her face. "I can't stay all night. My mother, um, hasn't been well lately and my sister needs help with her." She limped quickly out of the bathroom.

Where were her clothes?

The living room.

She headed that way. Ethan stopped her with a hand to her arm. "Wait a minute! What's your hurry? It's the middle of the night. At least wait until I've doctored your knee. Your family will be asleep, anyway."

"Not Mama. She . . . has insomnia." She pulled free and hurried into the living room, where she retrieved her bra from the chair back.

"Hey. You don't have to be embarrassed about that shower stall. Things happen. It's no big deal."

"I know." She buttoned her blouse.

"Okay, then, can I see you tomorrow night? That is, if nobody in my district gets shot or anything?" He chuckled.

She shook her head. "That's my night to watch Mama. My sister has a date."

"I could come out to your place. I'd really like to see you, Tess."

The yearning in his voice cracked her heart. Tess had been in love before, but there was something about this man which was different from any other she'd known. It wasn't *him* as such, as it was the *connection* between them. She knew he felt it too.

But something was poisoning her mind—her *life*—and she couldn't expect this good man and his child to be poisoned too.

"Ethan." She swallowed. "I think we need to . . . slow down. Things are happening too fast."

He stared at her, vulnerable in his nakedness. "I didn't mean to put any pressure on you," he said, his eyes sadly probing hers.

"You didn't," she said. "It's not you. It's me." She hesitated.

"What?"

"I just . . . have to work out some things in my mind."

He nodded. "Okay. Fair enough. I just want you to know that this wasn't a one-night thing for me."

"Me either." They stared at one another, then she broke eye contact and gathered up her things.

"I . . . I'll see you later, Ethan." She turned to go. At the door, she looked back. "I had a lovely, lovely evening."

He nodded, and she stepped out into the cold dark night, alone.

It wasn't until dawn slipped silent fingers beneath the curtains in Tess's bedroom in her mother's house, where she lay wide-eyed and staring, that she remembered her reason for getting together with Ethan in the first place: to tell him about the governor's apartment in Midland.

An exchange of information. That's all she had intended. A few laughs. A good time.

Instead . . .

It's just as well, she thought grimly. *He'd only find out that it was registered in my father's name, and I won't have that bastard's name step in between me and the first truly fine man I've ever met.*

It was a joke, of course.

Because *Rex Alexander* was already there, hidden by dim ghostly vapors of life-choking smoke, burning his way through his daughter's consciousness with an all-consuming fire.

CHAPTER FIFTEEN

"STATE YOUR NAME, please."

"John Tercell."

"Where do you work?"

"I'm a fire marshal for the state of Texas, based in Lubbock."

"And as a state fire marshal, what are your duties?"

"I assist local fire departments, on request, in the investigations of fires in which there are fatalities, or suspicion of arson."

"Why don't local fire departments take care of that themselves?"

"Because state fire investigators are highly trained and skilled individuals with a great deal of experience in fire and arson investigation, and because we have at our access sophisticated equipment and lab technology that might not be available in a small town."

"Could you please tell the court a little about your own background, Mr. Tercell?"

"I worked as a fire fighter and paramedic for the Houston Fire Department for fifteen years, and as a fire marshal for that department for five years."

"And in that capacity, you've also attended a number of special schools in fire investigation, have you not?"

"I have, and I continue to do so."

"You also contribute articles to *Fire Engineering* magazine, do you not?"

"*Objection.* Your Honor, I think the witness's competency has long since been established."

"Get on with your questioning, Mr. Baxter."

Deadline

"Certainly. Mr. Tercell . . . Were you asked by the Remington Fire Department to assist in the investigation of the fire at the ranch residence of Ross Chandler on October 24, 1990?"

"I was."

"And when did you arrive?"

"It was around midnight."

"And how did you find the house?"

"Completely engaged. The roof had already collapsed. There had been a problem finding enough water to fight the fire, and volunteer fire fighters were concentrating on protecting surrounding barns and outside animals."

"Were you aware that there were people inside?"

"I was. But the collapsed roof and lack of water made search and rescue difficult at that point."

"You say 'search and rescue.' Did you believe anyone could still be alive at that point?"

"No. I did not. I'm referring primarily to a search for bodies."

"And yet, Annie Mitchell *did* survive. Where did you find the child?"

"She was wandering in a nearby pasture, in a state of deep shock. She was also badly burned. If we hadn't stumbled on her when we did, she'd have collapsed on the spot and probably died."

"How did Annie manage to escape the flames, whereas other family members did not?"

"That's never been made entirely clear."

"You're saying you don't know."

"We don't know."

"Did she speak to anyone when she was found?"

"No."

"Your Honor, the people wish to enter into evidence photographs taken by Fire Marshal Tercell at the scene of the fire."

"Does the defense have any objections?"

"May we examine the photographs, please? . . . No objection."

"The state wishes to enter exhibit number one."

"So entered."

"Mr. Tercell, could you explain these photographs, please, and then we will allow the jury to examine them."

"These photographs were taken at first light the following morning. They are exterior shots taken of the house."

"Thank you. And these?"

"These are close-ups of the collapsed roof."

"Could you explain these photos?"

"We had parts of the roof removed to aid in our investigation, and also to make the site a safer one for the investigators."

"And what did your investigation reveal? Please refer to the photographs."

"These photographs reveal a distinct V-pattern spreading up from the direction of the stove."

"Could you explain for the court what that means?"

"A V-pattern is the distinct mark made by fire as it burns. Fire, you see, always burns upward, beginning at a narrow point and moving up and out. You can see, here, the knob for the back burner is locked in the 'on' position. This, here, is the burned remnant of the dish towel which lay on the cabinet next to the burner. From the position of the nearby window and the fire pattern, here, you can see that the stove caught the towel on fire, which then spread to the curtains.

"Thank you. Bailiff, if you'll hand these to the jury, please? Thank you. Now, Mr. Tercell, could you explain *these* photographs?"

"This indicates another V-pattern, at a low point near the ceiling of a back bedroom. We tore open the wall, and it pointed directly to a dead short in the electrical wiring, which was caused, we think, by a nail."

"Mr. Tercell, is there anything unusual about this finding?"

"Yes."

"Why?"

"Accidental fires do not have multiple points of origin."

"And what does that indicate to you, in your professional opinion?"

"Separate and distinct points of origin are always indications of arson."

A soft murmur rippled throughout the courtroom. Tess, who didn't know much more at this point than the rest of the

Deadline   119

spectators, was aware that arson had been suspected but never proved. Now she knew why. To have two such distinct and deadly fires occurring at the same time in the same house was a coincidence of astronomical proportions.

"Your Honor, the state wishes to enter into evidence photographs taken by Fire Marshal Tercell at the scene of the victims."

"The defense objects to this evidence, Your Honor, on the grounds that these photographs are unnecessarily inflammatory."

"Will the jury please be excused?"

Exchanging bewildered looks, the jury silently followed the bailiff out the door to a small room. The door closed.

Judge McKenzie glowered at Frank Baxter. "Is this necessary?"

Baxter nodded. "We feel that since this is a murder investigation, the condition of the bodies upon discovery bears significantly on that investigation."

Cameron Thornton wore a pained expression. "Your Honor, these photographs are grotesque. I see no reason to subject the jury to this."

"The people were still alive at the time of the fire. They were bludgeoned unconscious in their beds, and died as a result of the fire. The photographs are necessary to prove that."

"Let me see the photographs," demanded the judge. Baxter handed them over. McKenzie looked over the top of his spectacles at the lawyer and said, "Frank, these are gruesome and you know it. Don't you have any forensic evidence that can prove your case without having to make the jury sick?"

Grudgingly Baxter nodded. "Yes, Your Honor."

"Then let's stick to that. Objection sustained." The judge signaled to the bailiff, and the jury filed back into the courtroom.

"Mr. Tercell, based on your examination of the bodies at the scene of the fire, what would you say was the cause of their deaths?"

"*Objection!* Mr. Tercell is a fire marshal, not a forensic pathologist. This is out of his level of expertise."

"Sustained."

"Mr. Tercell, where did you discover the bodies?"

"In their beds."

"Were they clothed?"

"They were wearing pajamas or gowns."

"What was the condition of the bodies when you first discovered them?"

"The skin was badly charred, due mainly to the burning of the bedclothes around them; their skulls were split; there was soot in the mouths of the two adults; and what skin was not charred on the adults was a bright red color."

The jury members stirred restlessly. Some covered their mouths. A few coughed or looked away.

"*Objection!* Move to strike, Your Honor. Inflammatory."

"I'm simply asking for a factual description of the victims upon discovery, Your Honor. It's difficult to do *without* being inflammatory."

"Overruled. But don't milk this, Mr. Baxter."

"Mr. Tercell, could you explain the significance of the soot in the mouths of the adult victims?"

"*Objection.* Calls for a conclusion out of the witness's area of expertise."

"This witness has viewed many victims of fire, Your Honor. This is well within his area of expertise."

"Overruled. You may answer the question, Mr. Tercell."

"Soot in the mouth indicates smoke inhalation."

"Which means?"

"It means the victim was not dead at the time of the fire."

"And the cherry-red skin? What does that indicate?"

"Carbon monoxide poisoning. From the inhalation of deadly fumes and gases often released by a house fire."

"What about the split skulls?"

"*Objection!* Your Honor, if the state wishes to bring in a pathologist, let them do so."

"Sustained. Mr. Baxter, let's move to another line of questioning, shall we?"

"I have no further questions, Your Honor."

The throbbing started over Tess's left eye sometime during the questioning about the inhalation of smoke and deadly poisons during a fire.

A child, in her bed, inhaling death.

Deadline

She groped in her bag for a migraine pill and watched as the soft-spoken and courtly Cameron Thornton approached the fire marshal.

"Mr. Tercell, I'd just like to clear up a couple of points. First, have you ever found fire victims, in their beds, with evidence of smoke inhalation or carbon monoxide poisoning present on their bodies?"

"Yes, I have."

"Were those deaths ruled accidental?"

"*Objection!*"

"Sustained."

"Let me put it this way. Is there always a sign of foul play in such cases?"

"Not always, no."

"Tell me something, Mr. Tercell. When a house is filled with smoke from a fire, how quickly can someone be rendered unconscious?"

"Sometimes as quickly as three minutes or less."

"Three minutes or less?"

"That's correct."

"So, if someone is deeply asleep, they can inhale smoke or deadly gases and die in less than three minutes?"

"It's possible, yes."

"Let me ask you something about your earlier testimony. You said that if a fire has multiple points of origin, it always indicates arson, right?"

"That's right."

"Do you mean, absolutely, one hundred percent, *always*?"

"Are you asking for an absolute guarantee?"

"I'm asking if it is absolutely *impossible* that two fires could start simultaneously in the same house."

"Well, nothing's impossible, but—"

"Thank you. Mr. Tercell, could you define for the court the word *accelerant*?"

"An accelerant is a flammable liquid used to start or spread a fire."

"The presence of an accelerant at the point of origin of a fire is nearly always an indication of arson, isn't that correct?"

"That's correct."

"And did you find any traces of accelerants anywhere near the points of origin of the fire at the Chandler home?"

"Nothing conclusive."

"Why don't you *just say no*, Mr. Tercell?"

"*Objection.* Counsel is harassing the witness."

"Sustained. Just ask the question, Mr. Thornton."

"Did you find any accelerants which might have been used to start or spread the fire at the Chandler home?"

"No."

"No further questions."

"Your Honor, I'd like to redirect."

"Make it brief, Mr. Baxter. The court would like to take a break."

"I will. Mr. Tercell, in those fires in which there were smoke inhalation fatalities, say, while the family was sleeping, do you think they might have survived if they'd been warned?"

"No doubt about it. Working smoke detectors have been proven to save hundreds of lives every year. I've never pulled a body out of a bed in a house in which there was a working smoke detector—I mean to say, a body which was not dead before the fire or unconscious due to alcohol, drugs, or other causes."

"And did you find any smoke detectors in the ruins of the Chandler house?"

"I did."

"And did they appear to you to be in good working order?"

"They couldn't have been. The batteries had been removed."

Murmuring swept through the courthouse. The judge rapped his gavel.

"No further questions, Your Honor."

"The court will now recess for fifteen minutes."

The headache was getting worse. Nausea clenched at Tess's stomach. Gritting her teeth, she swallowed another migraine pill and gripped the edge of the sink in the women's rest room. In the mirror, her face was chalk-white, her freckles pop-up brown against her face.

Get a grip, she told herself. *You can handle this stuff. It's nothing compared to what you saw in Matamoros.*

But Matamoros wasn't personal.

This was, and she didn't even know why.

With shaking hands, she gathered up her things and headed back into the courtroom.

"State your name and occupation, please."

"Henry Rodriguez, M.D., Deputy Chief Medical Examiner Southwest Institute of Forensic Sciences, Director, Criminal Lab."

"Are you a forensic pathologist?"

"I am."

"Could you explain for the court just what forensic pathology is?"

"It is the branch of medicine which deals with the reaction of the body to disease or injury, and it is the application of that pathology to questions of law."

"As a forensic pathologist, what are your duties, Dr. Rodriguez?"

"I supervise autopsies which are performed as stipulated by law, in other words, in unusual or unexpected or otherwise questionable death, and I uphold the Code of Criminal Procedure in the death investigation."

"Could you explain for the court, please, what is the procedure in this investigation?"

"When a suspected homicide is brought in, the body is assessed, numbered, checked in, and examined; the clothing and other effects with the body are held until the autopsy; the body is photographed, fingerprinted, X-rayed, given an internal and toxicological examination, and the clothing is microscopically examined. Through these methods we determine the cause and manner of death."

"Dr. Rodriguez, can you tell me some criteria pathologists use to determine whether a person was alive at the time of a fire, even though the body is badly burned?"

"Yes. There are three signs: the presence of carbon monoxide in the blood, soot in the air passages and lungs, and vital reaction of the skin."

"What do you mean, *vital reaction?*"

"The skin responds to injury for some hours after clinical death occurs—up to twelve hours, actually."

"And how do you check for vital skin reaction?"

"Various tests. Some by the naked eye, some microscopically, some with enzymes."

"Did you supervise the autopsies of Libby Chandler, her daughter, Amanda Mitchell, and the child, Jenny?"

"I did. I have copies of those autopsy reports here with me."

"Did the three victims meet the three criteria for being alive at the time of the fire?"

"The two adult subjects did. The child, however, did not."

The courtroom rustled, restless leaves being swept by an unpleasant wind. Tess squeezed shut her eyes, put her head in her hands, and pressed the throbbing veins in her temples.

"And what did the forensic investigation reveal in the examination of the three victims?"

"Skull fracture, laceration of the scalp, some bleeding, and bone fragments embedded in the brains."

"So your findings were . . ."

"The cause of death in the two adults was carbon monoxide poisoning and smoke inhalation, but because of the blow which had been rendered to the skull by a blunt instrument, inducing unconsciousness prior to the fire, the manner of death was ruled homicide."

"And the child?"

"Trauma to the skull as the result of bludgeoning to the head with a blunt instrument caused her death, which was also ruled homicide."

"Could you give us a clinical definition of homicide, Dr. Rodriguez?"

"Yes. It is the death of an individual as a direct result of some action of someone else."

CHAPTER SIXTEEN

THE DEATH OF an individual as a direct result of some action of someone else.

"Jonathan's dead and it's your fault."

The words, as clearly as if they'd been spoken aloud, rang in Tess's mind. Her head was shrieking with pain, and the statement, *Jonathan's dead and it's your fault*, hung like a nail, holding up the pain.

The lights in the courtroom dimmed.

Tess jumped up from the spectators' bench and hurried out of the room.

She wanted to escape but the words came with her.

"What's wrong, Tess? Is Ross all right?"

Tess blinked, focusing her blurred vision on Bunni, who stood before her in a subdued dark dress with a Peter Pan collar.

"I couldn't stand it in there anymore. Ross told me during the break to wait outside for a while. It's so *awful*! The prosecutors are twisting around all that complicated medical stuff to make it look bad for Ross! Can they do that?"

Grinding her teeth, Tess tried to step around Bunni, but the frightened young woman grasped her arm. "Don't they *know*? Ross would never do anything to hurt those children. How could *anyone* hit a child in the head and then burn the house down around her?"

With a hard swallow, Tess closed her eyes and managed, "I don't know."

"You're going to tell the story right, aren't you, Tess? Ross says you're on our side. He says you'll tell the truth, and everyone will read your book and know that he is innocent."

Forcing herself to concentrate on the diminutive blonde, Tess said, "I'm not on anybody's side, Bunni. The governor knows that." She hesitated. "No. That's not true." Gazing over the top of Bunni's head, she said, "I'm on Annie's side."

Bunni's blue eyes widened. "But Annie says—"

"I'm going to tell the truth for Annie's sake, whatever that may be. Now, if you'll excuse me, I've got a splitting headache."

She staggered on down the hall, fighting waves of dizziness, and somehow managed to get herself home, where she fell into bed and slept the sleep of the dead.

"Well, I hope you got a good night's sleep."

Marah's angry words stung Tess as she left her room the next morning. She turned to see her sister, hands crossed over chest, glaring at her.

"I did. Thank you."

Marah stalked up close to Tess and spat, "You *said* you'd watch over Mama."

"When?"

"You don't *remember*?"

Tess tried to keep her expression blank, to hide the turmoil that churned in her mind.

"Last night. You got up for a while and said you'd be glad to watch Mama so that I could get some sleep."

"I did?"

"What's the *matter* with you? Yes, you did. Then *you* went back to bed yourself, and left her all *alone*!" The last part was a wail which, Tess recognized, was partly due to fatigue.

Strain as she might, she could not remember watching her mother at all the night before.

Sleepwalking!

That had to be it. Tess had read of cases where sleepwalkers carried on conversations with people in their sleep and did not remember them the next day. She stared helplessly at her sister. "I'm sorry, Marah."

"Just don't do me any more favors, all right?" Marah stormed inside her own bedroom and slammed the door.

Tess felt sick to her stomach. In her *sleep* she had offered to watch Mama! What might have happened?

It wasn't until she was getting ready to drive to court and

had just fit the key in the ignition that she realized the hilarity of the situation, which only someone with a black sense of humor could appreciate: a sleepwalker watching over an Alzheimer's patient in the middle of the night.

Tess put the car in gear.

She didn't laugh.

"State your name, rank, and occupation for the court, please."

"Sergeant Ethan Samuels, Texas Rangers. My office is located in Remington, but I serve a five-county area, including Windham County."

"In what capacity did you become involved in the Ross Chandler case?"

"The Windham County sheriff's department requested my assistance in the investigation as soon as the autopsy results came in and it became an official homicide investigation."

"So you have been working exclusively on this case for the last six months?"

"For the most part, yes."

"Would you please tell the court, Sergeant Samuels . . ."

It was no use. Tess couldn't concentrate on any of the testimony Ethan was giving, and hoped fervently that her tape recorder was picking up most of it. All she could do was watch his hands as he made an infrequent gesture, and remember his touch; or trace the line of his lips with her gaze and long to kiss him again. Like a desert traveler, she drank in his body and his voice.

She didn't snap out of her self-imposed trance until Charles Douglas got to his feet.

"Sergeant Samuels, during the course of your investigation, did you ever find any sort of *blunt instrument* which could have caused the alleged blows on the Chandler family?"

"No."

"Not even in the charred ruins of the fire?"

"Nothing that showed any traces of hair or blood under laboratory analysis."

"Nothing in the trunk of Ross Chandler's car?"

"No."

"Nothing on the grounds surrounding the house?"

"No."

"Nothing, say, thrown into a ditch on a nearby highway?"

"No."

"Thank you, Sergeant. No further questions."

Ethan unfolded his big lean body from the witness stand, stepped down, and walked down the aisle of the spectators' area, right past Tess, where she sat at the edge of the bench.

The scent of him made her want to weep.

"State your name and occupation."

"Eddie Yarborough. I'm a waiter at the Holiday Inn restaurant in Odessa."

"And were you working at the restaurant on the night of October 24, 1990?"

"I was."

"Tell us what you saw that night."

"I took some garbage out back around eight-thirty, and I seen the governor, there, get in his car and drive away."

"Where was his car parked?"

"In the back parking lot."

"How can you be sure of the time?"

"Because I get off at nine o'clock. I was finishin' up, you know, doin' all my little chores so's I could leave on time."

"Eddie, how did you know it was the governor?"

"Everybody knows what the guy looks like. I seen him on TV."

"Thank you. Your witness."

"Eddie, when you were taking out the trash, did you happen to see a wedding party head out into that same parking lot you mentioned?"

"Yeah. They'd had the reception and everything, I think. The bride and groom was leavin' and everybody was throwin' rice and stuff."

"I see. And where was the governor parked?"

"He was a few rows behind them."

"A few rows behind the wedding party?"

"Yeah."

"And you were standing behind the building, putting trash in the dumpster?"

"Right."

"So here comes this big gala crowd of people, jostling and

laughing and throwing rice, and somehow you saw *this* man walk through this crowd and get into his car, which was parked several rows behind? . . . Eddie?"

"Well, I'm pretty sure it was him."

"Thank you. No further questions."

Tess found the piece of paper, neatly folded in half, jammed beneath her windshield wipers. It was not a parking ticket, and it didn't look like a circular or advertisement.

She was on her way to lunch and she was in a hurry. Tossing her things into the car, she yanked the paper out from under the wipers, slid behind the wheel, and unfolded the paper. In a large, block printing style unfamiliar to her, the message read:

One, two, whatever you do,
Start it well and carry it through.
Try, try, never say die,
Unless you do something dire,
       and start a fire.

CHAPTER SEVENTEEN

THE ODD LITTLE poem looked familiar, and yet it didn't. Tess *knew* she'd seen it somewhere before, but at the same time, something didn't ring true about it.

Unless you do something dire, and start a fire.

What was *that* supposed to mean?

She craned her neck in every direction, straining to see who could have left the message, but most of the courtroom spectators and courthouse employees had either driven away or left on foot to eat at cafés scattered around the town square. Try as she might, Tess couldn't begin to imagine who would leave her such a message or why. She couldn't even figure out what it *meant*.

Putting the car into gear, she backed out of the parking space and headed away from the town square, toward the wide boulevard which was famous for fast-food joints. As she drove, the rhyme beat a refrain into her brain: *One, two, whatever you do.*

She pulled into a Dairy Queen parking lot. *Start it well and carry it through.*

She gathered up her handbag. *Try, try, never say die.*

She saw Marah.

What was Marah doing in Remington?

As Marah crossed the parking lot on the other side of the building and opened the door on the ranch pickup, Tess shouted her sister's name. No response.

Fumbling with the door handle, Tess sprang from her car. "*Marah!*"

Without giving any indication that she had heard, Marah got into the pickup and started the engine. Waving furiously,

Deadline

Tess jogged toward the pickup. It backed out of its parking spot.

Tess stopped. Marah *had* to see her. She was looking over her shoulder as she backed out of the space. She *had* to see Tess. She waved over her head at Marah.

With a cranky shift of gears, the pickup gathered momentum and drove away from Tess. Her hand fell to her side, and she stood in windy lonesomeness in the parking lot while her sister left. No doubt about it, her sister's snub stung. Funny how families can hurt us so much worse than friends, Tess thought, when they want to.

Head down, she turned toward the Dairy Queen and almost missed the tan flash in her peripheral vision of the plain government sedan Ethan drove while on duty. She glanced up and watched in astonishment as he braked, whipped into a car wash across the street, pulled a U-turn, threaded a quick needle through traffic, and drove up neatly next to Tess. Rolling down his window, he said, "Don't run off, now. I'll take you to lunch."

And she obeyed, standing right where she was while he parked, cursing her heart, which fluttered about inside her chest like a trapped butterfly, and her stomach, which did a neat somersault at the very sight of him.

She fervently hoped her face didn't betray her, because if it did, she would look like a teenybopper on her first crush.

"You look great," he said as he came up beside her, tilting his head into the wind so that his hat wouldn't blow off.

"So do you," she said, more wistfully than she'd intended.

Inside, he ordered a chicken fried steak platter while she ordered a burger and fries. (Sophia would be proud, mused Tess.) They took a corner booth away from the crowd. Ethan took off his hat and placed it upside down on the back of the booth. "So how've you been?" he asked.

"Lonesome." Tess looked away. Where had *that* come from? She hadn't intended to say anything at all like that. Why couldn't she have just said, "Fine," like most people and left it at that? Why did she have to tell him the truth?

He was smiling at her. "I can fix that, you know."

"I know." She couldn't help it. She smiled back. Suddenly she wanted him with a ferocity that caught her off guard. Plenty of time, she thought, to grab a quickie back at his place before the trial commences again. Cheeks flushing heat, she looked down at the Formica booth counter and said nothing.

"What are you thinking?"

She shook her head.

"I want to see you again, Tess."

She nodded helplessly, still staring at the table.

"I felt so bad about the way things ended the other night. I thought about you all weekend."

"Me, too. It's just—"

"What?"

"There are some things going on in my life right now. I don't . . ." She hesitated. "I just don't think I should get involved until those things are . . . straightened out."

He shrugged. "Don't worry about it so much. We'll just take it one step at a time." He smiled again.

Looking into his blue eyes, Tess hid the turmoil raging inside. She shouldn't even be having this conversation with Ethan Samuels, shouldn't even be seeing him, really. Every day Tess could see her mother slipping away further and further from them into a netherland no one could reach. And every day Tess felt as if she were confronting her own cruel fate. How could she subject anyone else to such a thing?

One step at a time.

Maybe Ethan was right. For the time being, Tess was healthy enough. As long as she held a part of herself back from this man—only giving so much and no more—they could be good for one another. For a while. Then, if her symptoms got worse, well, then she could just pull away.

So she told herself.

They could have a good time, right? So long as nothing got too "heavy," everything would be fine. She wouldn't have to be so lonely all the time, and neither would he. With her feelings so neatly compartmentalized and everything under control, Tess dazzled Ethan with a smile and was rewarded with a wink and a knee pressed solidly against hers.

"Did you know that Ross Chandler was keeping Bunni in an apartment in Midland before the house burned down?"

Ethan stopped a french fry halfway to his mouth. "Are you sure?"

"Checked it out myself. The Windridge Apartments." Tess busied herself with her burger and avoided his gaze. "He rented it under the name 'Rex Alexander.'"

"Then how did you know it was Chandler's place?"

She shrugged. "I asked him. He admitted it."

Ethan popped the french fry in his mouth. "I'll be damned."

Tess grinned. "I take it you didn't know."

"No. And as a matter of fact . . ." He grabbed his hat. "You done?"

"I guess so. Why?"

"Let's go." He scrambled to his feet. Tess followed, half running to keep up with his long, rapid strides. She got into the car with him and gave him curious looks as he screeched down the boulevard and maneuvered his way down some side streets near the courthouse to a smart set of offices marked, *Baxter, Jones, & Palmer, Attorneys-at-Law*.

"Wait a minute," she said. "You want me to tell the prosecutor?"

"You got it."

All three lawyers were munching pizza over a cluttered desk in Frank Baxter's "civilian" office. (Like most small-town prosecutors, Baxter had a private practice as well.) Ethan walked right in, grinned at their surprised faces, swept a hand toward Tess, and said to her, "Tell 'em."

She told them about the apartment.

Frank Baxter leapt to his feet. "Hot diggety dawg! This is great! Ethan, how soon can you get me a subpoena?"

"Half an hour. Forty-five minutes tops."

"Get on it."

"Will do." He headed out of the room.

"Wait! What about me?" Tess had no idea what was going on.

"Kristen, can you take her back to the Dairy Queen to get her car?" asked Ethan.

"You bet."

"Okay. Uh, see you later, Tess." He vanished.

Kristen gathered up a handbag and keys. "Let's go."

Like a confused sheep, Tess headed out the door. Frank stopped her. "Thanks a lot," he said. "Listen, you need any help with this book, I'll do whatever I can."

"What's going on?" Tess demanded.

"We're going to subpoena Bunni as a witness. Get her on the stand this afternoon. Blow the jury's minds when they hear about the governor's little love nest."

The news came as a surprise to Tess, followed quickly by the certainty that she should have realized the consequences of telling Ethan about the apartment. What made her uncomfortable was the feeling that somehow she'd drifted over to the "side" of the prosecution, when she was supposed to be strictly an objective observer. Now she was even helping their case.

Hadn't she warned the governor that this very thing might happen as she researched the book?

On the other hand, hadn't he cooperated fully with her in the first place because he trusted in her objectivity? Or did he simply trust that she was on *his* side? Bunni seemed to think he did.

Without speaking, Tess followed a jubilant Kristen out to a sleek cream-colored BMW 325i convertible. The top was down on this sunny spring day and the wind tossed Tess's wild auburn hair all around her face as Kristen raced to the first traffic light and came to a screeching halt at the red indicator.

"This is a super break for us," she told Tess. "It's not absolutely necessary for the prosecution to prove motive to a jury in order to win, but anything that can cast doubt on the defendant's innocence helps."

A spotless navy Cadillac Eldorado pulled up next to the convertible, on Tess's side. She turned her head and looked full into the eyes of Ross Chandler.

Then the light turned green.

"State your name, please."

"Walter Evans."

"What is your occupation, Mr. Evans?"

"I own my own insurance services company, Evans Insurance Services, Incorporated."

"And where are your offices located?"

"In Midland."

"Mr. Evans, has the defendant ever taken out life insurance policies on members of his family with your firm?"

"He has."

"Could you describe these policies?"

"About a year ago, Mr. Chandler took out life policies on his wife and his daughter, Amanda."

"And what was the amount of these policies?"

"There were two policies on Mrs. Chandler, valued at half a million dollars apiece, and there was one for half a million dollars on Amanda Mitchell."

"Mr. Evans, were there any special stipulations to these policies?"

"Stipulations?"

"Were there any special provisions?"

"Yes. Both policies were double indemnity policies."

"Could you describe for the court what a double indemnity policy is?"

"Certainly. In the event of accidental death of the insured, the beneficiary receives double the amount of the policy."

"So that would make the full value—in the event that Mrs. Chandler and Mrs. Mitchell died accidentally—that would make the full value, then, two million dollars for Mrs. Chandler and one million dollars for Mrs. Mitchell. Is that correct?"

"That is correct."

"And who was the beneficiary of these policies?"

"Ross Chandler."

"State your name, please, and your occupation."

"My name is Arnold Schultz, and I am a certified public accountant."

"Mr. Schultz, is one of your clients Mr. Ross Chandler?"

"Yes."

"How long has Mr. Chandler been a client of yours?"

"For twenty-five years."

"You were not a willing witness, were you, Mr. Schultz?"

"No, sir. I had to be subpoenaed to come here today. Mr. Chandler—I'd never testify against you if I didn't have to."

"Mr. Schultz, you will limit your remarks to the court. Just answer the questions as they are put to you."

"Yes, Your Honor."

"Mr. Schultz, you are here under a special arrangement with the prosecution, are you not?"

"Yes, I am."

"Could you explain for the court what that agreement is?"

"Yes. I will not be prosecuted for any wrong-doing under federal tax laws if I tell the truth about Ross Chandler's books."

"And by 'books,' you mean his general accounting of finances."

"Yes."

"The people wish to enter state's exhibit number two. It is a chart outlining Ross Chandler's expenses and income during the past five years."

"*Objection! This is immaterial and irrelevant!*"

"Oh, no. This is *very* relevant."

"Counsel, approach the bench."

While the lawyers whispered urgently to the judge, Tess studied the jury. None of them made eye contact with Ross Chandler, or even looked over his way. He sat ramrod-straight, impeccable in a tailored blue pinstripe suit and snowy-white shirt, relaxed and confident that his lawyers would take care of him, while the prosecution tightened the noose an inch at a time.

"Objection overruled. I will allow the chart. Mr. Baxter, you may proceed."

For the next hour, Frank Baxter demonstrated clearly and concisely the defendant's sharply declining oil royalties, poor investments, and unloadable real estate. By the time the gray-faced, stoop-shouldered accountant had stepped down and shuffled out of the courtroom, the pecan trees outside the windows were cloaked in long shadows cast by the building.

After a brief conference with Kristen, the prosecutor rose, and with just the slightest ring of triumph in his voice, said, "The state calls Bunni Layne to the stand."

Then all hell broke loose.

CHAPTER EIGHTEEN

"OBJECTION! YOUR HONOR, the defense is entitled to full right of disclosure. This is a surprise witness."

"We only recently became aware of the value of this witness's testimony ourselves, Your Honor."

"I respectfully submit that this is not TV, Your Honor, this is a court of law, and the defense has a right to prepare an adequate cross-examination for prosecution witnesses!"

"All right, all right. Everybody calm down here. Mr. Baxter, is this necessary?"

"We believe so, Your Honor. The testimony of this witness can show state of mind of the defendant at the time of the crime, and can contribute toward proving motive."

"Well, it's getting late. Tell you what, Mr. Thornton. I'll allow the prosecution to call and question this witness, and then we'll break for the day. You can prepare your cross overnight and begin first thing in the morning."

Good news, bad news, thought Tess. *The good news is that he can show up in the morning with both barrels loaded. The bad news is that the jury will have all night to mull over the impact Bunni makes as a prosecution witness.*

She watched as a pinched-face Bunni, dressed rather unfortunately in a softly revealing pink gauze peasant blouse and clinging skirt, made her way to the stand. Apparently there'd been no time to return to the ranch and put on her schoolmarm clothes.

Bunni was clutching a tissue in her hands, and during testimony, she shredded it into dozens of little damp pieces. She was obviously terrified of saying the wrong thing.

Through it all, Ross Chandler never flinched.

"State your name, please."

"Bunni Marie Layne."

"Is Bunni your given name or a nickname?"

"My given name."

"Where do you live?"

"Um, at the . . ."

"Please speak up."

"At the Bar-C Ranch."

"Ten miles north of Remington?"

"Yes."

"You live with former governor Ross Chandler, don't you?"

"*Objection.*"

"Overruled."

"Yes."

"I'm sorry. You're going to have to speak louder."

"*Yes.*"

"And what is your occupation?"

"I'm the governor's private secretary."

"Ms. Layne, do you have an office at the governor's suite in Midland?"

"No."

"Do you have an office at the governor's suite in Austin?"

"No."

"Then where *is* your office? In the governor's bedroom?"

"*Objection!*"

"Sustained."

"You may answer the question, Ms. Layne."

"What question?"

"Where is your office located? It's not a very hard question."

"*Objection.* Your Honor, the prosecutor is clearly harassing this witness."

"Limit your remarks to the questions, Mr. Baxter."

"Okay. I'll ask the question again. Where is your office located?"

"At the ranch house."

"And what kind of business do you handle for Ross Chandler?"

"Personal correspondence. Stuff like that."

Deadline

"Uh-*huh*. Ms. Layne, how long have you known Mr. Chandler?"

"Um . . . I'm not sure."

"Take a wild guess."

"Well . . . a little more than a year, I guess."

"Where did you meet?"

"Where did I meet who?"

"Ross Chandler."

"I think . . . I mean . . . it may have been at a New Year's Eve party. Last year."

"Where was this party?"

"Where?"

"Like, name a city, Ms. Layne."

"Austin."

"Is that where you're from? Austin?"

"Yes. Well, originally I'm from Houston."

"But you were living in Austin at that time?"

"Yes. I was a student at UT."

"You were a student. Tell me, Ms. Layne, how is it that a student would be attending such a high-profile party which would have as its guest a former governor?"

"*Objection*. Your Honor, this line of questioning is totally irrelevant and immaterial to this trial."

"If I am allowed to continue, Your Honor, I guarantee it will *become* relevant."

"All right. But get to it, Mr. Baxter."

"This party. How did you happen to be there?"

"Our sorority was acting as hostesses."

"I see. Tell me, how close to graduation were you at the time you served as hostess at this party where you met the governor?"

"Well . . . I don't know. I wasn't a very good student. I had a ways to go yet."

"Uh-huh. And what was your major?"

"*Objection*! Irrelevant and immaterial!"

"I don't plan on sitting here until midnight, Mr. Baxter. Get *on* with it."

"I beg the court's patience. This all has a bearing."

"Well, it won't have much of a bearing if I cut off the questions, now, will it? Hurry up."

"What was your major?"

"My major?"

"Yes. Your major. What were you studying at the university? What were your career plans?"

"I hadn't really decided on a major."

"So then you met the governor at this fancy New Year's Eve party. Isn't it true that, shortly after the new year, you moved to Midland?"

"Yes."

"Speak up, please."

"Yes."

"You lived in the Windridge Apartments, isn't that correct?"

"Yes."

"Those are very expensive apartments. How were you able to afford them? After all, you quit school, didn't you?"

"I did quit school, yes."

"What were you doing then, in Midland?"

"I . . . I was w-working for the governor?"

"You're asking *me*?"

"Yes. I mean no. I was working for him."

"In what capacity?"

"What do you mean?"

"What was your *job*, Ms. Layne?"

"Personal secretary. Just like I am now."

"And you had offices at his suite there in Midland?"

"Er . . . no."

"You worked as the secretary of a former governor of Texas from an *apartment complex*?"

"Yes."

"And how often did the governor visit you so that you could handle this . . . correspondence?"

"*Objection*! Your Honor, this has *nothing* to do with this trial!"

"Overruled."

"Ms. Layne?"

"What?"

"How often did the governor visit you in your apartment?"

"Several times a week."

"And what did he pay you?"

"What do you mean?"

"Your salary? What was your salary as his private secretary? . . . Ms. Layne?"

"Answer the question, dear."

"Well, I never really figured it up . . ."

"What's to figure? You got a paycheck, didn't you?"

"Well, not exactly."

"What do you mean, not exactly?"

"I mean . . . you have to figure in rent, and credit cards—"

"Wait a minute! Let me get this straight. Ross Chandler was paying your rent at this fancy apartment, and giving you credit cards to use?"

"Well—"

"So you weren't getting a salary at all, then, were you? You were being *kept* in a nice apartment, with all the credit cards you wanted, by a married man. Or was he taking out your services in trade?"

"Objection!"

"Sustained. Settle down, Mr. Baxter."

"Ms. Layne, were you or were you not having an *affair* with Ross Chandler, for at least six months before his wife died?"

"Objection!"

"Overruled. Answer the question, Ms. Layne."

"I'll ask it again. Were you then, and aren't you now, having an affair with the former governor of Texas? Remember now, you're under oath."

"Yes."

"Could you say that a little louder, for the record?"

"*YES*! I love him! There isn't anything in the world I wouldn't do for him! He's a good man, a kind man, and he would never—"

"That will be all for now. Thank you."

"But I just want to say—"

"You may step down, Ms. Layne."

"*Please*! You don't understand—"

"I'm sorry. Perhaps you'll have a chance to have your say tomorrow. For now, you are excused."

Sobbing, Bunni stepped down from behind the witness enclosure, and hurried, head down, out of court. Several reporters jumped up and dashed after her.

Then, for the first time since the beginning of the trial,

Ross Chandler moved. Swiveling slowly in his seat, he turned dead-cold eyes toward the spectators and locked gazes firmly with Tess.

Goose bumps broke out over her body and she suppressed a shiver. She lifted her chin in false bravado and he turned back to face the front of the court. Tess glanced from side to side but nobody else seemed to have been affected by it.

But it seemed to Tess as if she'd been stared down by Death himself.

When Tess pulled up wearily behind the old ranch house, one whole side of the sky was a nasty gray-green. Clouds roiled above, stabbing the horizon occasionally with wicked daggers of lightning. There was no wind.

"Goin' east of us again," muttered Juan as Tess climbed out of the car. "They say there's a tornado warning in the next county east of us."

"So we're not in any danger?"

"Nah. They'll get the rain, though, and we need it."

"But we don't need a storm like that, Juan."

"Mebbe not." A true rancher, Juan would have probably been willing to sacrifice a minor outbuilding or two in order to have a good drought-breaking rain.

Tess gestured toward a dark blue pickup. "Who's here?"

Juan shrugged. "Some guy."

Tess knew that was about all the information she was going to get out of her old friend, so she headed toward the house. The closer she got, the more she was able to hear sounds of a heated argument going on in Spanish between Sophia and an unknown male voice. Translating in her mind, Tess was able to make out the words, *"I'm not giving you anything! You talk to Tess about it or you get out!"*

She hurried into the house. "What's going on, Sophia?" she asked in Spanish.

Sophia was clearly relieved to see her. In English, she answered, "This guy says he works for Ross Chandler." She pointed at a squat-bodied Hispanic man standing nearby, his swarthy face glowering. "Says he's come to take back all his files and stuff that the governor gave you. But I wasn't gonna let him touch *nothin'*." She folded proud arms across her massive bosom.

For a moment, Tess stood in shock. When her mind unhinged, she could see what was happening, had even expected something of the sort. To buy herself more time to examine the boxloads of papers the governor had put at her disposal, she said, "Tell Mr. Chandler that if he wants these boxes and files, he will have to pick them up himself. Tell him I am not going to turn them over to a stranger."

The man cursed at her in Spanish. He took a step toward the door leading to the hallway. Sophia, moving on feet light as a dancer's, dashed over to a walk-in cupboard and emerged with a double-barrel shotgun aimed solidly at the man's midsection. "Get out," she said. *"Vamanos."*

With a final infuriated glance at Tess, the man left.

After the sound of the pickup had growled into the distance, Tess said, "You wouldn't have shot him, would you, Sophia?"

A broad grin cracked the woman's face. "Hell, it wouldn't've done no good. I never keep this gun loaded when the kids are around!"

That night, Tess spread everything out—papers, files, and photographs—over the dining room table, floor, and chairs. Her intention was to stay up all night, sorting through them and taking notes on as much as she could before the governor took them away from her.

At least, that was her plan.

At some point after two A.M., Tess fell asleep, but when the kids woke her up the following morning on their chatterbox way to the breakfast table, Tess discovered two of her spiral notebooks at her elbow, crammed with notes.

She could only assume that the notes were helpful, because she had no memory whatsoever of writing them.

CHAPTER NINETEEN

There was a little girl who had a little curl
Right in the middle of her forehead;
When she was good, she was very, very good,
And when she was bad, she was horrid.

In the muggy but rainless morning air, Tess stared at the note which she'd found folded neatly and placed in the ranch mailbox. She'd reached in to leave some bills and letters for mailing and had put her hand on this note.

This time, she remembered exactly where she'd seen the verse: it was an old nursery rhyme. And as soon as she realized that fact, she also recognized where she'd seen the poem she'd found beneath her windshield wiper the day before:

One, two, whatever you do,
Start it well and carry it through.
Try, try, never say die,
Things will come right you know,
      by and by.

At least, that's the way Tess *remembered* the rhyme. Someone had deliberately changed the last two lines to, *"unless you do something dire, and start a fire."*

Who in the world would be delivering old nursery rhymes to Tess? Who would doctor a cheerful little ditty and turn it into something macabre? And why? To frighten her?

"But it's not working," she declared, rolling up her window and heading down the road toward Remington.

It wasn't exactly the truth, though. The truth was that it *was* working. She *did* feel vulnerable and frightened. She just didn't want to say it out loud and tempt fate.

Still, the drive was long enough to give her plenty of time to think. Sending nasty little nursery rhymes as some sort of vague warning was just the kind of thing Tess figured Bunni might do.

Unless you do something dire, and start a fire.

But what about that line?

Because if the "you" was personal, then the only fire Tess could think of had to have something to do with Jonathan. And Bunni couldn't possibly know about that.

"We go way back. Rex and I knew him before he even thought about being governor."

Then again, Tess knew someone who could.

They came face-to-face on the courthouse steps.

"I am sending my lawyers to your house this evening as my personal emissaries. You will return all items belonging to me to my lawyers *tonight* or we will take legal action," said Ross Chandler in icy tones to Tess.

He was standing one step above her and she stepped up to lessen the advantage. "I don't mind returning your things to you, Governor, but I don't appreciate game-playing and I want you to stop harassing me."

"I have no idea what you are talking about," he said, turning to go.

"You've never seen these before?" She held the two notepapers containing the nursery rhymes in front of his face.

Charles Douglas closed an iron fist over the papers, crumpling them into a ball. "Keep away from him," he snarled, shoving open the doors and whisking the governor inside. Over his shoulder, he cried, "You've done enough harm!"

Tess smoothed the papers out against her skirt.

"You want to explain to us what just happened here?" a woman asked. A microphone was shoved into Tess's face. She looked behind her.

A TV news team had taped the entire exchange.

Fumbling to hide the notes from the prying camera, Tess stepped away from the mike. "No comment," she said, and escaped into the courthouse caverns.

Despite poor Bunni's rather pathetic attempts to detail the many clerical duties she claimed to perform for the governor, she wound up doing more damage to him in the long run.

It was just too late.

"State your name, please."

"Hilda Simpson."

"And where do you live?"

"Abilene."

"What was your relationship to the deceased?"

"She was my sister."

"Were you and your sister close?"

"We spoke on the phone once a week. Sometimes once a day. And we got together for lunch two or three times a month."

"Did your sister love her husband?"

"Very much."

"Did she know he was having an affair?"

"*Objection.* Hearsay."

"This is already a matter of record, Counsel."

"We don't know what the defendant's wife thought about it, and we can't know without hearsay evidence, or at the very least, speculation on the part of the witness."

"Your Honor, this is an explanatory statement which clearly shows the mental condition of the victim at the time of her death, and should be admitted under the res gestae exception to the hearsay rule."

"I'm going to accept it, Mr. Thornton."

"Then I'd like my exception to go on record."

"So done. You may continue, Mr. Baxter."

"To your knowledge, did Libby Chandler know her husband was having an affair with Bunni Layne?"

"Yes."

"And how did she know this?"

"She found out about the apartment in Midland where he was keeping her."

"Objection to the term 'keeping her.' Move to strike."

"Sustained. The jury will disregard references to the

Deadline

apartment in Midland as a place where the defendant *kept* the witness, Bunni Layne, and will refer to it as the apartment where she lived."

"Mrs. Simpson, when did Mrs. Chandler learn of the Midland apartment where Bunni, er, *lived*?"

"It was a week or so before the fire. She said she'd had it and she was going to divorce Ross."

"Objection."

"Overruled."

"Exception."

"Noted."

"Had she told Mr. Chandler of her plans to divorce him?"

"No. But she was planning to."

"Are you sure of this?"

"Positive. The last time I saw her, she told me she was going to invite Amanda to come visit for a while with the kids. She said she needed them for moral support when she asked Ross for the divorce."

"Thank you. No further questions."

Ethan was waiting for Tess outside the courtroom doors when the trial broke for lunch. Her heart constricted at the sight of him.

"Think you could stand soup and sandwiches at my place? You could kick off your heels and relax."

"Oh, that sounds so much better than snatching some fast food someplace."

Because Ethan was still on duty and pressed for time, and Tess had errands to run, they agreed to take separate cars to his place. After checking to make sure there weren't any more weird little nursery rhymes stashed someplace in her car, she followed Ethan to his house. As they walked in, he said, "I was hoping we could get together this weekend and you could meet Josh."

"I'd like that." She dropped her bag on the couch.

He hung his hat up on the rack near the door.

Then, as if on cue, they flung their arms around each other and melted together in a kiss that wound up taking up all the time they would have spent in the kitchen.

• • •

"I don't know what you do to me, woman," said Ethan as he sat on the edge of the bed, buttoning up his shirt. "I really did invite you over here for lunch."

"Liar." She grinned at him.

"Does sound lame, doesn't it?" He kissed her on the nose.

"I can't complain. I had the same idea yesterday." She buckled her belt.

"You *did*? Why didn't you say something?"

"You were too busy rushing off to hang Ross Chandler."

"Oh." He pulled on a boot. With a crooked grin her way, he added, "That *was* great, wasn't it?"

She shrugged. "I'm not so sure. The man's no longer speaking to me."

"No great loss." He tugged on the other boot.

A sudden wave of dizziness clenched at Tess's stomach and she squeezed shut her eyes.

"You are the most fascinating woman I've ever met. I never know what to expect from you," said Ethan.

Tess looked around. They were standing outside the house, in front of her car. Both were dressed for work.

"It's exciting," he added. "I never knew you could do that."

She swallowed. "Do . . . what?"

He rolled his eyes and broke out laughing. Squeezing her arm, he walked away and started to get into his car. "Don't forget about Friday night," he called.

Before she could say anything, he'd gotten into his car and driven away.

Trembling overtook Tess. Her knees buckled and she sat down hard on the edge of the driver's seat of her car. *How much time had passed during the blackout? What had she said? And what were they doing Friday night?*

Gripping the wheel with whitened knuckles, she leaned her head against it and struggled against the blind panic which had engulfed her.

She'd just lost another chunk of her life and no one but Ethan knew where it had gone.

Even worse . . . she couldn't ask him about it, either.

"Your Honor, the state requests an overnight continuance so that we may adequately prepare for the questioning of our final witness."

"And who would that be, Counsel?"

"The child, sir. Annie Mitchell."

"Haven't you had enough time already?"

"We've only been able to see the child in and around hospital regulations. We could use a little more time."

"Does defense have any objections?"

"No, Your Honor. We could use the preparation time as well."

"All right, then. But only overnight, you understand. No point in driving a sequestered jury nuts with unnecessary delays."

"Thank you."

"Court is adjourned until ten A.M. tomorrow."

When Tess walked in the back door several hours earlier than expected, there was no sign of Sophia or Marah.

Her mother, however, sat on the kitchen floor slowly rocking back and forth, and crying softly.

"Mama? What's wrong?" Tess knelt beside her mother and put her arm over the woman's unyielding shoulders. There was no response.

She went calling for Sophia but the big woman and her battered old pickup were gone. Marah was in the laundry room, pulling a load of clothes from the dryer.

"What's the matter with Mama?"

"She's got Alzheimer's," snapped Marah sarcastically.

"You *know* what I'm talking about. Why is she crying?"

"Because she's got Alzheimer's!" yelled Marah, slamming shut the dryer door. "You don't need any more explanation than that."

"The hell I don't."

"That's right. The *hell* you don't." Marah picked up the overfull laundry basket. "Now get out of my way."

Tess blocked the doorway and folded her arms over her chest. "Mama is sitting in the middle of the kitchen floor bawling and Sophia is gone. What is going on here?"

"What do you care?" Her sister narrowed her eyes.

"Oh, no. I'm not getting into this with you again, Marah."

"Fine. Now move." She shoved the basket against Tess.

Tess braced herself. "How can you just let her sit there and cry?"

Hatred blazed from Marah's eyes. "How? You ask me how? When you're never even around, and when you are, you're buried under papers and computer work? *How?* I'll *tell* you how, you selfish bitch. It's this way, see. *Nothing* I do, or Sophia does, or *you* do, is going to make any difference." She flung down the basket and took a menacing step toward Tess. Poking a stiff finger into Tess's chest to emphasize each word, she spat, "She's a *space cadet*. Her mind is *gone*, see. She's *out of it. Wacko.*"

"Take your hands off me."

"Bonkers."

"Don't touch me, Marah."

"Out to lunch."

"Stop it."

"A fruitcake."

"I'm warning you—"

"Crazy in the head. Just . . . like . . . you."

Tess wasn't sure what happened next. One minute her sister was shoving her backward, her face twisted and malevolent, and the next minute they were sprawled together on the hard narrow laundry room floor, yanking out handfuls of each other's hair, screaming and kicking and clawing.

It was almost as if Tess was watching herself from some other place, observing with cool detachment while this wild animal tried to tear out her sister's hair. She didn't even feel the pain of Marah's bloodred nails as they tore at her skin.

It wasn't happening to her, and yet it was.

Her own behavior should have appalled her; instead, she felt a sly sense of satisfaction at watching her sister yelp in pain.

Teach her to call me crazy.

"Oh, *madre mía*, what is goin' on here? Stop it! Stop it right now."

The sound of Sophia's horrified voice seemed to slice through the murderous atmosphere and stab into the fuzzed consciousness of both women. Like puppies caught squabbling at obedience school, they loosened their grips simultaneously and pushed away from each other without making eye contact.

"You girls should be ashamed of yourselves! And your mama so sick."

Tess examined a torn sleeve on her blouse. Marah dabbed at a bleeding scratch on the back of one hand.

Sophia's broad brown face was a picture in righteous indignation. She tsk-tsked loudly. "Rolling around on the floor like a coupla alley cats and your mama in there cryin'. I ought to bust both your butts, even if you *are* grown-up, because you're actin' worse than Molly and Cody. And that's another thing. What if they'd come home and seen you like this? What kind of example is that?"

Clearly Sophia was warming to a full-scale lecture. Marah sprang to her feet and brushed past Sophia, her face averted.

Tess got slowly to her knees and began picking up clothing that had scattered from the laundry basket in the fray. She sighed. "I'm sorry, Sophia."

"You better be. Your mama's gittin' worse. She needs you now real bad."

"I know."

Sophia reached down a gentle hand and patted Tess's stooped shoulder. "I know it's hard, honey."

Tess pulled a rumpled, worn, and soft cotton gown out from under a sewing table. It had a dirt smudge in one sleeve from the fight. She'd seen her mother wearing this gown during many happier times, sitting around the kitchen table, laughing over a cup of coffee. She pressed the gown to her face.

Crazy in the head, just like you, Marah had said.

Sophia turned to go.

"Sophia?"

"What, honey?" Their gray-headed old friend stopped and looked back at Tess, still kneeling on the cold floor.

Tess lifted her face and stared full into Sophia's dark eyes. It was time to get some answers. Things couldn't go on much longer the way they were without them. She took a deep breath.

"Sophia . . . Who was Jonathan?"

CHAPTER TWENTY

SOPHIA RECOILED AS if she'd been slapped. Shaking her head, she turned quickly away and mumbled, "I don't know."

Tess jumped to her feet and grabbed Sophia's arm before the woman could leave. "You *do* know, Sophia. You've got to."

"No."

"Sophia, *please*. You've got to help me."

The old woman would not look into Tess's eyes. "Why you wanna ask me this now?"

"I . . . I've been having dreams about someone named Jonathan. I just don't know who he is."

Sophia pulled away from her. "I say let sleepin' dogs lie." Her body was mountainous and impossible to stop once she'd made up her mind to leave. Tess trailed along after her into the living room.

"Sophia . . . wait."

When Sophia finally turned her smoldering gaze on Tess, it took her breath away. Her old friend's eyes glittered with a strange hardness. She whispered, "Why do you want to bring evil back into this house?"

Tess's mouth fell open. "What?"

"You start diggin' around in that stuff, you'll bring evil back, just like before. I'm tellin' you. *Leave it alone*."

The last words came out in a hiss. Setting her formidable back to a shaken Tess, Sophia turned on the TV.

Her mind reeling, Tess stumbled into the kitchen.

There in the middle of the floor sat her mother, still rocking, still weeping.

• • •

152

Deadline 153

"Tessie! Tessie! It's burning."

Oh God oh God *fire* oh God where was he how had he gotten here oh God it was burning—

Running blindly through the dark, groping, reaching, calling for Jonathan, but he didn't *answer*, he quit *calling*, oh God she couldn't *find* him where was he where was he—

Stumbling, falling, calling, searching and the heat, the *heat* where *was* he oh God oh God they were going to die they were both going to die oh God—

The smoke oh God she couldn't breathe couldn't breathe was *choking* and it burned oh it burned and stung and she couldn't *breathe* and *where* was Jonathan help oh HELP—

Help! HELP!

"Help! Please *help!*"—

Tess awoke in total blackness, beating her fists raw on bare wooden walls. Totally disoriented, she struck out wildly, banging her shins against sharp corners and struggling not to succumb to the screaming panic which possessed her.

Her heart jackhammered against her breastbone. Frantic shallowed pants threatened to render her unconscious. Taking great gulps of air, Tess lowered herself to the floor and wrestled with demons so deep within her soul they had no name.

Gathering fistfuls of tangled hair, she yanked until the pain brought her securely into the present. Powerful memories clamored at the frazzled edges of her subconscious, seeking a way into her thoughts. Terrified beyond belief, she shut them out.

Sleepwalk, she thought.

Then she said it aloud. *"Sleepwalk."*

She had to have been sleepwalking. Couldn't have gone far. Had to figure out where she was and get herself out, that's all.

Remember.

She remembered nothing after her confrontation with Sophia. Nothing, that is, except seeing the pathetic shell of her mother's tormented person, rocking and sobbing softly on the kitchen floor.

After that . . . blank.

Calm down.

It was dark now. Had to be night.

Breathe deeply.

Dust. The sneezy scent of dust. Raw wood. Pitch-black.
She had to be in the attic.
Okay. All she had to do was get her bearings and find her way to the light switch. There was nothing scary about it.
Was there?
No. He's gone now.
Who?
You know who.
He might come back.
If he does, you can kill him.
A deep shudder overtook Tess's body and she rode it out like storm-tossed surf.
Where were these thoughts coming from?
To escape them, Tess struggled to her feet and began stumbling around the room. Her head cracked against something that made a crisp *ting* in the darkness and swung away from the blow. She reached up and caught it.
It was a light bulb, hanging from a cord.
But the attic light came from a switch on the wall.
She reached up, caught the swinging bulb, fingered the switch, and pressed it with her thumb.
A tiny, coffinlike room, no more than six feet by six feet, sprang to garish life under the glaring light of the swaying bulb. Shadows rose and fell, rose and fell, alternately hiding and revealing the dust-laden trunk, and in a gloom-draped corner . . . a child's broken rocking horse, staring at her with one gleaming eye as the swinging light brought it to macabre life, moving it back and forth, and in and out, of her horror.

You can't get out. You'll die here, because you're a bad girl, just like he said. A horrid little girl.
A swarm of batlike terrors rose out of the caverns of Tess's mind and attacked her thoughts, driving her to another blind panic. Screaming, she flung her body against the walls, pummeling them until her knuckles bled. Finally, exhausted, she crumpled onto the trunk.
There once was a girl who had a little curl—
She squeezed shut her eyes.
Right in the middle of her forehead.
She shook her head.
When she was good, she was very, very good—

"No." Goose bumps crawled over her flesh.

And when she was bad—

She put her face in her hands.

She was horrid.

"No. No." She began to rock and cry. "Leave me alone. I'm not bad. I'm not."

She jumped to her feet again, hit the light bulb, and set up a wild dance of light and shadow, black and white—good and bad?

"Got to get out. Got to get *out*."

Frantic again, she made her way from corner to corner, shoving against the walls with all her strength until her shoulders were bruised and sore.

Then, just when she was about to give into the panic again, she stepped on a board which sank ever so slightly beneath her weight, and just like that—a panel in the wall swung outward. Tess fell forward, and found herself standing in the attic, staring at a blank wall.

It took the weight of an adult to spring the latch that opened the trapdoor. A small child would not have enough strength. And the light bulb, of course, would have been out of reach. Not only that, but the room was virtually soundproof, which explained why no one heard her screams.

Why no one had *ever* heard her screams.

Standing drained and exhausted before the sprung latch, feeling like the knight who'd just slain the deadly dragon, Tess understood the depth of her earlier panic. This was a room *he* had locked her up in, many years before, many times. And just as the room itself remained a secret from the rest of the house, so too had it been hidden from her own memory by some mysterious ability devised by the human mind to protect it from its own demons.

Still, it gave her the creeps. She didn't even want to turn out the light, not even with the larger attic light on outside the room, because then she'd be left inside in the dark. She would leave it on, she decided, and return later with more bulbs.

Not that she wanted to return. Not that she *ever* wanted to return. Wouldn't, in fact, if it weren't for the trunk. It was too heavy to move, and it was secured against all prying by a big, mean-looking lock.

There were answers, Tess was sure, hidden away in that trunk. For answers, she would return.

It was a crusade no fire-breathing dragon could stop.

CHAPTER TWENTY-ONE

AN ELECTRIC HUM of excitement coursed throughout the crowded spectators' seats, vibrated over the jury, reverberated against the lawyers' tables, and needled along Tess's veins the following morning as she readied her tape recorder for the day.

For some reason, the batteries in it kept fading out. This was her third replacement since the trial began.

Outside, April sunshine coaxed budding blossoms from the pecan trees, but Tess didn't notice anything beyond her own body. She could almost feel the blood rushing into arteries and out of veins, could hear the pounding of her own heart, for this was the day she would face, would see and hear for herself, the burned child accuse her beloved grandfather of murder.

Somehow, Tess knew her life was never going to be the same again. She had known it from that first phone conversation with her editor. It was as if she had a psychic connection with that child, an understanding that went beyond compassion; a bond.

A flash of crimson caught her eye and she glanced out the tall window. The pecan trees glittered green in the morning golden sunshine; a snappy breeze rustled through the leaves, though Tess couldn't hear it through the windowpane.

Another crimson blink and Tess recognized it as an ambulance light, swiveling slowly and soundlessly through the twinkling green of the newborn pecan leaves. As she watched, little picture mosaics revealed themselves through the patches of leaf and limb: TV cameras thronging to the square white vehicle, a breathless suspension of movement in their wake, a flurry of activity beneath the gentle pecan boughs, clumps of people surging up the walkway toward the entrance of the courthouse. An anticipatory hush fell over the spectators, although only a few were observing the activity below through the narrow windows.

Kristen Palmer suddenly burst through the courtroom doors, hurried down the aisle, and whispered to Frank Baxter. He nodded and got to his feet.

"The state calls Annie Mitchell to the stand, please."

Like a wedding crowd, everyone in the courthouse turned in their seats or otherwise craned their necks toward the double doors at the back of the room. Tess glanced over her shoulder at Ross Chandler.

He, alone, had not turned to see the child.

A clank and a thunk brought her attention back to the double doors. Someone held them open, and a wheelchair was pushed slowly into the room.

Though it was a child's wheelchair, scaled to size, she still looked incredibly small. Someone had been able to convince her to come without her baseball cap, and the effect was truly devastating.

Only slight wisps of hair clung to her scarred scalp. With no eyebrows, she looked like a startled alien, just emerged from her spaceship to view humans for the first time. She was wearing a light cotton sleeveless gown, and dark discolored patches of skin covered her arms, shoulders, neck, and parts of her face like wrinkled plastic.

In the heavy, pervasive silence of the room, the only sound was the soft rubber *whisk* of wheelchair tires on linoleum. Someone coughed. Someone else snuffled. No one moved.

The white pantsuited nurse pushed the wheelchair to just in front of the witness stand and turned it to face the courtroom and Kristen Palmer, who was waiting. Frank Baxter had made a wise choice for the questioner of this ravaged, frightened child, who took one look at her immobile grandfather and immediately began a soundless stream of tears that continued for the duration of her testimony.

Several jurors groped for tissues in handbags and handkerchiefs from back pockets. Tess began to tremble.

Ross Chandler never looked at his granddaughter.

• • •

Deadline

"Hi, sweetie. Do you think you feel well enough to talk to us today?"

"Yes, ma'am."

"Do you remember who I am?"

"Yes, ma'am. You're Kristen, the lawyer lady."

"That's right. Do you know where you are?"

"I'm in court. Like *L.A. Law*."

"Could you tell us your name?"

"Libby Ann Mitchell. But everybody calls me Annie."

"Annie, were you named after your grandma?"

"Yes, ma'am."

"Honey, do you know the difference between a lie and the truth?"

"Uh-huh."

"If I told you I played football for the Dallas Cowboys, what would you think?"

"I would think you were crazy."

(Laughter.)

"Would that be a lie?"

"Yes, ma'am."

"You understand that you must always, *always* tell the truth in court, don't you?"

"Oh, yes. Mommy always told us to tell the truth *all* the time, not just in court."

"Your mommy must have been very special."

"I miss her so much."

"I know you do, sweetie. And you are a very brave girl for coming here today and helping us to understand what happened to your mommy."

"*Objection.*"

"Sustained."

"Now, Annie, I know that this is hard for you, sweetie, but I'm going to ask you to remember back to the night when you got hurt in the fire. Can you do that for us? . . . Annie?"

"Counsel, do you need some time to help your witness regain her composure?"

"I'll see. Sweetie, do you want to take a little break and tell us about it in a few minutes? I could get you a Coke or something and you could get to feeling a little better."

"No, ma'am. I won't feel any better just because I drink a Coke. It still *happened*."

"I know. I know. But you are going to have to be very brave and tell us what happened, so that these nice people over here can decide what to do about it, okay?"

"Okay. Could I have a Kleenex?"

"Sure. Here you go. Take all the time you need, sweetie. There. Feel better now?"

"Not really."

"But you can talk about it?"

"Yes, ma'am. I think. I'll try."

"That's my brave girl. Now, the people wish to enter state's exhibit number four: a diagram of the home of Ross Chandler before it burned to the ground, including the ground floor and second floor."

"Any objection?"

"No objection."

"Annie, do you recognize this drawing?"

"Yes, ma'am. That's my grandma's house."

"Would you take this stick, here, and point to the room where you and Jenny were sleeping?"

"Right here."

"Okay. Now, where was the bathroom?"

"Here."

"And your mother's room?"

"Right here."

"Is this a fair and accurate representation of your grandma's house?"

"Ma'am?"

"Does this look just like what your grandma's house looked like?"

"Oh. Yes, ma'am."

"Now, tell the court: do you remember that night when your grandma's house burned down? . . . Sweetie, I'm going to have to ask you to say yes or no. See that lady there? She's writing down everything you say here and she can't write down when you nod your head, okay?"

"Okay. Yes, ma'am, I remember the fire."

"Could you tell us what happened that night?"

At that moment, Annie Mitchell turned her tear-brimmed gaze fully on her grandfather, who continued to stare straight ahead as though she did not exist, was not present in the room, was not breaking the hearts of every individual there.

Deadline   161

She put her face in her hands and sobbed, her thin shoulder blades poking out of the back of the gown.

The young prosecutor shot a worried glance at her boss, who, Tess knew, had long since learned the first rule of courtroom law: never show any emotion. The judge, old enough to have plenty of grandkids of his own, showed no sense of impatience or urgency in his expression. No one, in fact, desired to rush the child through this trauma.

Still, the governor's fate hung suspended in the hushed room, while a little girl wept.

"Annie, sweetie, I think it would be much easier for you if you just looked right straight at me while you tell your story. Just tell *me*, and the other people will be able to hear it, okay? Don't worry about *anybody else* in this room . . . Annie?"

"Okay. I mean, yes, ma'am . . . um, my sister Jenny and me, we went to bed and Mommy said . . . Mommy said . . . Sleep tight, and have . . . sweet dreams . . . and . . . ohhhh, I wish she hadn't died!"

"I know, sweetie. You have to tell us, though. You have to tell us what happened next. It's very important."

"Well, then we went to sleep, only I woke up because I had to go to, er, the rest room, and . . . I saw . . . I saw—"

"It's okay. You're doing fine."

"I saw . . . a man, in Mommy's room. He had a big stick, and he *hit* her. She was in her bed asleep and she didn't know he was there and he *hit* her! And so . . . and then . . . I ran back to my room to get Jenny. I tried to get her to wake up, I said, *Wake up! You gotta get up!* but she wouldn't get up! She said *Go away. Leave me alone.* She was mad at me because she was sleepy, and I *tried* to get her to wake up! I *tried*, Kristen, I *tried*!"

A soul-piercing wail shattered the courtroom silence as the child battled with her grief and guilt. Most everyone in the room, with the exception of those seated at the defense table, was weeping. Tess was screaming inside.

"It's all right, Annie. It's okay. We're almost through, sweetie. Just a little bit more, okay?"

"The man was coming and Jenny wouldn't get up and he was coming and he had that stick and so I *hid*! I hid in the closet, and I saw . . . I saw . . . I *can't*, Kristen! Please don't make me! Please don't make me say any more!"

"Counsel, do you wish to take a short recess?"

"I don't know, Your Honor. To tell you the truth, I actually think it would be better for Annie to get this over with all in one lump. Don't you think so, sweetie? Just tell it all out and get rid of it forever, okay? Can you do that? You've been such a brave, brave girl and you're almost through now."

"Okay."

"All right. Good girl. Now, you'll have to speak up a little so this nice lady here can hear everything you're saying, okay?"

"Okay."

"Now, what did you see from the closet?"

"The man . . . the man came into the room and he *hit* Jenny! He *hit* her real hard in the head!"

"What did you do?"

"I was so scared I just was like a bunny—I couldn't move or say anything. I was so scared, and then he turned around and he started *looking* for something; I thought maybe it was *me* he was looking for, and I *saw* him!"

"Who did you see, Annie?"

"Him!"

"Tell us his name, sweetie. Tell us who you saw."

"I saw . . . I saw . . . Granddad, why did you hurt us? Why did you hit Mommy and Jenny? Did we do something to make you mad? Were we bad? Granddad, why do you hate us?"

"Counsel, I'm going to call a short recess now and I want you to help this child calm down. I don't think any of us can stand to watch any more of this."

"I agree, Your Honor."

"The court stands in recess for one-half hour."

While the courthouse emptied, Tess bent over at the waist and put her head down between her knees to keep from passing out cold. Dark dots swarmed before her eyes; her hands tingled; her head felt disembodied.

Her body drifted toward a surreal state, an astral projection of consciousness. Part of her crouched on the hard courtroom bench, trying not to faint, while part of her hovered above, watching Tess Alexander make a fool of herself.

An explosion of her past sent memory shrapnel piercing into her brain: *I tried*, cried a voice from within her tormented soul. *I tried to save him.*

You killed him, said another. *You're a murderer.*

CHAPTER TWENTY-TWO

"Annie, are you feeling better now?"

"Yes, sir."

"My name is Cameron Thornton, Annie. I am a lawyer."

"You're my granddad's lawyer. You're going to try and get him off."

"Well, let's just say I'm going to try and help everyone find out the truth about what happened."

"But I *told* the truth!"

"I know, I know. You are a good girl and you would never tell a lie. I understand that. But I need to ask you just a few questions to help you figure out a little better what happened."

"I already know what happened."

"Okay. I understand. Now, would you tell me, Annie, did you and your sister sleep with a night-light?"

"*No*. A night-light's for babies."

"So, when you got up in the night to go to the bathroom, you didn't have a night-light to help you find your way?"

"No, but that's all right, because I knew where the bathroom was."

"So, when you came out of the bathroom, did you turn the light off or did you leave it on?"

"I left it on."

"Are you absolutely certain? Very, very sure?"

"Yes, sir. I left the light on."

"All right. I believe you. Now, your mommy's room was right here . . . and your room was *here*, right?"

"Right."

"And the bathroom was in the hall, at the end of the hall, between the two rooms, is that right?"

"Yes, sir. It's right there on the picture."

"I see. I see. Now, Annie, would you take this pointer, here, and show us where you bedroom closet was?"

"It was, um, over here."

"So the closet was here. You hid in the closet. Did you close the closet door?"

"Just a little. Not all the way."

"And you watched a man come into your room?"

"Yes."

"And when he turned around, could you see him very clearly?"

"Yes."

"But Annie, it was the middle of the night. You didn't have a night-light, and the bathroom was down the hall. How could you see so clearly in the dark?"

"I don't know. I just could."

"But you were sleepy and scared, weren't you? How did you know it was your granddad?"

"I just knew."

"But how? How did you know?"

"*Objection*. The child knows her own grandfather."

"Overruled. Restate the question, though, Counsel. I'm not sure the child understands."

"Okay. Annie, what made you so sure that the man was your granddad?"

"He was tall, like my granddad, and he had silver hair, like my granddad, and . . ."

"But could you see his face, like it had a light on it?"

"It didn't have a light on it."

"No further questions."

Ladybird, ladybird, fly away home!
Your house is on fire, your children all gone,
All but one, and her name is Ann,
And she crept under the pudding pan.

Tess turned panicked eyes to the lobby receptionist. "Who did you say left this note for me?" she asked the pretty young woman.

"I don't know. I'd gone to make some copies for Judge McKenzie, and when I got back, this note was here with your name on it. I *loved* your book, by the way."

"Thank you," said Tess vaguely. "Um, if anyone else leaves me any messages, try to get their names, will you?"

"You bet."

A throbbing set in over Tess's left eye. Mechanically she swallowed a migraine pill. Nausea churned her stomach, and she decided to stretch out in the backseat of her car until it passed. She had to think. Who was doing this to her, and why?

Once she was lying flat, she began to feel a little better. Someone was obviously harassing her, not just about the trial, but about her own past. Who could know?

In spite of the fact that she denied it, Marah could know. Marah had always been jealous and envious of Tess's success, but since Tess had been living at home, the tension between them had risen to a level of vindictiveness on Marah's part that surprised even Tess. Maybe the stress of taking care of Mama was making her crazy. Maybe she wanted to bring down Tess, watch her fall, then, what? Stand over her sister and gloat?

Maybe.

Then there was the governor himself. Between such a powerful, vengeful man and his love-besotted girlfriend (emphasis on the word *girl*), who knew what havoc they could cause Tess? A man like Ross Chandler was in a position to find out more about Tess's past than even *she* seemed to know.

Then there was one possibility that was so petrifying to Tess it paralyzed her to even consider it, but she must.

Rex.

What if the governor had lied to her? What if Rex *had* been renting that apartment in Midland for the governor's use? What if Rex *worked* for the governor as some sort of . . . what? Henchman? He certainly had the nature for it.

And if the governor was still in touch with Rex Alexander, then Rex certainly knew Tess was back home. Hell, since that AP news story, everybody in the country knew it.

Anyone could find her.

• • •

Deadline 167

Crises awaited Tess at home.
First was the letter from David Feldman:

> Dear Tess,
>
> I was really sorry to hear you'd decided to drop the Ross Chandler book. I understand he hasn't been the most co-operative of subjects, but you can handle that. I've talked to the publisher about it, and he wants us to go ahead with the project, even if you don't do it yourself. He's asked me to contact Joe McGuiness—you know he's one of our writers. If he's unavailable, we still have some good talent at this house, but to tell you the truth, I really thought nobody could do the story quite like you.
>
> I'll let you know when galleys are ready for *Blood on Their Hands*. Until then,
>
> Take care,
>
> David

"What?" shrieked Tess. She'd torn open the letter from her editor while still sitting in her car by the rural mailbox, engine idling.

"What the hell is he talking about?" She reread the letter. He'd said he *was sorry to hear*.

Who told her editor that she was dropping the project?

All the way to the house, Tess pondered the whole situation with the fury of the righteous. She'd never backed out of a project before. *Never*. She wouldn't do that to David— wouldn't waste the time of either of them.

As difficult as this entire situation had been, it had never even occurred to Tess to drop the project. And she certainly hadn't said anything to him about it.

But someone had.

"I'll call him first thing in the morning," she vowed. And as she pulled up behind the brooding old house, she tried not to think just how out of control her life was becoming, how *frightening*.

The phone call came just as Tess was finishing another strained, silent meal opposite her mother, who seemed to be forgetting how to eat; her sister, who refused even to look at

Tess; and her niece and nephew, who stared big-eyed at their grandma and finally convinced their mother to let them eat in front of the TV. Tess thought it just as well. That way they wouldn't have to bear the brunt of the tension. Still, she missed their playful rivalry and school yard gossip. It was the only lightheartedness in her life.

Tess answered the phone, longing to escape from the table as much as the kids, hoping it was Ethan.

"Is this Tess Alexander?"

The voice had a familiar, Asian accent. "Yes, speaking."

"This is Bic Tran."

"*Bic*! Yes, how are you? I got my copies of *Texas Monthly* today, but I haven't had a chance to read through the article yet. What do you think?"

"I think you killed me, man."

"What?"

"I'm a dead man. Why did you do this to me? *Why?*"

"Do what? Bic, what are you talking about?" Even as she asked the question, stretching the phone wire around through the doorway to hunch over the receiver in the hall for privacy, she felt cold fingers of fear grip her heart.

"You published my *real name*! *My real name, man!* You *promised* me you wouldn't do that! I *trusted* you."

"No, Bic, you must be mistaken. I would *never* put your real name in that story! I used another name for you. I called you Ngyen Thuey Loc."

"You *didn't*! Check it out. You'll see. You screwed up!"

While needles of dismay prickled her skin, Tess let the phone dangle on its cord and fumbled through the day's mail where it still lay on the counter. She picked up a copy of the magazine and shuffled frantically through it.

Marah watched her.

There. She found it, scanned it, and dropped the magazine in cold horror. She'd written an article about a Vietnamese crime ring in Houston, promising her informant confidentiality, and there for all the world to see was his published name.

She'd killed him.

"Oh my God, what have I done?" Leaning against a chair for support, Tess's glance fell to her sister's face and the expression was unmistakable.

Deadline 169

Marah was gazing at Tess with a gleam in her eye of pure malicious satisfaction.

Tess stood over the trunk with a crowbar. Working the heavy steel bar between the clasp and the lock, she pushed against it with all her strength, prying, struggling, pushing, until finally, with a loud crack, the clasp broke free.
Now.
Now she would learn the secrets of her past, the reason for her torments, the truth of her life.
Her lips were dry and she licked them. Heart hammering, she squatted before the trunk and slowly, carefully, lifted the lid. It fell back with a cloudy clunk of dust.
Worms. Writhing, seething, crawling—huge, fat, slithering worms with undulating bodies—hundreds, no, thousands of worms squiggled free from their bondage and immediately attached their slimy bodies to Tess, sticking to her, crawling on her, tangling in her hair, searching for her mouth, her nose, her eyes . . .
A scream, rising from so deep in her diaphragm that it hurt her chest and made raw her throat tore itself from Tess and woke her up, sweating, panting, deep in the wind-howling night.

CHAPTER TWENTY-THREE

BEFORE LEAVING FOR court, Tess placed a call to the offices of *Texas Monthly* in Austin and spoke to her editor there, Mike Harris. "What's the deal, Mike?" she asked. "Why did you run Bic Tran's real name in the Vietnamese crime ring story?"

"It's the name you had in galleys, Tess. You'd blocked out whatever name was there with a thick black marker, and wrote in the name 'Bic Tran' with a red pencil above. We figured 'Bic Tran' was the alias and we went with it."

"But that's impossible, Mike! I was very careful *never* to refer to Bic by his real name. I've got it right here on disk."

"Well, that's not what you put on galleys."

"Mike, this is very serious."

"Yeah, I know. We may be talking mega-lawsuit here."

"We may be talking the man's *life*."

"Shit."

"I put Bic in touch with a friend of mine in Houston, an ex-cop who's a private investigator," she said with a weary sigh. "He's going to help Bic vanish."

"Sort of like the Federal Witness Protection program?"

"Just like that."

"You think it'll work?"

"It has to, Mike. If anything happened to Bic I'd feel like a murderer."

The confrontation with her sister was considerably more difficult.

"You jacked around with my galleys before I mailed them

Deadline 171

in to the magazine, didn't you?" she asked over a cup of bitter black coffee.

"I don't even know what galleys are." Her sister turned a freezing glance her way, then turned back to the sink.

"Don't play dumb with me, Marah."

Marah said nothing.

Suddenly overcome with rage, Tess sprang to her feet, grabbed Marah by the shoulder, and spun her around. "Because of your little childish prank, a man could *die*," she hissed. "Do you understand that? He could *die*, just so you could have the satisfaction of seeing me squirm."

Marah knocked off Tess's hand and narrowed her eyes. When she spoke, the tone in her voice stunned Tess like a splash of ice-cold water in her face. "You ever touch me again," Marah said quietly, "I'll kill you."

"It was just a letter," said David Feldman when Tess was finally able to track him down at his New York offices, managed, even, to drag him away from a meeting.

"Was it handwritten?"

"Nope. Typed."

"On my usual computer printer script?"

"Hell, I don't know, Tess. I don't even have the letter anymore."

"Did I sign it?"

"Typed your name."

"You didn't think that was strange?"

"Yeah, I thought it was strange, but I'm used to strange behavior from you."

"Very funny." She grinned. "You're not going to let me forget that, are you?"

He laughed. "Well, I never received a telegram in Spanish before."

"Just because I'd been in Mexico for three months working on *Murder and Madness*—it was easy to forget to speak English."

"Yeah, like you forgot your deadline."

"What're you complaining about? I got it in six months early."

She knew he was smiling. Sometimes she did get forgetful

when she was working extra hard. Then his tone turned serious. "Hey—what's going on here?" he asked gently.

"I don't know," said Tess truthfully. "But I think someone may be trying to sabotage my work."

"That sounds crazy!"

"I know. But take my word for it."

"I can't imagine anybody wanting to do something like that to you, Tess."

"You'd be surprised. There seems to be a waiting list."

The state rested its case against Ross Chandler, former governor of Texas, for the murder of his wife, daughter, and granddaughter, without fanfare.

The defense's first witness, testifying reluctantly under subpoena, was Dr. Ellyn Frazier, therapist to the governor's granddaughter, Annie.

"Dr. Frazier, what was the purpose of your first consultation with Annie Mitchell?"

"I was called in by her attending physician as soon as it was ascertained that her muteness was not a physical disability, but a psychological one."

"And how soon after the fire were you first called in?"

"About a week after she emerged from the coma."

"How often did you meet with Annie?"

"At first, I went to see her every day. After she began talking, I dropped our sessions down to three times a week."

"And are you seeing her now?"

"Yes."

"How often?"

"Once a week."

"She seems to be speaking well enough now. Why do you keep seeing her?"

"Mr. Thornton, this child has endured a terrible trauma. She needs help coping with the grieving process."

"I see. Dr. Frazier, do you read the newspaper?"

"Sure."

"Watch TV news?"

"Of course."

"So, you had to be aware that Ross Chandler was under suspicion for the murders of his family, is that correct?"

"That's correct."

"It would be only human nature, then, wouldn't it, for you to take this prejudice with you into sessions with the child?"

"Human nature, possibly, but therapists must sometimes dissociate themselves from normal human response in order to be the most help to their patients."

"Do you expect the court to believe, Dr. Frazier, that you *never once* suggested, or even intimidated, to Annie that her grandfather could be responsible for what happened to her?"

"Never."

"And yet, it is my understanding that, when Annie first began to speak, she suffered from amnesia, isn't that true?"

"Regarding the night of the fire, that's true. She still doesn't remember how she got out of the house."

"How is it, then, that you were able to help her remember the events of that night?"

"Through hypnosis."

"*Objection!* Permission to approach the bench, Your Honor."

"Yes. Will both counsels please approach."

While the gallery buzzed, Tess was flabbergasted that a man of the experience of Cameron Thornton would let such a gaffe occur. The decision had already been made to disallow the hypnosis tapes as evidence. Now he had opened the door to allowing those very tapes by bringing the subject into testimony. The prosecutor could now argue vigorously to allow the tapes to be viewed by the jury after all.

She could see the judge shaking his head. After all, the hypnosis tapes were almost a moot point since Annie herself had testified. Besides, Tess could remember no leading questions on the part of the therapist. She wondered what the crafty defense lawyer had in mind.

She doubted that a man like Cameron Thornton really *would* make a big mistake for a client such as Ross Chandler. She watched as Charles Douglas leaned over and whispered into Chandler's ear. For the first time during the trial, a ghost of a grin played on Chandler's face.

When testimony resumed, no mention was made of the tapes.

• • •

"Dr. Frazier, you were explaining to us that you used hypnosis as a viable tool to trigger the child's memory of traumatic events."

"That's correct."

"And what is your professional opinion of hypnosis?"

"I believe it to be a powerful mechanism to unlock the subconscious and reveal secrets hidden from the conscious mind."

"So you believe that everything admitted under hypnosis is accurate and truthful?"

"I do."

"Isn't it true, though, that a number of individuals have given explicit detail—while under hypnosis—of experiences they supposedly endured after having been kidnapped by aliens in UFOs?"

"Well . . . not in *my* office."

"And isn't it true that many people spin long and colorful tales while under hypnosis of past lives they've lived, say two or three centuries ago? . . . Dr. Frazier?"

"Dr. Frazier, I'm afraid you must answer the question."

"Yes, but—"

"Do you believe in UFOs, Dr. Frazier?"

"No."

"Please speak up."

"No."

"Do you believe in reincarnation?"

"Not exactly."

"Then, do you think that the people who are under hypnosis are lying about those experiences that they claim to have had?"

"No."

"So then . . . is it possible that a hypnotic experience *could* actually be like an incredibly realistic dream . . . or even a nightmare?"

"I don't . . . know."

"Could it be that, under hypnosis, our subconscious could unravel a long, colorful story of *our worst fears*, rather than a *true and actual representation of fact*?"

"All I know is that I have used hypnosis with great success."

"But how do you *know*? Can you be absolutely *positive*

that what an individual reveals under a hypnotic trance is the final truth?"

"There are no absolutes when you are dealing with the human mind."

"Yes or no, Dr. Frazier?"

"Not absolutely positive, no."

"Dr. Frazier, isn't it true that some children have trouble separating fantasy from reality?"

"Some *very young* children, yes."

"But if, say, a child awakens in the middle of a horrible, but very believable, nightmare, and a close adult told that child that what he just dreamed was *real*, that child would believe that adult, wouldn't he?"

"It would depend on the child and the relationship."

"Yes or no, Dr. Frazier."

"I can't give you yeses and nos!"

"Then let's take a hypothetical situation, shall we? A child, severely traumatized by a life-altering situation, awakens badly injured to discover that he or *she* has just lost his or *her* entire support system—his whole family, practically, is dead—and a kind, grandmotherly sort of lady visits this child *every day*, building up the trust of this grieving child . . . Let's say that, upon awakening from a hypnotic trance, this child is told by this trusted woman that the nightmare visions the child saw while in a trance are *true*, wouldn't that child then *believe* what this trusted adult says?"

"I suppose so."

"Is that a yes?"

"Yes!"

"What if that adult, say, *believed* in UFOs?"

"What are you asking me?"

"I'm asking that, if the adult believed in UFOs, and this child claimed under hypnotic trance to have been kidnapped by a UFO, then the adult would encourage this child to believe the truth of that trance, wouldn't she?"

"You're twisting this all around. That's not the way it happened."

"Yes or no, Dr. Frazier."

"Yes, but—"

"No further questions."

• • •

"State your name, please."

"Booker Washington Smith, M.D."

"And what is your occupation?"

"I am a consulting forensic pathologist."

"Before you became a consultant, where were you employed and what was your position?"

"I was deputy chief medical examiner for the city of New York."

"And how long were you employed in that position?"

"Nineteen years."

"During your tenure as deputy chief medical examiner in New York City, how many autopsies did you perform in which the manner of death was listed as homicide?"

"I'd say the number runs into the thousands."

"And how many fire-related deaths did your office investigate during that same period of time?"

"Again, I'd have to say thousands."

"Dr. Smith, have you had an opportunity to study the autopsy reports prepared by the Southwest Institute of Forensic Sciences on the bodies of Libby Chandler, Amanda Mitchell, and Jenny Mitchell?"

"I have."

"And do you concur with the findings of your colleagues?"

"In the method of death, I do concur that the two adults died of smoke inhalation and carbon monoxide poisoning. However, I do not agree with the finding of blunt trauma on any of the three victims, and I believe the child also died of carbon monoxide poisoning before she had the chance to inhale smoke."

"Are you saying that none of the victims was struck in the head by a blunt instrument?"

"By studying postmortem photographs and examining the toxicological studies and other findings, I believe the fractured skulls were caused by heat hematoma."

"Could you refresh the court's memory, Dr. Smith, as to the definition of heat hematoma? In layman's terms, please."

"The intense heat from the fire causes the brain to expand, pushing onward on the skull with enough pressure to actually split or fracture it. Sometimes it even resembles an explosion."

"For the sake of our more sensitive jurors, Doctor, would you please reassure us on one matter: do the victims feel any pain?"

"Oh, no. This usually occurs long after the death—or at least the deep unconsciousness—of the victims. They feel nothing."

"Dr. Smith, if you had performed these autopsies, what would have been your findings as to manner of death?"

"I would have ruled these deaths as accidental."

CHAPTER TWENTY-FOUR

THE BLARE OF the jukebox made an effective cloak for Tess and Dr. Ellyn Frazier. They sat at a back booth of a highway truck stop outside Remington, dissecting the day's events, while men with lined faces and long sideburns cracked jokes with the thick-waisted waitress and a loud cash register rang up payment for food that would give a cardiologist nightmares: ham and eggs, fat juicy burgers, onion rings, steaming bowls of chile, sweet pie, and coffee.

Tess poked at a huge fluffy slab of coconut cream pie. It looked delicious, but she realized, idly, that she could not remember the last time she'd been truly hungry. She was even having trouble remembering having eaten. Dr. Frazier had given her a long interview on her involvement with Annie Mitchell, being careful not to reveal the particulars of any of Annie's sessions, but giving thoughtful, generous information on her impressions of the child and her belief that what Annie saw in hypnosis is what happened the night her mother, sister, and grandmother died.

"Do you think there's a valid point to what Thornton was saying about hypnosis?" Tess asked her.

"Reluctantly, yes. I have to admit that he does have a point." Frazier sponged up apple pie crumbs off her plate with her fork. "But I think you have to take into consideration the qualifications of the therapist, the mental state of the patient, and the subject matter of the session, as well as the reactions of the patient while under hypnosis to what he or she sees."

"Can hypnosis work, say, with memories that have been

suppressed for many, many years?" Tess avoided looking into the kind doctor's eyes.

"Absolutely. In fact, hypnosis is often the only way those memories will ever be released."

"And what if . . . the patient . . . doesn't really want to remember?" The restaurant seemed suddenly to be very warm, the sounds of the music muffled.

Dr. Frazier studied Tess's face before answering. "We're not talking about Annie anymore, are we?"

Tess began smushing up her pie with her fork. "No."

"Powerful unconscious memories can influence everything we do in life: our reactions to others, our intimate relationships with the opposite sex, even our physical health. It can be like a festering wound that can infect the entire body. Only when that wound is lanced, drained of all the unhealthy cells, and treated can the body begin to heal."

Tess chopped the pie slice into smithereens. "Won't the infection just clear up on its own?"

"No. It can cause a sort of mental blood poisoning, so to speak. Even death."

The therapist's voice seemed to be coming from someplace far away. Sweat broke out on Tess's forehead. Her mouth was dry, and when she reached for some ice water, it sloshed over onto the plastic tablecloth.

Dr. Frazier placed a warm hand over Tess's own. "Tess, why don't you come in and see me in my office? I think I can help you."

"I thought you just worked with kids." Tess looked in wonderment at her demolished pie.

"I'd be happy to make an exception in your case."

"Maybe sometime." Tess wiped sweaty hands on a paper napkin. "I'm so busy with the trial and this book. Maybe when the trial's over . . ."

She didn't want to admit just how terrified she was of her own memories. If the dreams and sleepwalking were any indication of the secrets hidden deep within Tess—like seeing a shadow before a person steps out from behind a wall—then Tess didn't think she could handle confronting the cause of that shadow face-to-face.

Dr. Frazier patted her hand, gave her a wise look, and began gathering her things. "Well, I still have to drive back to Lubbock, and I've got a full day tomorrow." She pushed a loose strand of gray hair behind her ear.

"I really appreciate all your help. The book just wouldn't be complete without your input."

"Well, I'd probably make a better impression if I hadn't made such a fool of myself on the stand today." She gave Tess a wry, twinkle-eyed smile, looking more like a grandmother than a shrink.

Tess shrugged. "Defense posturing. Don't be surprised if Frank Baxter hauls in some expert on hypnosis when Thornton's through. He may even convince the judge to allow those tapes after all. If the jury could see that poor child . . ." Her voice broke and she swallowed. She seemed to have no objectivity whatsoever where Annie was concerned.

Dr. Frazier got to her feet, hesitated, then pulled out a business card. On the back, she jotted down a number. "This is my home number," she said, handing the card to Tess. "It's unlisted and I don't use a service with this number. If you ever feel like you are ready to talk, you call me *anytime*."

"Why, thank you. I probably wouldn't disturb you at home, though."

"If I minded, I wouldn't give you the number." With a final, knowing smile, the therapist left.

For a long time, Tess sat, staring at the card. Finally she stuffed it into her wallet and turned to look out the big plate-glass window beside the booth. It was very dark out. Tess glanced at her watch, but it had stopped. Had the battery gone out on it, too?

They'd arrived at the truck stop during the dinner hour, when the lot was full. Tess's car was parked out of the range of the tall yellow lights ringing the building. She could see the behemoth trucks hulking in a distant row.

Bad memories were a festering wound, Dr. Frazier had said.

Tess focused on her own reflection, staring back at her with huge hollow eyes, but the person she saw in the window was a stranger to her.

Weariness dogged Tess's steps as she crossed the long parking lot of the truck stop to her car. Her mind was numbed with fatigue so profound it seemed as if she were disembodied, watching herself do the necessary things like walk and drive. The interview with Ellyn Frazier had left her emotionally exhausted, mostly, she knew, because of the last five minutes of the conversation.

Even *discussing* Tess's past, just *thinking* about discussing it, seized at her chest like a vise grip, compressing it until she thought she might suffocate.

Let sleeping dogs lie, Sophia had said.

She also had said that Tess had brought evil to the house at one time.

Evil.

Maybe now the evil is inside you, came a voice from deep within.

She stopped at the car door, hands shaking, and fumbled for her keys. She hadn't locked the car—it was seldom necessary in a small town. It was so dark she had to feel for them within her bag. After a clumsy grapple, she dropped them to the pavement and stooped over to pick them up.

Suddenly Tess felt a thud, as if someone's fist were striking her from behind. Her knees buckled. At the same time, she heard what sounded like the crinkling of paper. Something seemed to be tugging at her back. Reaching her right hand underneath her left arm and back around as far as she could, Tess felt, unbelievably, first a piece of paper and then the handle of a knife, protruding straight out of her back.

Her hand came away hot and sticky.

The breath seemed to go out of her in a whoosh, whether from shock or the injury, and when she tried to breathe again, a hot poker seemed to stab straight through to her side, and the breath, when it came, was shallow. Nausea roiled in her stomach.

Desperately, still on her knees on the hard pavement, she twisted from side to side to see if she could see anyone. Were those footsteps she heard, running away? There was a hollow roaring in her ears. She strained toward that direction to see someone, *anyone*, who could have attacked her. There were clusters of cars here and there, closer toward the building . . . could he be hiding amongst them?

This can't be happening to me. A quavering rush of pain and nausea rolled through her disbelief, followed by a wave of disorientation. She had to get help. Peering toward the building, which seemed exaggeratedly far away now, she thought dully, *I'll never make it*.

For the first time in her life, it occurred to Tess that she might be going to die. It was a feeling, more than a thought, a hazy sort of aura on the periphery of her fluttery panicked thoughts. Part of her didn't accept the feeling—couldn't, really—but part of her flirted with it, considered it, weighed it. It was getting harder and harder for her to breathe, and she knew she was bleeding.

Her life didn't "flash before her eyes," as she'd always heard about. Rather, sad regret at all the things still left undone in her life pierced her. She had never held a child of her own in her arms. Had never, even, committed herself to any one man permanently.

Strange that her work had always had such a high priority in her life; had, in fact, been everything to her. And yet all those magazine and newspaper articles were mere fodder for the incinerator. Even her books could hardly be expected to attain the literary legacy of a Shakespeare or a Thoreau. But to come to the end of her life without love was almost unendurable.

She coughed; tasted blood. Pain clenched her chest. She cried out, hoping someone, somehow, would hear her, but the only sound which emerged from her lips was a weak kittenish mew. Blackness closed in on her peripheral vision.

No. Please. Help.

Then the blackness was total. She didn't even feel herself slump to the pavement.

The high-pitched sound of a horn pierced her consciousness. Gradually Tess became aware that it was her own car horn. She awoke to find herself half in, half out of the automobile, which was careened crazily onto the lawn of a house.

For a moment, she did not know whose house, and for the life of her, she did not know how she had come to be here.

"Tess! Oh my God, Tess!" Then she knew.

It was so much easier to be unconscious, and it didn't last nearly long enough. Tess opened her eyes to Ethan's frantic face and almost unimaginable pain. He was pulling her from the car, where he stretched her out on the grass on her side.

Deadline   183

Though Tess hazily recalled that Ethan's house was located only a mile or so down the road from the truck stop, she still had no idea how she had managed to drive herself there.

"Can you hear me? What happened? Who did this to you? Oh God."

His voice drifted away and she closed her eyes. It was too much trouble to think. She didn't even care anymore how she had gotten here. All that mattered was that she had.

Screaming sirens were the next thing Tess noticed. There was lots of confusion around her, and something fitted over her face that she tried to take off.

"Punctured lung," someone said. "We'll let the doctors remove the knife."

"What the hell is this?" asked someone else.

"It's a fucking *murder* note." Ethan's voice. "I haven't exactly taken the time to read it all yet."

"Jesus."

"I'll take care of Josh." A woman's voice. "You go on. We'll just keep him overnight. I'll get him to school, don't worry."

Her body was manhandled and she groaned.

"I'm right here, sweetheart. I'm not going to leave you." A big, strong hand took hers and she gave it a little squeeze. She wanted to tell him something very important, but she couldn't remember what it was.

Time was suspended, passing by in a slow-motion, surreal blur. None of it seemed to be really happening: the race to the hospital, the stone-faced doctors and nurses, the deafening rush of pain when the knife was removed, Ethan's distant voice, the tubes and machines, the warm, welcome, wonderful blur when the drugs took effect and, at long last, there was no more pain.

She opened her eyes. Sunlight streamed through a venetian-blind-slatted window and backlit the big man prone in a chair next to the bed, his head thrown back, arms hanging limp, legs akimbo. She smiled at him, then grimaced. Her whole upper torso ached, and breathing, while easier now, still hurt.

Tess was lying on her right side, and when she started to roll over on her back, she almost cried out and bit her lip to keep from waking Ethan. Her back was heavily bandaged.

An IV dripped from an overhead bottle into the back of her left hand, which felt leaden and heavy when she tried to lift it.

She decided to stay where she was.

Ethan shifted position uncomfortably, adjusted his body, then opened his eyes, looking straight into hers. "You're awake!" He sat up, put his elbows on his knees, and rubbed his eyes with the palms of his hands. Then he reached out and closed his big hand over her limp right one. She squeezed his hand and he folded both hands over hers.

"How do you feel?"

"Like hell." She smiled.

"You don't know how lucky you are. A few millimeters and that knife might have done some *real* damage."

"Thank you—" Her voice caught. "For taking care of me."

"I want you to tell me everything that happened."

She started to heave a sigh, thought better of it, and nodded. "Okay."

She told him about the attack.

He shook his head. "No. I want *everything*."

"I don't know what you mean." She glanced away.

Ethan reached inside a jacket pocket and withdrew a Ziploc bag. Inside the bag was a crumpled, blood-smeared piece of paper with a bloody slash in the middle and words written on it in block printing.

"Tess, I want you to read this note, and then I want you to tell me *everything*." He handed her the bag.

Adjusting her position painfully, Tess forced herself to read what was written on the note; and though her heart was filled with dread, it in no way prepared her for this:

Who saw her die?
"I," said the fly,
"With my little eye,
I saw her die."

Who caught her blood?
"I," said the fish,
"With my little dish,
I caught her blood."

Who'll make her shroud?
"I," said the beetle.
"With my thread and needle,
I'll make her shroud."

Who'll dig her grave?
"I," said the owl.
"With my spade and trowel,
I'll dig her grave."

CHAPTER TWENTY-FIVE

"It's a nursery rhyme," she said stupidly. "I think they changed it."

"How do you know? Changed it how?"

"I don't know for sure. It's been a long time since I've read nursery rhymes, but I think this is a poem about the death of Cock Robin. Cock Robin is a he, not a she." She closed her eyes.

"Tess, have you ever seen this before?"

She opened her eyes. Ethan was holding out another Ziploc bag. This one contained a mean-looking knife with a wooden handle—darkened and sticky-looking with blood—and a curved, bloodstained, serrated blade about five inches long. She shook her head and stared, fascinated.

"We couldn't get any prints except from your own hand, which was bloody when you grabbed the knife. The assailant was probably wearing gloves." He stuffed the bag with the knife back into his roomy inside jacket pocket. "This is kind of an all-purpose knife. I mean, it's not necessarily a hunting knife. It could even be a kitchen knife." He leaned forward. "Now, talk to me."

Defeated, she looked around the room. "Where's my purse?"

"Over there, in the closet. Why?"

"You'll find some more poems in it."

"You mean, you've gotten some more of these?" He got up and went around the bed to the closet, retrieving Tess's tote bag from an inside hook. "Why didn't you tell me?"

"I didn't consider them dangerous. Just annoying."

He dug around in the bag. "My God, woman. You've got a whole office in here."

"I use it when I'm working."

"Okay. Here they are." He withdrew the notes carefully, holding them by the corners. "Are they in order?"

"Yes."

After he'd scanned the rhymes, she told him when and where she'd received them.

He shook his head. "This is really weird." After producing another plastic bag from a pocket, he slid the notes inside it. "We'll check for prints. Probably won't have much luck, considering the wear and tear they've endured since you got them." He gave her an accusing look and pocketed the notes. "Why nursery rhymes? And why you? What's going on here?"

"I wish I knew."

"Who do you think could be doing this? Maybe if we started there, we might have a better idea as to why they might be doing it."

She was silent. She didn't really want to discuss any of the possibilities that had occurred to her. The governor? She had no proof. Her father? *Let sleeping dogs lie.* Marah? Did she really want Molly and Cody's mother to go to jail?

"I don't really have any idea," she said finally.

He gave her a long, doubtful look. "You know, in the law enforcement business, when something like this happens, we always start with family."

She rolled over on her back, stifled a cry, and looked away from him.

"I've been thinking about something you told me," Ethan persisted. "It didn't register at the time but it occurred to me later. You said that Ross Chandler had rented an apartment for Bunni under the name of Rex Alexander. Did you know a Rex Alexander?"

She squeezed shut her eyes. "Yes," she said. "I knew him." And then, against her will, a long, cold shudder shook her body.

The door whooshed open. Marah stood there. "Oh, Tess." Her posture was awkward, and she held a small overnight case in her hand. "Ethan called me," she said with a nod in his direction. "I couldn't come until Sophia could take care of Mama."

Tess nodded. "It's okay, really."

Marah approached the bed. "Are you all right?"

"I'll be fine."

Her sister gave her an awkward hug and set the bag on the floor. "I brought you some things. A gown, toothbrush, you know."

"Thank you." Tess glanced at Ethan. He was watching them with an unreadable expression in his eyes. "How's Mama?"

"The same. *Tess*, what happened?"

Tess shrugged, then gasped. Each little movement extracted a price. "I guess I got mugged."

"It was a little more than that," put in Ethan.

"What do you mean?"

"We'll talk later." He did not show Marah the note or the knife.

Although Ethan was an attractive man, Tess noticed that Marah made no attempt to flirt with him; in fact, she seemed uncomfortable in his presence, nervous, even.

Marah shifted her weight from one foot to the other. "The doctor said it was a close call."

"I guess so." To Tess's surprise, Marah took her hand. "I don't know what I'd do if anything happened to you," she said quietly.

"Probably rejoice." It was out before Tess even thought, and even though she meant it as a joke, Marah's lips stiffened and she let go of Tess's hand. Tess wanted to take back the remark, but she didn't know how.

Marah turned away from her and asked Ethan, "Did they c-catch the guy yet?" He seemed to intimidate her.

Ethan shook his head.

"I couldn't give them a description at all," explained Tess. "It happened so fast, and it was so dark. I guess I was in shock—I just didn't see anything, really. Pretty pathetic for a crime writer." She attempted a smile, then cried, "Oh, no! The trial! What am I going to do?"

Cowboys had a term for projects that didn't seem to go well from the beginning and only got worse as time went on. They called it "snakebit." It seemed to Tess that the book, the trial, indeed her whole life, seemed snakebit. She brought her right hand up to her eyes.

"That trial should be the last worry on your mind," scolded Ethan. "You just concentrate on getting healed."

"I *can't* miss the final days of testimony, Ethan. Not to mention closing statements."

"Don't you work from a trial transcript?"

"Later, yes. But I want to *be* there."

"Well, you can't, that's all." In any other situation, the masculine finality of his statement would have made her laugh.

She chewed on a bottom lip. "Do you think you could find a spectator who wouldn't mind taping it for me, maybe giving me a few impressions of the day?"

"I'll talk to the editor of the *Remington News*. I'm sure he'd be happy to help you any way he could."

"Tess?"

They both looked at Marah.

"Maybe you shouldn't write this book." She licked her lips. "I mean, maybe this is a warning."

"What do you mean?" Ethan's voice was sharp.

"Well . . . they didn't kill her, did they? It just seems to me that if they wanted to kill her, she'd be dead, right?"

No one answered.

Marah looked directly into Tess's eyes. "If it were me, I'd back off."

But I'm not you, thought Tess, *and I don't back off*.

"I'm going to run a computer check on your dad," said Ethan after Marah left.

"Don't call him that."

"What?"

"My dad."

"That's what he is, isn't he?"

"No. He's *Rex*. That's all."

Ethan sat down again and took Tess's hand. "Tell me about him."

"He was a bastard. He's gone. Hopefully dead." She closed her eyes.

"C'mon, Tess."

"I don't like to talk about him!" she cried. "Ouch."

"You're going to have to, anyway."

"Please. Not now."

He sighed. "All right. I can see how tired you are and how much you're hurting. I'm going to leave you now so you can rest. I'll be back later." He got to his feet.

Suddenly she clutched at his hand. "Don't leave me."

He leaned down and kissed her tenderly. "I've got to. I have some things to check out. Besides, I need to grab that editor before trial begins this morning, right?"

She nodded reluctantly. "Right." She shivered.

"You cold?" He fretted with the blankets.

Down deep in my soul, she thought.

He kissed her again. "I'll be back," he whispered, and walked out, leaving a huge vacancy in his wake.

The pain was getting worse and beginning to throb, but Tess did not request any medication. A drug-induced sleep would make her much more vulnerable, should the parking lot phantom decide to bring her any more messages.

"State your name, please."

"Sam Dickens."

"And your occupation, Mr. Dickens?"

"I was lieutenant governor of the state of Texas. I resigned that position in order to devote full-time to the gubernatorial campaign. I am currently involved in a runoff election for the Democratic nomination."

"Do you know Ross Chandler?"

"I certainly do. I have served with him in government, and we have known one another for many years. I consider it an honor to know Ross Chandler and be considered his friend."

"Do you remember the night of October 24, 1990?"

"Indeed I do. I was attending a fund-raiser in my honor at the Holiday Inn in Odessa."

"Did you see the former governor, Ross Chandler, at that fund-raiser?"

"He sat right next to me at the dais. I'm sure his presence had a great deal to do with the amount of money we were able to raise that night. Mr. Chandler is well thought of in this state, particularly in his home area of West Texas."

"What time did the fund-raiser end that night?"

"Oh, 'bout nine, nine-thirty."

"And when was the last time you saw the governor?"

"Ross went back to my room with me that night. We had a drink and talked about old times. He left sometime after ten."

"So you were personally with Ross Chandler until past ten P.M. on the evening of October 24?"

"I was. No doubt about it."

"Mr. Dickens, have you ever been a guest in the ranch home of Ross Chandler, near Remington?"

"I have."

"How far would you say the ranch is located from Odessa?"

"If you drove like a bat out of hell and didn't meet any po-lice along the way, it'd still take you at least an hour to get there."

"No further questions."

"State your name, please."

"Bobby Williams."

"And your occupation?"

"I work for the Remington Fire Department."

"Were you on duty on the night of October 24, 1990?"

"I was."

"Could you tell us the time when the call first came in from the Ross Chandler car phone?"

"It was eleven-fifteen P.M."

"Do you remember who placed the call?"

"Yes, I do. And we have it on tape, too. It was Ross Chandler."

"Are you sure?"

"No question."

"Do you remember what he said?"

"Objection!"

"Shows state of mind, Your Honor."

"Overruled."

"What did Ross Chandler say when he called in the fire?"

"He said, 'Please help me. My house is on fire and my wife is inside. Please hurry.' "

"How did Mr. Chandler sound to you?"

"He sounded hysterical."

"Thank you. That will be all."

"State your name, please."

"Preston Havery, M.D."

"What is your occupation?"

"I am a physician."

"Did you have emergency room duty at the Remington hospital on the night of October 24, 1990?"

"I did."

"Could you explain for the court the condition of Ross Chandler when he arrived at the emergency room?"

"He was in shock. There were first-degree burns on his hands and lower arms, plus some abrasions and a bruise on his head."

"Did he say anything about his family?"

"Objection."

"Overruled."

"Yes. He kept saying, 'Are they all dead? Are they all dead?' He kept resisting medical care and trying to get up or get away from us. He was completely hysterical. We had to sedate him."

"Thank you, Doctor. No further questions."

Tess pushed the "stop" button on the tape recorder and stared up at the corner of the night-shrouded hospital ceiling. A nurse passed down the hall, her rubber-soled shoes squeaking on the polished floor. Otherwise, the hospital slept.

All except for Tess.

She lay on her side, refusing all pain medication, her back pulsating so hard her chest hurt, and listened to the tapes the newspaper editor had brought her. Listened over and over, trying to drown out the sound of Ross Chandler's voice saying to her, *"I'm innocent."*

Doubts, Tess found, could sometimes scream louder than pain.

CHAPTER TWENTY-SIX

"I HAD A little talk with your sister," said Ethan, settling his big body into the too-small chair next to Tess's bed. Until Ethan arrived, Tess had spent the day wallowing in despondency, feeling helpless and victimized about every situation in her life, but too sore and exhausted to know how or where she could begin to take control. Just seeing him walk through the door, though, had renewed her energy and given her hope.

That is, until he mentioned Marah. "It was a very revealing conversation," he added.

"I'm sure it was," Tess snapped. "Marah never did know when to keep her mouth shut."

His smile was patient. "Now, see? That kind of remark from you doesn't surprise me at all. Oh, it would have yesterday, but today, I spoke to Marah."

"Great. Let's call a national holiday."

"My, my, aren't we testy today?" He gave her a mock-patronizing pat on the hand. She jerked it away. He chuckled. "So the two of you don't get along. Through my superb investigatory skills, you see, I'd already figured that out."

"What'd she tell you?" Tess wasn't just curious; she was worried. Marah was a talker, and not everything that came out of her mouth was, as Cameron Thornton would say, a true and actual representation of fact.

"For starters, she told me your mom has Alzheimer's, and it's getting much worse recently." He leaned forward and forced her to look into his eyes. "You could have told me that yourself, you know. It's nothing to be ashamed of."

I'm not ashamed, she thought, *I'm terrified.*

"And she told me you beat the crap out of her the other day."

"She *told* you that? I can't believe it."

"And that you're always on her case."

"I am not."

"She says you accused her of messing with one of your articles and getting a guy in trouble. Is this true?"

"It's true she did it. There's no other way those galleys could have been changed."

Ethan rubbed his chin. "Tell me about it."

She did.

"This guy could be another suspect, you know. Getting revenge on you for screwing up his life."

"Bic would never do that." She adjusted her position with a painful grimace.

"He might. If he was desperate enough. I'm going to check it out, anyway." He cocked his head at her. "This is just a question. Don't get pissed off or anything. But do you think your sister would be capable of hurting you this way?"

Tess started to say, *Damn right*, thought of Molly and Cody, and said nothing.

He watched her a moment, then said, "Tell me again where you found the notes, and when."

When she mentioned the first note, found beneath the windshield wiper on her car in the courthouse parking lot, he said, "Do you have any way of knowing whether Marah could have been in Remington that day?"

Tess remembered seeing Marah in the pickup at the Dairy Queen parking lot, backing up, looking right at her. Still, she said nothing.

He pretended not to notice her reticence. "Okay. You found the next note in the mailbox. Had it been mailed?"

"No. It was just stuffed into the mailbox," she said. "Anyone driving down the road could have done it."

"True. So could anyone living at the ranch. What about Sophia or Juan? Any problems with them?"

Tess's stitches from the knife wound in her back felt tight and hot. "Why are you interrogating me?" she said irritably.

"Tess." His voice was gentle. "I'm not interrogating you. But someone tried to kill you. Someone has been harassing you and threatening you. I'm trying to *help* you here. You might still be in danger."

"Marah and I don't get along, that's true," she said, thinking, *She hates me*, "but she's my sister. She would never do anything violent to me."

Ethan's eyes were sad as he shook his head. "Honey," he said, "I wish I had a quarter for every time I've heard a grieving family member say just that, right after a domestic shooting or stabbing. I'd be a rich man."

That night, Tess listened to the tapes of Dr. Smith, forensic pathologist from New York, admit under Frank Baxter's careful rebuttal examination that no, he had never examined the bodies of the three victims; he had only studied the autopsy reports prepared by the Dallas team; and that yes, a blunt blow to the skull could be much more readily proved by studying firsthand the concave fracture of bone, and the fragments embedded in the brain, which was considerably different from the outward skull fracture caused by heat hematoma. And yes, he had performed autopsies during his career which had been overturned by a second, independent study of the bodies. And that yes, he was being paid a great deal of money for his testimony.

Was it the *swish* of jean-clad legs walking away that woke her, or the soft *whoosh* of the door closing, or perhaps sneaker soles treading with sinister secrecy on the immaculate floor? Tess's eyes flew open and she was at once atingle and fully awake.

All of the lights in the room, save a small one over her bed, were off. Struggling to one elbow, Tess peered through sleep-grained eyes into shadow-draped corners. Nothing. Maybe it was a dream, then, and nothing real at all.

Although the IV had been disconnected, Tess was still quite uncomfortable. There was no position in which she could rest that did not tug at her wound and send tentacles of pain crawling through her ribs. She spent a lot of time awake and when she slept, her rest was fitful, dream-tossed, and episodic. Interruptions from nurses compounded the situation, so that she actually felt more tired than when she first arrived. Still stubborn about pain medication, she had relented to taking Tylenol, but was getting little relief from it.

With a soft moan, she managed to sit up and reach for her water pitcher to get a drink. It was empty. She'd been so thirsty, it seemed, feverish. The doctors, murmuring about infection, had her on a stiff regimen of antibiotics. Regarding the pitcher with a frustrated expression, Tess knew she could call a nurse for more water, but it seemed like a lot of trouble. Besides, she had to go to the bathroom, anyway. She'd refill the pitcher from the sink.

Easing herself gingerly to the floor, testing her weight, Tess moved slowly and uncertainly toward the bathroom, clinging to things for support. She hated the weakness, it seemed, much worse than the situation which had provoked it.

In the bathroom, she snapped on the flickering fluorescent light and stooped over the sink to refill the pitcher. Ice would be so nice, she reflected dully, but surely the overworked, underpaid night nurses had better things to do with their time. Her eyes burned and her mouth was dry.

Setting the refilled pitcher on the back of the toilet, she leaned over the sink and splashed cool water into her face and eyes, straightened, reached for a towel, and froze.

In the mirror over the sink, block-printed in bloodred marker, were the lines:

As I walked by myself,
And talked to myself,
Myself said unto me:
"Look to thyself,
Take care of thyself,
For nobody cares for thee."

Cool, wet grass under her feet did nothing to put out the fire that raged through Tess's body. A power drill bored through her back, pulsated into her chest, and throbbed through her shoulders and neck. Still, she put one foot in front of the other. Step. Step. Step, step away. Get away. Get away.

Like the rhythm of a boot camp drill, the refrain beat through her brain. Grass gave way to slick pavement but still she kept going away. Moist, dark wind pressed its body seductively against her, kissing her face and caressing her hair. It felt good, but her teeth began to chatter, anyway.

Away get away. Away get away.

With a wrench to her ankle she stepped off a curb, cried out, and kept going. Something fat and wet struck her head, then again, then again and again and again. A shower of cool water drenched her body and put out the fire and then she was so, so very *cold*, cold like a corpse.

Away get away. Away get away.

A cold cloak of darkness wrapped itself around her and gave no comfort. Something sharp bit into her bare foot but she did not slow down. Violent shivering made her stagger but she did not stop, no, she did not stop for anything.

Away get away. Away get away.

With her soaked gown stuck to her body, she began to slosh through ankle-high water. Following it like the River Styx, she continued into the cloying shroud of black, hugging herself with cold fingers, mumbling to herself little nonsense words that came out of her own mouth and yet did not register in her brain.

Away get away. Away get away.

Water streamed off her long bedraggled hair and pooled in the cleavage of her breasts. The drill bored through her back, cracked against her breastbone, and went to work on her lungs. The fire blazed up again, converting her own body into a boiling cauldron so hot that steam began to rise from her skin.

"The burning hosts of hell itself live inside you," said a voice. *"Evil, lying murderer."*

She put her hands over her ears.

Away get away. Away get away.

The voice was deep and low and sounded familiar, but ancient and far away. Who spoke with a voice like that? And when had she heard those words before?

Her toe cracked hard against something and she went down. Her back ripped open, shooting flames into the night so bright the whole world lit up.

Away get away. *Away get away!*

She started to crawl.

Flames rose higher out of her body, bright yellow smokeless flames.

She heard another voice. "What's the matter, lady? Did you get hit by a car? Good Lord, Edith, look at her."

"She's wearing a hospital band on her wrist. It's just about a half a mile away, Harold. Let's take her to the emergency room."

"She might be dangerous. Maybe we should call the police."

"Oh, for heaven's sake, Harold, does she *look* dangerous? She's burning up with fever and soaked to the bone from the rain. *Hurry!* Help me with her. What's your name, honey? Hmmm? Can you tell me your name? Hold the door open, Harold."

"Oh my God—there's blood all over her back."

"Would you just help me here? Can you do that?"

"The fire. You'll get burned."

"What did you say, honey? What'd she say, Harold?"

"How do I know? Oof."

"You're going to have to help us, honey. That's a girl. We're going to take you back to the hospital."

"No! No!" She wanted to struggle, tried to struggle, but her body was just too weak. Didn't they understand? Couldn't they *see*? She had to get away! Her teeth began to chatter so hard her jaw ached. Black dots swarmed in front of her eyes.

Smoke from the fire, probably. Couldn't they see it? Couldn't they feel the *heat*?

The jaws of hell clamped onto her back and chest and began to chew with shark teeth.

"You poor, poor child. What on earth were you doing out in the rain like that? Did you wander off? You're just *on fire*."

They *could* feel the heat!

"We're almost there. *Don't hit those speed bumps so hard, Harold!* She's torn open a wound of some kind. What's your name, my dear?"

Through rattling teeth, Tess heard herself say, "Theresa."

Then all the black dots swarmed together like a cave full of bats, and there was no more light.

CHAPTER TWENTY-SEVEN

". . . INTRAVENOUS ANTIBIOTICS . . . she's not responding to medication by mouth . . ."

". . . morphine . . ."

". . . keep her sedated . . ."

". . . What the hell *happened* here? Somebody must have got to her. Have you seen the bathroom mirror? . . ."

". . . *mi pequeña niña* . . ."

". . . Is she going to die? . . ."

Tess opened her eyes. Sophia was sitting in the chair by her bed, reading a *National Enquirer*. "Can I have a drink of water?" she asked.

As if someone had goosed her, Sophia started, dropped the paper, peered at Tess, and broke into a beaming smile. "Sure you can, *mi pequeña niña*."

"I'm not your little baby."

"Then what are these rails doing on the side of your bed?" Still grinning, she poured Tess a drink and helped her sip, then gulp it. She was impossibly thirsty. And hungry. "Is it time for breakfast?" she asked.

"*Breakfast?* It's eight o'clock at night, *niña*." She leaned forward. "Do you know what day it is?"

Tess stared at her old friend. "I have no idea."

"Do you remember leavin' the hospital in the middle of the night in your gown and wanderin' down the road in the rain?"

Tess gaped. "I did that?"

"You really don't remember?"

Tess shook her head.

"And these nice people saw you on the side of the road and they picked you up and brought you back to the hospital. You don't remember any of it?"

Tess blinked.

"You told them your name was Theresa. Since that name got put on your birth certificate, I never heard anybody call you that." She shook her head. "You been unconscious for two days." Reaching out to squeeze Tess's arm, she added, "We thought we were gonna lose you for a while there, *niña*. You had a bad infection, and you busted open your stitches, too." She tsk-tsked.

"It doesn't hurt too bad," said Tess, round-eyed. How could she not remember *any* of it?

"I guess not. They had you so doped up I thought they'd kill you with drugs." She shook her head. "You was delirious with the fever. It got up to a hundred and seven, I heard. They put all these ice cubes around you in the bed." Gathering up her massive black plastic purse, she said, "I'm gonna go down to the snack bar and get you something to eat, *niña*. I'll call your sister, too. She's been worried sick about you."

I'll bet.

Laying her weary head back on the pillows, Tess knew there was something very, very important that she should be remembering. She strained to recall through the clouds in her head, but it was too much effort. Exhausted, she closed her eyes.

By the time Sophia had returned with the food, Tess was asleep.

"How ya doin'?" Ethan's kiss was tender, his face worry-lined.

"Much better. It still hurts, but I made them quit doping me up with morphine."

"Sophia says you don't remember anything about that night."

She shook her head.

"You don't even remember the note?"

"What note?" A little needle of fear pricked her heart.

"There was another poem, written on your bathroom mirror with a red marker."

"What did it say?"

He withdrew a photograph from his shirt pocket and showed it to her.

The needle went deeper. "Oh my God," she whispered.

"If you don't remember the note, then I don't guess it does any good to ask you if you saw anyone who could have left it, does it?"

She raised her hands, palms up.

"I've talked to the night nurses. They've just had a major turnover. Two quit, and one was sick that night. There was only one nurse to take care of the whole floor and she was away from the desk more often than not. That's why you were able to wander out without her seeing you. There's an exit door just down the hall, and this is a first-floor room. Probably didn't take you five minutes to vanish. She hadn't even missed you when they brought you in to emergency."

"I'm so sorry I worried everyone, Ethan. I can't imagine what got into me."

"You kept saying you needed to get away. I think you may have caught a glimpse of the person who left the note, and it scared you so bad you just took off."

"You'd think I'd remember a thing like that."

"That high fever made mashed potatoes out of your brain. It's a wonder you didn't come out of it with brain damage, seriously." He leaned forward, locking gazes with her. His eyes had never been more earnest. "I've been trying to track down Rex Alexander, Tess. Now, don't freak out on me or anything, but he's still alive. He gave a bogus address on his driver's license, but that was some time ago. We think he may be using an alias now."

More needles of fear pincushioned her heart. "What do you mean, 'bogus'?"

"It's a vacant lot. I had a Ranger in Dallas check it out for me."

"He lives in Dallas, then?"

"Not necessarily. The address is fake, you see." Shifting his weight, he glanced away from her.

"There's more, isn't there?"

He nodded, then said reluctantly, "There's an outstanding warrant out on him. It's an old one. He's wanted in connection with a stabbing in El Paso." He cleared his throat. "It was a woman. Witnesses say he stabbed her in the back after she accused him of molesting her daughter."

A dark chasm opened before Tess and there was no way back. She had to plunge in. "He's come after me, then, hasn't he?"

Somehow, she'd known it. All her life, she'd known that she would never, ever be free of Rex Alexander.

"Tess, I don't know what is going on here, but I do believe you are in danger. I want you to come and move in with me and Josh."

"I can't do that!"

"You're too vulnerable out at the ranch. Too isolated. If he has returned and is threatening you, he'd never think to look at my place. And if he did . . ." Ethan left those consequences unspoken, but Tess could imagine.

She shook her head. "I can't. You've got a little boy and it wouldn't be right. Ethan, I've never even *met* Josh!"

"That doesn't matter. I expect he'll be as impressed with you as I am. And don't worry. We've got three bedrooms. You can stay in the guest room. It won't bother Josh. Of course"—he leered at her—"what he doesn't know about what goes on late at night in that guest room won't hurt him."

"But *Josh* could be in danger!"

"If I thought that, I'd never suggest this in the first place."

"But—"

"Tess, listen to me. Your sister wasn't home the night you left the hospital."

"What?"

"She asked a friend of theirs to stay with your mother a little while and she went into town."

Tess stared at him.

"I have to tell you, honey, she's more of a suspect in my mind than some guy you haven't seen in what? Twenty years?"

"Eighteen."

"Now, just to be on the safe side, I've put his description and all other information I could gather into the Crime Bulletin. It gets circulated to all law enforcement agencies in the state. If anyone has arrested a man fitting his description for any crime, they'll get back to me, no matter what he's calling himself these days."

For one horrifying moment, Tess tried to picture her father in front of her.

Blank. Total blank.

She could not remember what he looked like.

She *could* remember what he sounded like.

She shuddered. "How did you know what he looked like?"

"Sophia gave me a description of how he looked back then. I had a computer expert who works for the Rangers in Austin give me an idea of how he might look now." He hesitated. "Would you like to see the picture?"

"No!"

"Okay, okay." He waved his hands in a gesture of calming. "I don't want you to get upset, as sick as you've been."

Her heart fluttered and batted against her ribs.

"Anyway, the thing is . . . I don't trust your sister, especially now, as weak as you are. I don't want you staying with her until this gets cleared up."

"She needs my help with Mama and the kids."

"She'll just have to manage without it."

Tess lay in gloomy silence, staring at the bland beige hospital walls, a butterfly pinned to a board.

Ethan reached for her hand, toyed with her fingers. "It's not true, you know."

"What?"

"The note. What it said. How nobody cares for you. It's not true."

She sighed. "When your mother lives in La-La Land and doesn't even remember your name, and when the police can't figure out just exactly whether it's your *father* or your *sister* who wants to kill you, well, it's starting to feel like that note's making pretty good sense."

He squeezed her hand tightly. "Not good sense. *Nonsense*. Tess—" He took her chin and gently turned her face so she was forced to look into his eyes. "*I* care for you."

She wanted to believe that, but she couldn't help wondering how long it would be before she somehow managed to poison this relationship, just like she'd done all the others in her life. An unbidden tear welled up in one eye, pooled in the corner, and then spilled over, dribbling slowly down her cheek. Ethan raised his hand and tenderly brushed it away.

"I won't let anything happen to you," he said.

But in spite of his solid, strong, reassuring presence at her side, Tess knew that Ethan would not be able to be with her every minute of every day. Sooner or later, she would be alone.

Even worse . . . whoever it was who liked to spend time flipping through Mother Goose books knew it, too.

On Friday, the last witness was called in the Ross Chandler trial. Final arguments were scheduled for the following Monday.

On Saturday, Tess Alexander was released from the hospital with an armload of antibiotic prescriptions and stern orders to remain in bed for at least two weeks. Ethan drove her to the ranch and helped her collect her things, even loading up all her computer equipment. Juan and Sophia promised to drive her car out to Ethan's for her.

Molly and Cody begged her not to leave. She promised to come visit and hugged them with a stone-heavy heart.

For a long moment, she held her mother, kissed her, told her she loved her, and wept. With her mother's soft hair against her cheek, she wondered, really *wondered*, what had happened to her on the night she left the hospital. Was it fever? Really? Or could she expect such a thing to happen again?

She found Marah shoving a vacuum cleaner across the living room floor with ferocious energy; tried shouting at her, finally unplugged the machine. Marah turned furious eyes upon her.

Ethan was outside, loading the computer into the car.

"Marah, please forgive me. I'm not abandoning you—really I'm not."

"Oh, yeah? Who gives a shit, anyway?" She yanked the cord from Tess's hand and started to plug it in.

Tess stopped her. "This is too much pressure for you to handle alone," she said. "I think it's time we, well, started looking for some kind of help for Mama."

"You'd like that, wouldn't you? Hide her away in some smelly nursing home where they'd tie her to her chair and leave her all day."

"*Marah!* That's not fair! I *love* Mama."

"You don't love anybody but yourself." Marah took back the cord.

"Marah, *look* at me, please!"

Her sister stood still, staring at the floor.

"If you just *knew* me, you'd know that isn't true."

With a bitter chuckle and shake of her head, Marah said, "How can I know you, Tess? You don't know your*self*."

Stung, Tess stepped back. Sensing the advantage, her sister Tess smirked at her. "You keep lording it over me, like you're so great and I'm shit."

Tess shook her head, stepped back. "No."

"You think *I'm* fucked up! Look at your *own* life! It's a shambles." She narrowed her eyes and leaned closer to Tess. "You're scared of Mama. I can see it in your eyes. *Scared* of her! Isn't *that* a joke!" She laughed mirthlessly.

"You're wrong."

"Oh, yeah? Am I? Maybe so, but I know one thing. You and Mama were always two peas in a pod. Just alike."

Tess's back began to throb.

"I think you look at Mama, and you see some kind of futuristic mirror. Like, your fate or something. Like you're going to wind up like her. Only Mama's got people who love her." She turned disdainful eyes away from Tess. "And you'll wind up all alone."

The vacuum cleaner growled and roared. Marah brandished it at Tess like a weapon.

Her sister's prophetic words screaming in her brain, Tess turned and stumbled out of the room, getting away, away, as fast as she could.

CHAPTER TWENTY-EIGHT

"This is Josh," said Ethan proudly, holding open the door for Tess to limp through. Her back was hurting so bad it was affecting her ability to walk.

A handsome, brown-haired little boy with great solemn dark eyes approached Tess and somberly shook her hand. "Daddy said you got hurt and needed a place to stay," he said matter-of-factly. "We got an extra room."

"Thank you," said Tess, easing herself gingerly into a chair while Ethan said good-bye to the neighbor lady who'd kept the boy.

The boy stood close by, staring at her. "You're pretty," he said.

"Why, thank you again." She smiled at him.

"Would you like to see my dinosaur collection?" he asked.

"Not right now, Josh," scolded Ethan. "Tess needs to rest."

"I'd love to see them," she said, quirking an eyebrow at Ethan. She trailed along slowly behind Josh as he scampered down the hall. His room was an explosion of brilliant primary colors and the clutter of a little boy. She exclaimed over his crowded shelf of plastic dinosaurs and commented on all the books jammed into more shelves. The backs of the books were well-worn, a good sign that he was being raised to love reading. She sat on the edge of his bed.

"I have some pretty rocks," he said, handing her a heavy shoe box. Sorting through them, he pointed out his favorites. At last, as though he'd been looking for it, his fingers closed over a rock that resembled pink quartz. "You can have this one." He held it out to her.

Deadline   207

"Oh, Josh! Are you sure?"

He nodded. He had Ethan's dark eyes, but there was a sadness in them that bonded to the child in Tess, something he seemed to sense at once in the almost clairvoyant way of children.

Taking the rock, she turned it over and over in her hands. "I love it," she told him seriously. "I'll cherish it."

He smiled, and her heart melted.

"Do you like crazy eights?" he asked.

"It's my favorite game."

While Josh dug through the debris on the floor, searching for his deck of cards, Tess looked up and caught Ethan leaning against the doorjamb, watching them. In the smile they gave one another, it almost seemed as if they were just a normal family, sharing a normal day, smiling at one another over the head of a child in the normal way of parents.

If it weren't for the throbbing in her back and the ache in her soul, she could almost believe it was true.

Almost.

When Tess slid between crisp clean sheets in the guest room of Ethan's house later that evening, there was a shy tap at the door. Sleep tugged at her aching body. "Come in," she called.

Josh entered the room, holding a raggedy stuffed dinosaur whose head flopped back and forth. "I thought you might be lonely," he said, holding out the toy to Tess.

She took the dinosaur. "You don't need him?"

He shook his head. "I have some others. I thought he might make you feel better."

She folded her arms over the stuffed toy, hugging it. "This is the nicest thing anybody ever did for me, Josh. I appreciate it very much, and I'll take good care of him."

He nodded, gave her a long, searching look, and left the room, closing the door softly behind him.

Tess settled on her side, the dinosaur clutched in her arms, and fell immediately into a deep, exhausted sleep.

"Tessie! Tessie!"

In one fluid motion, Tess had flung back the covers and

was out of bed. It was Jonathan again. She had to find him. She *had* to.

"*Tessie!*"

Tess staggered to a stop. It wasn't Jonathan. It was *Josh*!

Oh God, she had to hurry. She could smell the smoke already, could *feel* the heat! She couldn't lose him. Ethan would blame her. It would be all her fault again!

"Josh! Where are you?"

Smoke filled her eyes and burned her nostrils. Choking, coughing, she stumbled from room to room, slamming back doors, searching, crying.

No no no no it can't be happening again!

Sobbing, groping through the smoke, she grasped something square, heavy, and solid. She shoved it aside, creating an enormous racket and a hail of hard things raining onto her feet and legs.

"Tess! What's going on?"

Someone had grabbed her arms. *Him!* It was him! Screaming, she fought against him, flailing her arms, striking out, struggling to get away, *get away* so she could find Jonathan—or was it Josh?

He shook her, cried out her name, shook her again—

And she looked around, in disbelief. She was standing in the middle of Josh's room, surrounded by rocks, which littered the floor around her. Ethan, standing in front of her in his underwear, had hold of her arms while Josh, white-faced, cowered in the corner of his bed.

"How long have you been sleepwalking?" Ethan, now clad in a terry-cloth robe which was too short for his long legs, handed Tess a cup of coffee. "Decaf."

She nodded and took a sip. It was bracing. "What did you tell Josh?"

"I told him you'd had a bad dream. He understood, sympathized, and went right back to sleep."

"Resilient kid."

"He's had to be." He studied her across the kitchen table over his own steaming mug. "You were sleepwalking that night you strolled through my shower door, weren't you?"

Miserably she nodded.

"Why didn't you tell me?"

Deadline   209

She shrugged.

"Have you always done it?"

"When I was a kid, I used to do it a lot. I haven't for a long time. But lately, with all the stress and everything . . ." She passed a hand over her eyes. "I'm sorry, Ethan. I was hoping it wouldn't happen again."

"You were screaming," he said. "Terrified. I was afraid I wasn't going to be able to wake you up."

Some nightmares never end, she thought.

Josh seemed none the worse for wear the next day, and Tess felt surprisingly well. The pain in her back had subsided to a dull but bearable ache and she was more rested—in spite of the sleepwalking incident—than she'd been in days.

Ethan mixed up a whopping batch of pancakes and told her funny stories about his job. It was so nice to sit back and let him wait on her, to read the Sunday comics to Josh, to watch Sam Donaldson drive some politician crazy on a news program, to be with Ethan.

Not until she'd gotten out from under the oppressive atmosphere of her mother's house had she realized just how stressful it had been to her. For the first time since coming home, she found herself beginning to relax.

"You look so much better," said Ethan, as if reading her mind. He sat down beside her on the couch and put his arm around her.

"You're like a tonic for me," she said truthfully, glanced around to make sure Josh wasn't in the room, and turned up her face for a kiss.

"I didn't think you'd feel like doing that so soon after getting hurt. You just got out of the hospital."

"Like doing what?"

Ethan frowned at her. "What have we been talking about for the last twenty minutes?"

A cold fist seized Tess's stomach. "Er . . . you tell me." She tried to smile, as if she were teasing him.

He pulled away from her and swiveled his body so that he was facing her. "What's the matter with you?"

"N-nothing." She struggled up from the couch. "I have to go to the bathroom." Hurrying down the hall, she locked herself into the small room and stood, shivering, in front of the mirror. *Twenty minutes*. She'd lost twenty minutes, *again*. Her own bewildered eyes stared back.

This wasn't going to work. Ethan was going to figure out that something was wrong with her. He and Josh didn't need this. Not now. Not from her. She was going to have to leave. Stay in a motel or something.

Pulling open the door, Tess jumped. Ethan was standing right in front of it, waiting for her.

"I'm g-going now," she said. "I can't stay with you."

Taking her right arm in a firm grasp, Ethan half dragged her down the hall and back into the living room, where he pressed her down onto the couch, taking care not to hurt her wound.

"Talk to me," he commanded. "Right here, and right now. You *tell* me what the *fuck* is going on with you!" His voice cracked like a whip.

She had no choice but to obey.

She told him everything, beginning with her first night back home again.

When she was finished, he was silent for a long time.

"Daddy, can I watch a movie on the VCR?" Josh's appearance in the room startled both of them.

"Not just yet, Josh. Why don't you draw a picture for Tess instead?"

"Okay!" He skipped from the room.

Ethan got up from his chair and paced the floor, looking everywhere but at Tess. Her soul withered. It was just the reaction she might have expected.

Finally he asked, "What do you think's causing these problems?"

"I think it's obvious, don't you?"

"No, I don't."

She laughed bitterly. "Let's just say I'm following in my mother's footsteps."

He gave her a baffled look, then cried, *"Alzheimers?"*

She nodded, then hung her head.

"But that's *crazy*! You're only thirty-four years old. No way you could be exhibiting Alzheimer's symptoms this early."

She sighed. "I don't see why not."

"Tess." He approached the couch, knelt down on one knee

in front of her. "Don't you see? You are not elderly. This is an old person's disease, or at least a postmenopausal one. The kinds of symptoms you described to me could be *any-thing*—a series of small strokes, for example, or—" He glanced away.

"Or what?"

With haunted eyes, he whispered, "Brain tumor. You could have a brain tumor, Tess. Memory loss, blackouts, severe headaches, dizziness—even the sleepwalking—could be caused by that or, or maybe even you're having some kind of seizures, like epilepsy."

She stared at him. "A brain tumor?" An almost hysterical desire to laugh seized her, because the thought of possibly having a brain tumor was actually a relief, compared to Alzheimer's. Brain tumors could often be *treated*, shrunk through radiation or removed by surgery. Alzheimer's, on the other hand, was irreversible.

He clasped her cold hands. "You've got to check yourself back into the hospital—one up in Lubbock that is equipped for it—and have tests run. CAT scans, things like that."

"No." Just like that, the word popped out. She knew he was right, but just the thought of lying in another antiseptic hospital bed filled her with dread.

He pulled back a little. "What?"

"No more hospitals."

"Tess—"

"He can get to me in the hospital. He's already done it once."

"But Tess, this is the kind of thing you can't put off. Believe me, I know."

"It won't do any good!" She looked away from him, blinking back tears. "I've been watching Mama deteriorate ever since I got here, Ethan. The children of Alzheimer's patients have a one-in-two chance of contracting the disease, and I've had the *very same* problems she did. They can run all the tests in the book on me, and the results will be the same." Tess knew she was being unreasonable, but she couldn't seem to help herself.

He let go of her hand and stood up. "Tess, I'm not going through this again."

She began to tremble. "I know."

"By the time I dragged Linda to the hospital, it was too late. I'm not going through that again. I'm not putting that boy through it again, either." He began to pace back and forth in front of her. "Either you check yourself into the hospital and have the necessary tests run, or at the very *least*, make an appointment with a reputable neurologist and have the basic tests run as an outpatient, or . . . or—" He faltered.

Slow tears began working their way down her cheeks. "I'm scared," she said. And that, she knew, was the simple truth.

He sat next to her and took her in his arms. "I know." She quivered all over and he tightened his hold on her.

"I just can't go into the hospital, Ethan. He can *find* me there."

"Okay. All right. We'll figure out something."

His embrace was comforting, but it wasn't enough.

By dawn, Tess had already been found again.

CHAPTER TWENTY-NINE

*There was a little man, and he had
    a little gun,
And his bullets were made of
    lead, lead, lead.
He went to see Tess, and found
    a big mess,
And shot her right through the
    head, head, head.*

Josh found the note.

A knife—identical to the knife which had been used on Tess—was stabbed through the note, forcibly affixing it to the front door facing. While scampering around on the front porch, waiting for his dad to take him to school Monday morning, the child found the macabre message.

Because he was unaware of what had been going on in Tess's life, he was more curious than scared.

It was the adults who panicked, each after their own fashion.

A grim-faced Ethan went immediately into his law enforcement mode. Since he lived just outside the city limits, he called the chief deputy of the sheriff's department to come out and assist in the investigation. Then he called the highway patrol and arranged to have a speed trap set up on the Dryton highway; not to watch for speeders, he explained to Tess, but to keep a sharp eye out for Marah's white Ford pickup.

As soon as they spotted the vehicle, they were to notify the sheriff's department so that she could be put under immediate surveillance. Meanwhile, Ethan would try to figure out a way to keep the ranch house under observation—not an easy task in an area where even a cloud of dust kicked up by a vehicle a mile away is visible from the house.

Throughout Ethan's phoning and ordering, Tess stood in the middle of the living room floor, clutching her arms to her chest, trembling, and clenching her teeth.

Finally she spoke. "It's not M-Marah."

"I'm not so sure of that." Ethan was busy dialing the number of a neighbor who could pick up Josh and take him to school.

"Listen to me!" She put white fingers on his arm. "She's my *sister*."

"All the more reason to make her a key suspect." He finished dialing, spoke briefly, and hung up.

Josh was standing by, big-eyed. Ethan said, "Sally's going to take you to school, son. I have some work to do right now."

"Is somebody going to hurt Tess?" asked the anxious child.

His father cuddled the small boy. "No way," he assured him. "I won't let anybody hurt Tess." He smiled at her over Josh's head.

She did not smile back.

As soon as the boy had left for school, she turned furious eyes toward Ethan. "I'm telling you. It's *not* Marah!"

"What makes you so sure of that? I thought she hated you."

"She does."

His eyebrows quirked.

"Ethan, I have never *once* seen my sister lay a hand on those two kids. She's been a loyal caretaker to my mother for months now, even though they never really got along that well."

"That's her kids. That's her mother. This is different. I don't know that Cain ever smote Eve, either, but he killed his brother Abel, didn't he?" He leaned forward. "You'd be amazed what violence rivalry between siblings can produce in families."

"You're not *listening* to me!" she shouted. "I *know* who's doing this. *Read the note.*"

"I read it."

"Read it again."

"Tess—"

"It says, 'There was a little man, and he had a little gun,' right?"

"Right."

"Ethan, it *has* to be Rex."

Only after it had been photographed for evidence and thoroughly documented did the men pull the knife out of the wall and bag it for evidence.

Through it all, Tess shut herself up in the bathroom, dressing carefully. After a while, Ethan tapped on the door. "I've arranged for you to spend the day with a friend of mine," he said. "I'm not leaving you here alone in this house. You'll be safe there."

She opened the door. He gawked at her. "What the hell—"

She pushed past him. He followed. "Tess—what's going on? Why are you dressed up?"

"I'm going to court," she said. "They're having final arguments today." She threw her tape recorder and extra batteries into her tote.

"No way," said Ethan. "First of all, you heard the doctors. You need at least two weeks of complete rest. Second, I have work to do away from the trial. I can't protect you there."

Tess dug through the room which was cluttered helter-skelter with her things, found a notebook, tossed it into the tote. "I already lost almost a whole week. I've had to listen to testimony by tape. Nurses, for example, who testified that Ross Chandler came to see his granddaughter only once, when she was comatose. I'm already working at a disadvantage because I can't record facial expressions and body language from such testimony, or Chandler's reaction to it. Don't you see? I have a *job* to do, and I'm going to do it." She riffled through her wallet, counting cash.

"Tess." He grabbed her arms, stopping her. "You can't do this. It's crazy. It almost makes me wonder if you *want* to get shot."

"Do you know what I want? Do you *know*?" She hurled the tote across the room where it slammed against the wall, spilling an avalanche of contents onto the floor in a loud rattle, wincing as she did so from the pain in her back. *"I want my life back!"* She was screaming into his bewildered face, screaming, not at him, but at the deterioration of all she held dear—her family, her work, her mental stability, her health, her freedom, her *life*.

The confusion on Ethan's face changed to anger. "I'm trying to *give* you back your life, you idiot! Are you *blind*? Why won't you let me *help* you? Why do you keep fighting me?"

She whirled away from him and he grasped her arm again. The next thing she knew, she was pummeling him, flailing against his chest like a weak and futile moth against a light bulb.

He stood rooted like a tree, absorbing the blows of her frustration, staring aghast at the madwoman this bright, talented person had become.

Exhaustion set in soon; after all, she was still recovering from a grievous wound. Chest heaving, back throbbing, arms aching, she stepped back, too horrified at herself to speak.

Ashen-faced, jaw clenched, Ethan turned wordlessly away from Tess and left the room. Down the hall, she could hear a muffled exchange between Ethan and the silent deputy who'd been tactfully waiting, then the front door slammed shut. Through the window by her bed, she could see the two men climb into the deputy's car and drive slowly away, leaving her alone.

It was, after all, what she wanted.

Wasn't it?

The spectators' gallery was packed. Media representatives from all the major networks, AP, and UPI were so numerous that the judge was allowing them to stand against the back walls, to take notes only. Cameras were not permitted in the courtroom. A courtroom artist furiously sketched the taciturn Ross Chandler, his busy attorneys, the brow-furrowed district attorney, the patient jurors, and the stern judge.

A dose of maximum-strength Bayer had dulled the throbbing in Tess's back, but there didn't seem to be much to do about the ache in her heart. She had hurt the one person in the world, it seemed, who truly cared for her, had angered him and pushed him away.

I knew it wouldn't take you long to screw it up, just like you do everything else, echoed the ghost voice that seemed to crop up with greater frequency in her mind lately.

With an anvil pressing her chest, Tess forced herself to face the realization that she was going to have to move out of Ethan's house, for sure this time. Josh had found the note. *Josh*. She couldn't afford to take the risk that something worse could happen to him.

She wanted to cry.

Instead, she busied herself with preparations for closing arguments, popping another set of fresh batteries into the tape recorder, flipping to a clean page in her notebook and recording the date and the—

Her watch had stopped again.

Her skin crawling with frustration, Tess wanted to rip it off and fling it across the room as she'd done her tote earlier, but contented herself with sneaking a peek at someone else's watch who sat close by on the crowded wooden bench.

Fatigue settled on her shoulders like a heavy cloak. Tess had underestimated how much energy her wound drained out of her just from the healing process. She'd already burned up most of her reserves for the day and still had a very long time to go.

Settling her aching body as comfortably as she could on the hard seat, Tess struggled to concentrate her frazzled attention on the task at hand.

Frank Baxter made it easier by waiving his right to opening arguments.

He was saving his big guns for last.

Cameron Thornton was every inch the country gentleman lawyer, soft-spoken, polite, nonthreatening. His Texan accent told the jurors he was one of them; they didn't know he was a Princeton graduate and a Rhodes scholar. His very bearing defined the word "dignity."

His gentle smile put them immediately at ease; and none of the twelve good men and women before him had ever earned enough money in their lives to even know what an Armani suit was, or to recognize that he was wearing one. Most of them, however, were well aware that Ross Chandler could afford the best. They were curious to see what "the best" was.

Still athletic in his sixties, Thornton moved gracefully, walking slowly up to the jury box, taking hold of the rail, and leaning into his hands. He smiled at the jury.

They smiled back.

With a soft shrug and a slight shake to his head, Thornton said, "Ladies and gentlemen, I wish to apologize for the fact that your valuable time has been wasted in this courtroom. For the past several weeks, you could have been busily employed at your trade, enjoying time with your families, entertaining friends. Instead, you've been here, wasting your time."

Turning away, he crossed to the defense table, stepped behind Ross Chandler, and placed his hands on the man's shoulders. "You've been wasting your time because the man seated here should never have been here in the first place." Stepping out from behind Chandler, he gave a disparaging glance toward the prosecutor. "Ross Chandler should never have been here because the prosecution never had a case! And that, my friends, is why you have been wasting your time, and you've no one to blame but *them*."

Disdainfully he crossed back over to stand in front of the jurors. "During the past several weeks, you've been subjected to an emotional ringer. Why, you've had sobbing children placed before you! It makes you want to kill somebody, doesn't it?"

Several of the women, caught up in Thornton's melodic presentation, nodded.

"But as jurors, your job is to evaluate *evidence*. Cold, hard facts. The prosecution *knows* they have not one smidgeon of evidence that would justify dragging the former governor of the state of Texas through the mud.

"Let's look at all the evidence they *don't* have. First of all, they have no evidence that the house fire which killed Ross Chandler's family was even caused by arson! Isn't that ridiculous? There was not *one trace* of accelerant found *anywhere* in the burned ruins of that house. No gasoline. No kerosene. No *nothing* which any self-respecting arsonist would use to ensure that a building will, indeed, burn to the ground."

A male juror nodded.

"Second, there is no hard evidence that the victims of that

Deadline 219

fire were murdered before the fire occurred. You have two esteemed experts in forensic pathology *arguing* about whether those people were even struck by a blunt object. A blunt object, I might add, which *never showed up*, was never found by law enforcement officers who crawled over every inch of that place, searching."

While detailing the points, Thornton had been pacing. He stopped and faced the jurors. "But let's just say, for the sake of argument, let's just say you believe the prosecution's version of the story. Let's say the victims *were* bludgeoned in their beds. Okay, where's the proof that the governor was responsible?" He leaned against the rail. "Ladies and gentlemen, the governor *wasn't even there*! We have a *whole roomful* of witnesses who can place him a hundred miles away that night! We have an esteemed member of our state's government who stated, under oath, that Ross Chandler didn't even leave the Holiday Inn in Odessa until after ten P.M. One hour and fifteen minutes later, a fireman testified that Ross Chandler called in the fire. He was, say many witnesses, *hysterical*, his own body covered with burns from his pitiful attempts to save his loved ones."

He shrugged, lifted his hands palms up. "You tell me how the man was supposed to get from Odessa to his ranch outside Remington, murder his family, set fire to the house, wait for it to become fully engaged—*without accelerants*—burn himself, then call in the fire in, oh, about an hour's time."

Pursing his lips momentarily, Thornton continued. "Now, I know you heard some disturbing testimony from a woman who claimed to have been having an affair with Ross Chandler at the time of the fire. And you heard some testimony that he was having financial problems." Shaking his head, he said, "So what? Now, don't misunderstand me. I'm not excusing the immorality of what my client did in having an extramarital affair, but ladies and gentlemen, that *does not make him a murderer*. And let me tell you, if all of us who had financial woes then opened ourselves up to accusations of *murder*, well, then, we would *all* be in serious trouble, wouldn't we?"

The jury laughed.

Thornton turned away, paused for dramatic effect, then in a sad, gentle voice, said, "I know many of you are concerned about little Annie Mitchell. Poor, poor child. She's been victimized, you know, and not just by tragedy. Losing her mother, her sister, and her grandmother was horrible enough for any nine-year-old to take. Suffering terrible burns made her recovery even worse. But that wasn't enough suffering, it seemed."

He turned back, his voice ringing with righteous indignation. "No, my friends. This child had to be victimized *again*, first by a bloodthirsty law enforcement establishment who were so determined to prove their own ridiculous theories that they had to suck the life out of an injured child to justify it, and second by well-meaning health-care professionals who seemed unable—or unwilling—to allow nature to take its course in the healing process. No. They had to help things along a little, didn't they? By resorting to quackery, chicanery, and manipulation, they took this pitifully traumatized little girl and *forced* her to back up their lopsided idea of vengeance."

His voice fell. "Well, you know what the Bible says about vengeance. *'Vengeance is mine, saith the Lord,'* and ladies and gentlemen, I *pray* that God takes His vengeance on the individuals who have tormented this poor family just to make their careers in the media, to satisfy a headline-addicted public, and to keep from having to admit to the whole world that *they have no idea what happened to Ross Chandler's family*!"

Releasing clenched fists, the normally soft-spoken lawyer allowed his voice to rise a decibel. "Ladies and gentlemen of the jury . . . I can tell you what happened that night. A good man, a fine man, a man who had *given his life* to public service, who had stayed married to the same woman for thirty-five years, who loved his child and his grandchildren . . . this good man left his family to perform an obligation which he considered it his responsibility to perform, an obligation to offer his considerable respectability and reputation to a man who had once worked side by side with him in the legislature of our fair state.

"And while he was gone . . . tragically his home caught fire by sheer, freak accident. His sleeping family never knew what hit them. They were unconscious or dead within minutes of carbon monoxide poison—a deadly gas which is released in almost every house fire from chemicals present in plastic, nylon, and other artificial fibers.

"But we can thank God, ladies and gentlemen; we can thank God that one child had to go to the bathroom that night. Because of that simple call to nature her life was spared."

With a sad sigh, Thornton said, "And here comes Ross Chandler, driving himself home late in the evening. Imagine the *horror* he must have experienced, spotting the orange glow on the distant prairie right where he knew his home to be; just imagine his panic, his frantic efforts to urge his car faster, ever faster, hoping, *praying* his beloved wife would be safe, only to arrive and find his *worst fears* had come true! Imagine his futile, hopeless, desperate attempts to get to her, his hysterical call to the fire department, his unmitigated *horror* as he stood in the cold black night, waiting for help, watching his home burn to the ground. And his overwhelming grief when he learned, in the hospital emergency room, that he had lost—not just his wife of thirty-five years, but practically his entire family!

"And then, and *then*, to discover to his shock and disbelief that the authorities are going to arrest *him* for this tragedy! And to sit here in this courtroom, day after day, watching the prosecutor *waste the time* of everyone in this room with a ridiculous excuse for a case, ladies and gentlemen . . ." He paused for breath. "I urge you, in the name of good, common *sense*, to consider the *evidence*. You will find that *there is none*. And *this* will be the fact that will give you reasonable doubt. One reasonable doubt is all you need. You will have no choice but to do the right thing.

"You will have *no choice* but to find Ross Chandler *not guilty* of all the charges against him."

CHAPTER THIRTY

When Frank Baxter rose to talk, some of the jurors who'd been sitting forward leaned back in their seats. Others visibly relaxed. After all, Frank Baxter *was* a country lawyer. He *was* one of them. In fact, next to the likes of Cameron Thornton, that was more a detriment than a plus, the idea being that a small-town attorney who chooses to stay in a small town to practice just might not be quite as good as the sophisticated and cultured Thornton; might not, in fact, have all that good of a case, just like Thornton said.

The district attorney for a town the size of Remington who practiced private law on the side made a good living, but not good enough to have a closet full of Armani suits. As if sensing that, Baxter shuffled when he walked, but his solid physique gave off an air of a bulldog not about to let loose of his prey. And when he spoke, they gave respectful attention.

"The first thing I have for you, ladies and gentlemen, is a question. If Ross Chandler is so sterling a character and has been so horrendously wronged, then why doesn't he speak for himself?" He paused to let that sink in. "Granted, he does not have to testify. It is not required by law. But, speaking personally, if *I* had felt so terribly wronged, and if *I* were so devastated by personal loss, *I'd* be *itching* for my day in court, wouldn't you?

"But Ross Chandler's well-paid and well-prepared attorneys wouldn't dare put their client on the stand, ladies and gentlemen, because if they did, you would be able to see for yourselves just what a cold fish he really is.

"You want facts?" He held his fist up in the air. "Fact." He raised his forefinger. "Ross Chandler was a philanderer

Deadline

and a womanizer. He'd been carrying on elicit affairs for years and was, in *fact*, keeping a sweet young thing half his age in a fancy apartment in Midland at the time of his *beloved* wife's death.

"Fact." He raised his middle finger. "He was broke. A combination of bad business ventures and tough economic times had combined to drain his considerable fortune nearly dry.

"Fact." Up went the ring finger. "He conspired with his accountant to hide his various dealings from the Internal Revenue Service, something I am sure that office will want to investigate. That makes him a cheat.

"Fact." The little finger went up. "Ross Chandler took out multimillion dollars' worth of life insurance policies on his entire family just *six months* before they all died. To this day, the insurance company has failed to pay out those policies, obviously because *they're* not buying his accident story, either.

"Fact." He held up his thumb. "We have a witness, and in spite of the defense's attempts to convince us that this child has been conned, I draw your attention, not just to her story, but to the manner in which it was presented. There was absolutely no doubt or hesitation in how she told what happened to her. And as for the reliability of hypnosis to aid in recall, law enforcement agencies around the country have relied on this method for years in order to jog the memories of witnesses of violent crime for descriptions of suspects, license plate numbers, and other valid testimony; *all of which* is recognized by every court of law in the land.

"Fact." Baxter held up the forefinger on his other hand. "Ross Chandler and Sam Dickens have been political cronies for years in an area in which favors are routinely exchanged for favors. Sam Dickens is currently involved in the election campaign of his life. Do you think Ross Chandler could help him win? And, if so, do you think he might want to win badly enough that he would *lie* for Ross Chandler? Have you ever in your lives *heard a politician lie*? I would consider these questions very carefully before I swallowed that man's testimony hook, line, and sinker; because, ladies and gentlemen, I smell a fish story.

"Fact." The other middle finger went up. "Some of you

on this jury have grandchildren, so this might make more of an impact on you, but if, say, this tragedy happened to you . . . if you lost your spouse, your only daughter, and one granddaughter, and if your sole surviving family member was a small child, helpless, traumatized, and severely burned, I ask you . . . wouldn't you plant yourself next to that child's bed? Wouldn't you pray for her, bring her gifts, watch over her lovingly and tenderly, *give your life* to bringing her back from the edge of death? Yet it is a *fact* that Ross Chandler visited his grandchild's bed *once*, while she was comatose, for a total of *five minutes*, and he *never* went back to see her again." His calm, rational voice rose to a commanding shout. *"He abandoned her! In her hour of deepest, darkest need, he didn't care whether that poor child lived or died!"*

He waited for his words to reverberate throughout the silent room. "And yet, while that pathetic little waif fought for her life, Ross Chandler was busy building an expensive new home for himself and his college-girl lover, moving in with her, living as if nothing had happened."

After a long pause, he said, "Fact," and brought up his second ring finger. "The defense team paid off an outside expert to come in here from *New York City* to razzle-dazzle you poor ignorant country bumpkins. Without *even seeing the bodies*, he claimed that their deaths were accidental. *Come on*, don't let yourselves be bamboozled and insulted by that! It doesn't take an expert to know when a bone has broken *outward* or *inward*, and when a pathologist picks skull fragments out of three brains, it's pretty easy to tell that somebody *bashed their heads in*!"

Whirling, pointing at Ross Chandler, he cried, "Who had the motive? Who had the opportunity? And who was *coldhearted* enough to do such a thing? I'll tell you who! A man who has *made a lifetime* out of conning the public, trading on image, and playacting respectability . . . a man who never gave a damn about anybody in this world except himself . . . a man who never bothered to honor his wedding vows, and didn't even have the common decency to allow a mourning period for his dead wife before publicly shacking up with her young replacement . . . a man who can afford to pay back in tremendous favors someone to *lie* for him on the witness stand . . . a man who can jiggle the books to come up with enough money to build a small mansion and pay off a top defense team just until he finally collects on the life insurance money he's waiting for . . . a man who would leave *his own flesh and blood* to rot in a hospital bed and then sit back, *completely unmoved*, while that maimed and mutilated child *sobs her heart out* on the witness stand!"

With a dramatic drop to his voice, Baxter, standing with solid calm before the jury, said, "I know many of you might wonder why a man who *seems* to be one thing on the surface, who can project such an all-American image on the outside, can be such a monster on the inside; or how someone who seems to have everything one day can throw it all away the next, without so much as a backward glance. I can't answer that.

"But I can tell you that there is a borderline we all walk . . . a thin line between sanity and madness, between civilization and anarchy, between self-control and chaos . . . and I think Ross Chandler crossed that line."

Holding out his hands cupped, as if full of water, he said, "Ladies and gentlemen, you hold in your hands the ability to send a clear message to this man, that *he cannot get away with murder*! He cannot cross over that borderline without paying a price. The *facts* are all there. Consider them carefully, and you will find Ross Chandler *guilty*, on all counts."

The Mustang churned up a cloud of dust on the hard white caleche road, blotting out the view from behind. Static blared from the radio. Mechanically Tess reached down and turned it off. Save for the crunch of the tires on the rocky road, silence enveloped the car.

Tess did not know where she was or how she had gotten there. She did not remember leaving the courthouse, getting into the car, or driving out into the country.

Her head swam and there was a metallic taste in her mouth. Nausea clenched at her stomach. She was surrounded by nondescript ranching country which did not look familiar and yet evoked a strange, arcane feeling of déjà vu. Since she had no sense of time, she was trapped in a twilight zone of suspended present, surrounded by a haunted past.

She came to a weedy cattle guard and slowed, her tires rattling over the metal pipes like a skeleton's bones. Brooding clouds lurked overhead, blanketing the sun and robbing from her any sense of direction. When the road curved, she followed the curve as if she had no choice, as if it were somehow impossible for her to stop, back up, turn around, and return . . . where?

Down the road dipped, over a rickety little bridge which forged a creek, a bridge which jolted Tess's spell like a hypnotist's clap, *a bridge she knew*. Up over the rise rested a small, abandoned house.

Tess broke out into a cold sweat.

She drove up to the house, parked, got out of the car, walked up to the creaky wooden porch; a robot, programmed to overlook the hammering of her heart and the overwhelming urge to run away.

The front door was ajar.

The sky growled.

She walked in.

Sand layered the floors and had drifted in the windowsills to an inch thick in places. Corner cobwebs wafted in the air currents stirred by Tess's body. Something skittled across the dusky room. She moved through the house. There were only four rooms. In the kitchen, linoleum rippled; the old, deep sink was rusted. Under her step, floors groaned. Thunder menaced at the window.

One bedroom was cluttered with a few things left behind by the former occupants. A couple of mismatched socks, hangers in the closet, the torn cover of a child's book. She picked it up.

Mother Goose.

Skin crawling, she threw it down.

Tessie, read me a poem!

She put her hands over her ears.

Daddy said you'd read me nursery rhymes.

She squeezed harder against her skull.

What's the matter, Tessie? Daddy likes nursery rhymes. Don't you?

She ran from the room and out of the house and stood, panting, in the back, looking for the barn.

There was a barn here. She was *sure* there was supposed to be a barn here.

She used to play hide-and-seek in the barn with Jonathan.

Deadline

Trembling, hurrying now, she jogged a little ways out back, past the dead fruit trees, past the old cistern, past the corrals—*there*. It should be right there.

Stumbling a little, she ran around behind the faded, tumbledown pens, caught her foot on something, and sprawled headlong.

Buried in the weeds was a long board, flush with the ground. Ignoring her filthy hands and knees, her torn stockings, her dusty pumps, she followed the board to a corner and along the line . . . It was a foundation.

The foundation for a barn which no longer existed.

A powerful wave of memory, surging up from her subconscious, washed over her, drowning her in the truth she'd never faced all these years:

Tess Alexander, nine years old, set fire to the barn herself.

A howl of agony, wrenched from a wound so deep within her soul that the grief was fresh-opened, echoed across the deserted landscape to the storm-laden emptiness beyond, as Tess cried out to her three-year-old brother, *"Jonathan! God help me! I didn't know you were in there!"*

CHAPTER THIRTY-ONE

LIGHTNING SPLIT OPEN the sky, shattering the air, followed by a crash of thunder, deafening Tess from her own anguished cries.

Jonathan wasn't the only one who liked to play hide-and-seek in the barn. How many times had Tess cowered in a shadowy corner deep behind a dusty hay bale, *praying* that her father wouldn't find her?

But he always did.

He liked to stuff his handkerchief in her mouth so that she couldn't scream, and after he was done with her, he would put her on his lap and read the most violent nursery rhymes he could find, often substituting Tess's name in ways designed to terrify her into silence.

The hot, musty, shadow-cloaked barn became a torture chamber. Tess knew Rex wouldn't dare do anything to her in the small cramped house, where her mother was always present, nursing her new baby sister and taking care of Jonathan. With the logic of a child, Tess surmised that, if the barn were no longer there, he would never again be able to hurt her. She didn't know they would move into her grandfather's house; couldn't know about the attic.

The updraft of the approaching storm produced a phenomenon peculiar to the Southwest: it sucked up a solid curtain of red dust about a mile from where Tess crouched at the old barn site, forming a moving bloodred wall which reached up to the boiling angry gray sky. Far above towered a mountain of cumulus clouds which resembled the eruption of Mount Saint Helens.

Jonathan. She squeezed shut her eyes.

They all doted on him. Rex, especially, was proud to have a male heir. All the love he'd starved from his older daughter he lavished on the boy. She should have been jealous but it was impossible to hold a grudge against Jonathan, so full of sunlight and smiles was he.

Her mother, distracted by problems with her philandering, gambling, womanizing husband and a difficult pregnancy with Marah, had simply entrusted the boy to young Tess, a responsibility she never minded. He followed her everywhere, unless, of course, he was ordered away by Rex.

Marah's birth, far from bringing about an improvement with her mother's state of mind, seemed to send her spiraling into a depression so deep the bewildered Tess found herself the grown-up more often than not, which was a natural progression, considering the rites of passage to which she was being subjected by her father.

Jonathan was her only bright spot, her only cuddly companion. In many ways, he was like her own child.

The arriving updraft caught Tess in a stinging swarm of wind-driven sand that battered her. Hidden in the wind seemed to be thousands of voices whispering, *Murderer. Murderer. Murderer.*

Arms crossed over her stomach, Tess began to rock back and forth.

As quickly as it came, the sand went away, and the full force of the storm-tossed wind slammed into her, buffeting her with moist fists, reaching slick fingers underneath her clothes, exposing her like the soft underbelly of a cowed animal to the ferocious fangs of its predator.

Dry sobs caught in her throat and were torn out by the wind.

A mile away, a creeping silver curtain obliterated the rolling plains, cedar breaks, and arroyos of Tess's childhood home. Shivering, still kneeling prayerlike in the ruins of her brother's death, she watched with numb fascination as snakes of lightning forked down and exploded a gnarled mesquite not half a mile away. Off to her right, the sky had a pale green cast to it, an undersea grayness that never failed to strike fear in the hearts of those who scanned such horizons with worried brow, searching for funnel clouds.

Soon a solid wall of water smacked into Tess, sending her

reeling facedown into the weeds and rocks, pummeling her with fat pellets of rain driven almost sideways by the fierce and mighty wind. Lightning sizzled so close her hair stood on end and she could smell an acrid burning. The resultant *crack* hurt her ears.

She couldn't go on anymore. Couldn't carry the burden.

Die, said a voice within.

Beaten and ravaged by the storm within and the storm without, Tess pushed herself up to her knees and then staggered to her feet, standing to her full height, praying that lightning would strike her and she would at last get the justice she deserved.

Against her will, her feet began moving, first slowly, haltingly, stumblingly, then faster in an awkward jog. *What's the matter with you?* cried another voice from deep inside. *Jonathan's death was an accident! You didn't mean to kill him! You loved him! It wasn't your fault!*

"But I *did* kill him!" she sobbed.

That's right, said another voice. *You were a horrid little arsonist. You burned down a barn and murdered that poor little boy. You deserve to die.*

Around her the storm raged, blinding her with torrents of water, deafening her with crashing thunder and crackling lightning. She staggered to the car. The door handle was slippery and she fumbled with it.

You know what to do, said the second voice.

Don't be foolish, said the first.

"God help me!" cried Tess, yanking open the door. "I'm going crazy!" Sobbing, she sank into the driver's seat and closed the door. Sheets of water poured down all windows, and almost immediately her breath fogged up the insides of them. Thunderous beatings of storm rains reverberated off the car roof.

She was alone.

Rivulets of water streamed off her clothes and puddled on the rubber mat on the floor beneath the steering wheel. Tess sneezed. Groping in her bag for a Kleenex, she heard the crinkle of paper.

Immediate dread seized her heart.

She knew what it was. She also knew that she had not put it there.

Deadline

It could mean only one thing: she had run like a rabbit straight into the coyote's den.

She hadn't gone into all the rooms of the house. Someone could have easily camped in that second bedroom, and Tess would never have known it. And if that was true, then *he* was here, now, watching her, waiting.

Without even turning the ignition, she sensed, she *knew*, that her car wouldn't start.

A perfect trap.

With trembling hands, Tess slowly withdrew the paper.

For every evil under the sun
There is a remedy or there is none.
If there be one, seek till you find it;
If there be none, never mind it.

Hail began smacking against the car with violent *cra-cra-cracks*. Tess jumped and strained to see out from her cocoon. Rubbing a Kleenex in a circle on the misty window beside her, she saw the sudden, blurry form of a man approaching the car.

With a scream half choked in her throat, Tess frantically fumbled with the key, desperately trying to start the ignition, but though the little car groaned, it wouldn't turn over. Whimpering, she locked all the doors.

No. Too much like a trap. Like those hay bales in the barn. He could always get to her when she cowered in a hole.

Ice missiles crashed into the car with a thunderous roar. Tess gave in to panic, flung open the door, and sprang out—straight into the hands of her pursuer.

Screaming, fighting, clawing, kicking, biting, adrenaline-spurred to greater strength, Tess tore loose from him and ran blindly down the road, which was now a raging torrent of water, pouring down across it from a nearby draw. Her impractical heels bogged her down, and when she stopped to kick them off, she was hit from behind, knocking them both down with a *splash*.

Choking, sputtering, Tess struggled with all her strength to escape the man, whose body covered her own, weighing her down. It was no use. He was much too strong for her.

Suddenly the fight went out of her. Her body went limp, her face sagging into the water.

Better to drown than face Rex Alexander.

Powerful hands grasped her shoulders, dragged her out of the water, and turned her rag-doll body around. As a last, desperate resort, she shut her eyes and cringed, waiting for the blows to come.

"Tess! What's the matter with you, for God's sake?"

Shivering, gasping, Tess opened her eyes and stared, bewildered, into the drench-haired, muddy face of Ethan Samuels.

They drove back to town in virtual silence. Ethan promised to send sheriff's deputies to pick up her car, which started the first time he cranked it. For some mysterious reason, he refused to let Tess drive, insisting that she ride back with him.

He'd been following her, he said, for the better part of the day. Though he claimed it was for her own protection, Tess sensed that he was withholding something crucial from her.

Both of them were soaked to the bone, mud-covered, and sore from their struggle and from the blows from hailstones. The car heater helped some. Tess heard over the radio that a funnel cloud had been spotted two miles from where she'd been, and that the county was under a tornado watch.

She asked him if the jury had come to a verdict in the Ross Chandler trial; he said no.

Ethan's attitude toward her was extremely awkward and strained; he might have been a stranger. In a small voice, she apologized for her behavior, including her morning tirade, but it didn't seem to help matters much. Clearly there was something deeply serious on his mind, and he was one of those infuriating men who could keep his counsel in a stony silence which even torture wouldn't budge.

Finally, as they drove into the Remington city limits, he said, "I think you should know, I've been notified by the Amarillo sheriff's department that Rex Alexander is wanted in that city in connection with an arson incident."

Arson.

Chill bumps crawled over her skin.

"Ethan—" She put her hand on his arm. "Do you think he could have had anything to do with the Chandler fire?"

He shrugged. "We're looking into it."

She pulled her hand away. "Are we going to your place to clean up?" she asked.

"No."

She looked at him curiously, but he might as well have been a mannikin.

He drove up to his office building, parked, and came around to open the door for her. Rainwater poured off his soaked and dingy hat as he leaned down. Tess realized the hat was ruined. It would be expensive to replace. She found herself apologizing, again, but he shook his head wordlessly and led her into his office. Ernest Carter, the chief deputy, was waiting for them. And there, in a corner chair, sat Dr. Ellyn Frazier. Even more shocking, to Tess, was the other person in the room.

"What are *you* doing here?" squawked Tess.

Marah said nothing.

She turned to Dr. Frazier. "What's going on?"

"You called me. You said it was an emergency. Don't you remember?"

With mute misery, Tess shook her head. There was so much she didn't remember, and so much she did. She looked at Ethan, who was watching her in that guarded way of his that saddened her.

"We know who's been sending those notes," he said. "And we know who stabbed you."

CHAPTER THIRTY-TWO

HE TOLD HER.

Shock brought on tingles in her hands and feet. Knees buckling, she sat down in one of the hard chairs facing Ethan's desk.

"No." She shook her head. "It can't be." She appealed to Marah. "It doesn't make any *sense*. It's *crazy*."

"On the contrary," put in Dr. Frazier. "It's really quite sane, when you put it in perspective."

"I don't *want* to put it in perspective!" Tess sprang to her feet and would have bolted from the room if Ernest Carter, an older man with a shopworn face and kind, sad eyes, hadn't taken gentle hold of her arm.

"Better sit back down," he said.

A violent shiver worked its cold track down her spine. "C-could I have some coffee, please?" she asked.

"Sure." He called out the door to a deputy down the hall to bring a coffeepot, some cups, and whatever else they might need.

Tess's head swam. Nausea crawled in her stomach. Suddenly she snapped up her head, straightened her back, and tossed her wet hair out of her eyes like a defiant dog. She couldn't see her own eyes, but the others in the room saw them make a sudden, startling change from silver to slate gray. Her voice, when she spoke, cracked like the snap-lash of a whip. "You don't have any proof!" she spat. "And until you do, you can get the fuck out of my face."

Stunned faces stared at her, all except for Dr. Frazier's. She leaned forward, keen-eyed. "Who are you?" she asked.

"None of your damn business."

"Would you rather I called you Tess?"

"That's a stupid, weak name. A name for losers."

"All right, then, what shall I call you?"

A sly smile worked its way over her face. "Alexandra."

"A beautiful name," said Dr. Frazier.

"A *strong* name." She glanced lasciviously at Ethan. "A sexy name."

He blushed and looked away.

"Why have you been trying to kill Tess?" asked Dr. Frazier.

She narrowed her eyes at the doctor. "I'm not saying a goddamn word until I see some hard proof."

Ethan cleared his throat, stammered around, and then said, "Your fingerprints were on the knife which had been stuck in my door. Yours and no one else's. Your fingerprints were also on the knife found in yo—er, Tess's back. And I saw you write the last note earlier today. By that time, I'd found the stationery which was used for the other notes in, um, Tess's things."

Giving him a hostile, suspicious look, she said, "That thing on?" and pointed to the camcorder perched on a corner tripod.

Ethan nodded.

She laughed, a hollow chuckle that brought chills to the others. "Okay. I confess. So what are you going to do, *arrest* me?" She leaned back in an arrogant pose, her lip curled into a snide smile.

"Alexandra." Dr. Frazier was not going to get sidetracked. "Surely you realize that if you kill Tess, you are effectively committing suicide, don't you?"

She shrugged. "You never heard of kamikaze pilots?" She sneered at the room. "Killing that stupid little bitch would be *worth* it."

Dr. Frazier leaned back. "You've done everything you can to wreak havoc in Tess's life, haven't you? You've tried to terrify and humiliate her with those nursery rhymes. You've tried to injure her in her sleep. You've sabotaged her work—it was you who wrote the letter to her publisher, wasn't it?"

Alexandra gave her a wicked little grin.

"And you are the one who changed the article galleys, endangering Bic Tran."

Alexandra shrugged. "Little snitch deserved it."

Marah's mouth dropped open. "You blamed *me* for that!"

"Not me," said Alexandra, grinning. "That was Tess. I had fun watching, though."

Dr. Frazier shook her head. "Not only have you tried to kill Tess, you've even tried to destroy her family life."

"*What* family?" she snarled. "You call *that* pitiful excuse for a human being *family*? Marah's nothing but a three-time loser, and that's all she'll ever be."

Marah gasped. "Those are the kinds of things she's been saying to me ever since she got here." She took a step forward. "I don't care *what* you call yourself! I could tear you apart with my bare hands!"

"Go ahead. I whipped your butt before. I could do it again."

"*Ladies!*" implored Dr. Frazier. "You're behaving worse than some of my youngest patients. Now, Marah, watch her closely. Did she look like this during those ugly episodes, or all the time?"

Marah shivered and clasped her hands over her arms. "She could be so nice sometimes, and then she would change, just like *that*!" She snapped her fingers. "It was like . . . well, two different people." She brooded at her sister. "I finally just stopped talking to her altogether. I thought she hated me."

Alexandra smiled mirthlessly at Marah. Marah broke eye contact first. "I usually hate anything that gets close to the body. These other two bore the shit out of me. If I could, I'd get rid of them both."

"What body?" demanded Ethan. "What other two?"

Dr. Frazier seemed unfazed. "When she says 'the body,' she's talking, literally, about the body which serves as host for the various personalities. It's my guess that the 'other two' refer to Tess and someone else . . . Marah, this person, here, hates you, but not Tess."

Ethan groaned and rolled his eyes. "This whole thing . . ." He couldn't seem to finish the sentence.

"I know. It's very hard to take, or even believe," said Dr. Frazier. "There have been experiments done with hired actors, trying to get them to emulate what a multiple personality does—and they couldn't do it. It's not just *behaving* differently; it's *being* different, altogether. Each personality can have her own handwriting, her own dreams, her own memories. One can have allergies and another not. One can even be right-handed while another is left-handed. In some miraculous way, the brain actually seems to split."

Alexandra, who'd been uncharacteristically silent, gave a disdainful snort.

The coffee arrived. Ernest handed Alexandra a cup first. "What's *this* swill? I didn't ask for any coffee!"

"Yes, you did." He looked around at the others.

"I did not, you stupid old fart."

"It's okay," said Dr. Frazier to the bewildered officer. "Just set it there on the desk. She may want it later." She resumed her thoughtful, probing manner. "Tell us why you want Tess Alexander dead."

"She deserves to die. She's a murderer. A *child killer*."

Ethan sucked in his breath. Dr. Frazier waved a warning signal at him. "Who did she kill?"

"Why, Jonathan, of course."

Marah's head snapped to attention. "Who in the world is Jonathan?"

"You ought to know. He's your brother. She burned him up. So you see, it's worth it to me to get justice done here, no matter what the repercussions to myself. I nearly pulled it off with that stabbing, until . . ."

"Until what?"

"Until . . . somebody . . . intervened."

"Who? Who intervened?"

"Oh. My head hurts." She buried her face in her hands. Her shoulders slumped, and her whole demeanor was transformed into the very picture of humility. Her eyes gentled to the color of mist, and her voice was soft and sweet. She looked up. "Dr. Frazier. Thank God you've come."

"I'm so glad you called, Theresa."

"Theresa?" Ethan and Ernest spoke together.

Everyone in the room got chill bumps all over again as they watched.

"It was getting to where I couldn't control Alexandra anymore. She was getting stronger all the time. I figured the only thing I could do was take Tess back to the old house, back where it all happened, and *make* her remember."

"You've protected her from those memories all these years, haven't you?"

She nodded. "They were just too painful. If I gave them to her all at once, well, I wasn't sure how she'd be able to handle it."

"What happened?" Dr. Frazier's manner with Theresa was much more relaxed and conversational.

"It's this trial, Dr. Frazier. It's just too similar to what happened all those years ago. It brought Alexandra out with a vengeance. I was so afraid she was going to kill us all."

"Could I ask a question?" Ethan, blushing as he asked.

Theresa turned gentle eyes his way.

He stared at her. "Um, when Tess and I were, um, *together*, who was I with?"

She smiled. "Tess was the one who fell in love with you. We stayed out of it. But lately, well, Alexandra decided that she liked you. She was jealous of the attention Tess was getting, so every now and then she would pop out for a little while."

"But, how do I *know* . . . who . . . ?"

"Well, let me put it this way. Alexandra has a very wild streak in her."

He flushed darkly and turned away.

"Theresa." Dr. Frazier got back to business. "Have you and Alexandra been breaking through lately to Tess?"

She nodded. "I got her help the night she ran out of the hospital. She could hear Alexandra some then. And when Tess got stabbed, well, I felt no pain, you see. I knew that Ethan lived very nearby and it was no trouble to drive her there. The body, though, was getting weak from loss of blood, so Tess came back just as we got there, thank goodness."

"Was there any other time that you thought Tess could hear the both of you?" asked Dr. Frazier.

"Yes. Today, back at the old house, she could hear both of us—in her mind, I mean. Not out loud. I mean, we're not crazy or anything."

"Of course not."

"Wait a minute." Ethan's voice was sharp. "You've . . . all . . . got me confused. Who was Jonathan and what happened to him?"

Theresa told them the whole story. Somewhere along the

line, Marah sat down and put her face in her hands. "So you see, Tess couldn't live with the guilt. The whole thing was a terrible tragedy. She was only a child, and she had no idea that her little brother had followed her into the barn. Once it caught fire, she could hear his screams but she couldn't find him." She reached for the cup of coffee Ernest had put on Ethan's desk, took a sip, and said, "Thanks so much. This is just what I needed."

Ernest raised his eyebrows.

"After that, Rex called her a murderer and a child killer whenever he had the chance. The fire department ruled the fire accidental—they said kids had caused it by playing with matches—and Rex went along with that publicly, but not in private. Not when they were alone. Mama . . ." Her quiet voice broke. Marah's eyes filled with tears. "Mama had what they used to call nervous breakdowns. She refused to leave her room for weeks—Tess had to take care of you, Marah; the baby. Then, when Mama was ready to come out, Jonathan's name was never mentioned again; it was *forbidden*. The family moved into Papa's house, but Rex tormented Tess worse and worse. That's when I came out. I always came out when the pain was too great for her to bear. Eventually I hid everything from her."

Dr. Frazier smiled. "You kept her sane, Theresa. You kept her functioning. Without you, she'd have gone catatonic, or worse."

She looked at the good doctor sadly. "I'm so tired, though, Doctor. I'm getting weaker. I'm trying to help Tess grow strong so that she won't need me anymore. Unfortunately Alexandra is also growing stronger." She shuddered.

"Don't worry about that," said Dr. Frazier. "Alexandra just acts out Tess's own suicidal impulses. In therapy, we'll work through her guilt, not just over Jonathan, but over the whole incest and child abuse thing."

Marah began shaking her head. "This is all so hard to believe. I mean, Daddy never, ever did anything to hurt me. In fact, he spoiled me, and I know I took advantage of that. It's just, I feel like I should have *known* if he was harming Tess that way."

"You were very young," said Dr. Frazier. "And it is not uncommon for a child abuser to select one child to abuse in a family. Remember the case of the six-year-old who'd been left in the bathroom to live for almost four years before finally crawling out of the window and escaping? He was one of four children, and yet he was chosen for the most horrendous abuses. There are other cases, cases in which a child has literally been beaten to death in a family while the other children were unharmed."

"It doesn't make sense, though," said Ernest. "With sex abuse cases, usually they'll start in on the other little girl when the first one outgrows it."

Dr. Frazier shrugged. "Rex left when Marah was still very young. Who knows what might have happened if he'd stayed?"

The room was silent for a moment. Finally Marah said, "Tess is never going to believe all this." She seemed to be growing more comfortable with the whole idea.

Ethan, however, was not. "I don't know," he said. "This is all so weird. Lots of kids get sexually abused. They don't wind up like . . . like *this*."

"It takes more than simple sexual abuse—if there *were* such a thing—to cause this kind of defense mechanism," said Dr. Frazier. "Severe and prolonged emotional trauma produces this; the kind of abuse that is not just discipline gone out of control, but sadistic, measured torture which goes on relentlessly."

"But why . . . *this*?" he persisted. "Why not some other form of mental illness?"

"I don't know that it can be considered an illness; but I will say that it takes an extraordinarily intelligent, highly creative, and very sensitive individual to create such a perfect form of escape."

"You talk about us as if we're not here," said Theresa in her soft, gentle voice. Her use of the plural "we" instead of "I" caught the others in the room by surprise. She smiled, and it was as if the vindictive Alexandra and the bewildered Tess had never existed at all, except in the fevered imaginations of those watching.

Marah considered her seriously. "Can't you, well, *tell* Tess? Write her a letter or something? It worked for Alexandra."

Theresa shook her head sadly. "I can see what Tess does,

as if through a window, but I can't always break through to her consciousness. Only once in a great while can I break through and take over her body while her consciousness is still out."

"Out?" Ernest was totally lost.

"Well, we all have to use the same body. Only one of us can be out at a time. Occasionally, I've been able to take over, and I know Alexandra has, too, but Tess never understood what was happening to her."

"We'll work through that in therapy," insisted Dr. Frazier.

"Then what?" asked Ethan scornfully. "They going to take turns or something?"

"The goal of therapy in these cases is usually to merge the personalities into a whole entity," said the therapist.

Theresa sighed. "Then Alexandra will get her wish."

They all looked toward her. Shoulders slumped, she said, "For us, it will be the same thing as murder."

Ethan punched the "stop" button on the VCR and the screen went blank. They were all gathered in a plain, almost austere room, watching Tess's tape on the television set there.

For a long moment, nobody spoke. After a while, Tess said, "So it's true. I really am crazy."

"No." The shake to Dr. Frazier's head was emphatic. "Multiple personality is an exquisite, creative, intelligent way for a victim of torture to preserve her own sanity."

Tess shook her head. "I'm so out of control, though. It's awful. I mean, how do I know Alexandra might come out and scream at Mama again, or call Marah vile names, or . . . try to kill me?"

Dr. Frazier leaned forward. "Your best defense is *remembering*. Dig up those memories and *let yourself experience the pain*. Then put it behind you. Only then can you heal."

Tess shook her head. "I can't remember. I've tried."

"I'll help you," said Dr. Frazier, pushing a gray strand of hair behind her ear. "Through hypnosis."

Marah asked, "Dr. Frazier, do you think . . . Alexandra . . . might hurt one of my kids?"

"No," said Dr. Frazier with an empathic shake of her head. "You heard Theresa. The only one Alexandra wants to hurt is Tess. She would never hurt a child. None of the personalities would."

Chewing on the inside of her cheek, Marah seemed to come to a decision. "Then I think you . . . all . . . should come home. We've got to keep an eye on Mama, anyway. We'll make sure Tess doesn't . . . hurt herself."

"Are you sure?" Dr. Frazier asked.

Marah nodded. "She's my sister," she said. "And I love her . . . especially now that I know she wasn't really responsible for all the things she said."

"Oh, Marah," said Tess. "I've been—I mean—this has all been so hard on you. I feel terrible. I'm so sorry for the things I must have said . . ."

Marah shrugged. "It's okay. You weren't yourself."

There was a brief pause, both sisters exchanged glances, then suddenly burst out laughing. Others in the room visibly relaxed. After a moment, Tess's brow furrowed. "How long will all this take?"

"Once you're *willing* and have the courage to face these demons, and once we start intensive therapy several times a week using hypnosis, it's possible to work through this in only a few weeks," promised Dr. Frazier. "It all depends on how cooperative you are. In your case, you are already having memory flashes on your own. I think you're ready."

Tess nodded. Then she said, "What will happen to Theresa and Alexandra?"

"I think that, as you remember and are able to handle those memories on your own, you won't need them to function anymore. The eventual goal in most therapy with multiples is an eventual merging of all the personalities into a whole."

Tess shook her head. "I can't believe I've got something like an Alexandra inside of me." She shuddered.

Dr. Frazier smiled, a sweet, kind smile. "Oh, child," she said. "Don't you realize that we *all* have an Alexandra inside of us? We *all* have a Theresa? Each day of our lives, we operate on a multiple-personality level. We behave one way with our three-year-old and one way with our boss—as if we are two almost entirely different people. And I suppose, if there is a dark guilty secret inside of us, then we are all capable of being self-destructive, and all capable of protecting ourselves from our own bad impulses.'' She chuckled. "We all hear voices in our head, telling us to do this, or not to do that.

"It's just that your situation was so totally out of control in your childhood, so threatening, so terrifying, so *hopeless*, that you found a brilliant way to deal with it."

"Real brilliant," scoffed Tess. "Sticking a knife in my own back." She felt a hot flush work its way up her neck. "It's so humiliating."

"But don't you see?" coaxed Dr. Frazier. "It *was* brilliant; a brilliant cry for help when the stress from this trial became too personal, too overwhelming, too memory-provoking. A part of you wanted to die, and another part devised a wonderful little set of warning signals, cries for help."

She held out a strong hand toward Tess, and Tess took it. "The truth, Tess, is that you don't really want to die. You want to *live*; you've been fighting to live all your life. I—we—can all help you to start life all over again."

Marah sat down next to her sister and put an arm around her. "I'll help," she said.

Tess hugged her and was hugged back with a ferocity that caught her by surprise. Finally, pulling back a little, she wiped a tear off her cheek and said, "I guess I'll be like Phoenix, then, rising from the ashes."

CHAPTER THIRTY-THREE

MARAH AND TESS stood in the hot little hidden attic room, peering down at the trunk.

"I never knew this room was up here, Tess."

"Me neither. At least, I never remembered it. Theresa brought me up here one night to help me remember."

"It's so strange, the way you talk about them like they're people."

"In a way, they are." Tess pushed at the trunk with her foot.

"Spooky."

"Yeah."

"Was it true that you got so sick from the knife wound because one of your, well, people . . . didn't respond to antibiotics?"

"Yeah. And another strange thing about this is that it's taken such an incredible amount of energy for me—or I guess I should say, us—to keep going that I've actually drained other power sources, like my tape recorder batteries."

Marah shivered. "It's cold in here." She glanced away. The topic of conversation was an awkward one, to be sure, but they were both avoiding the real reason for their attic visit. Marah said, "What are you going to do about the book? I mean, the jury was hung. No verdict. How do you end a book like that?"

Tess shrugged. "Nine jurors voted guilty. Three others just wouldn't give down. They're going to have to do the trial all over again—this time in a change of venue. It's terribly frustrating." She sighed. "And when I think of what they put that child through, and then, imagining her going through it *again . . ."* She shook her head. "I don't have much choice, though. I'm going to go ahead and write the book like it is and add an afterword after the new trial."

Marah nodded. "How long do you think you'll be staying with us?"

"Another few months. It would have taken me that long to finish my interviews and research for *Firestorm*, anyway. And Dr. Frazier seems to think things are going well in therapy. It's a little embarrassing, though, having to wait for appointments with all these little kids." She grinned.

"Don't worry about it. She told me that she was having to treat the hurt child in you."

Tess nodded somberly. "I've got to do this, you know."

"I know." Marah stood back while Tess wielded a crowbar, snapping the lock on the trunk easier than either of them expected. They crowded close.

Black-and-white snapshots littered the top tray. Tess picked one up. A happy, handsome little boy smiled up at her. Her vision blurred and she passed the photograph wordlessly over to her sister.

Small boy's clothes and a few toys were packed underneath the photographs. Tess's silent tears blotched the clean, neatly folded little overalls and tee-shirts.

"Who do you think packed this stuff up?" asked Marah.

"Probably Sophia, don't you think?"

Marah nodded. Reaching underneath a worn teddy bear, she pulled out a marriage license for Rex and their mother, dated January 3, 1958. Something about that didn't ring right to Tess, but she was too distracted by the teddy bear. She cuddled it close. *Let the memories come as they will,* Dr. Frazier had said. But oh God, how it hurt, picturing Jonathan bouncing into his little bed every night, clutching this bear close.

"Wait a minute." Marah's voice jolted her. "Look at this, Tess."

She glanced over her sister's arm idly, and froze. It was a birth certificate for a Theresa Sophia Powell, dated September 23, 1957.

"Powell?" She jerked the paper from her sister's hand. "That's Mama's maiden name. And look at the *date*. I mean, I was always told that Mama married Rex in January of *1957*."

"Look here, where it says to write in the name of the father."

Tess peered closer. "What does *NA* mean?"

"You're the journalist. You should know. It means *no answer*."

They stared at one another. After a stunned moment, a huge grin broke out on Tess's face. "*Marah!* Do you know what this means?"

Her sister laughed. "Yeah. It means you're a bastard."

"She was havin' an affair with a married man," grudgingly admitted Sophia. "Very prominent in town. When she got pregnant, he took his family and moved away. Nobody knew where he went."

Tess couldn't seem to stop grinning. "Oh, Sophia, why didn't anybody *tell* me? You can't imagine what it would have meant to me. It means . . . well, it means everything."

Sophia shook her head and tsk-tsked. "Your mama was ashamed. She was afraid if you knew, you wouldn't respect her. And then Rex, he didn't want you to know."

"Why did he marry her?" Tess asked.

"That's easy. Her daddy's money. She didn't really know, though. Oh, that Rex, he was a charmer. She just thought he was the sweetest thing, courting an unwed mother. This was a long time ago. To be an unwed mother was just the worst thing—it killed her papa, it really did, especially when she up and married this no good—" She glanced at Marah. "Sorry."

Marah shrugged. "You live and learn."

"Why didn't she leave him, Sophia?"

"This is her home. She threw *him* out a few times but always he come back. She was scared of him. Scared of what he might do. And she wasn't strong like you."

"Strong?" Tess shook her head.

Sophia folded her large arms across her ample chest and said, "Just about the toughest person I know. You'll figure that out, one of these days, and then you gonna be all right."

The dogs set up a cacophony and they all heard the sound of an automobile crunching up the drive out back. Marah squinted up at the clock. "It's not time for the school bus," she said. "I wonder who that could be." She went out to the mud room, glanced out, and pushed open the back door. "Hi, Ethan!" she called.

Tess's stomach froze. Ethan had been avoiding her ever since that fateful day in his office, wouldn't even look into her eyes when they did meet, as they had on the day the jury came in with their nonverdict for the Chandler trial. It was clear he didn't know how to relate to her anymore. On the one hand, she figured it was best—her life was in too much of a mess at present to try and deal with a new relationship; on the other hand . . . God, how she missed him.

Marah bustled back into the kitchen, and Ethan's big body seemed to fill up the room behind her. He took off his hat and ducked his head in greeting. He was looking awful good. She sighed.

"I have some news," he said, and his tone was ominous. "They arrested Rex Alexander in Midland, and when they searched his car, they turned up a bloody baseball bat. The blood matches that of the victims in the Chandler fire. He's willing to turn state's evidence on Ross Chandler, for conspiracy to commit murder, in exchange for dropping the capital charges. That way Alexander won't get the death sentence for the murders and arson."

"What?" screeched Marah. "Are you saying *Daddy* did it?" Her wild eyes glanced from Sophia to Tess to Ethan. "No. That can't be true."

"I'm sorry, Marah," said Ethan. "I'm afraid it is true. Rex had been working for Ross, doing his dirty work, for years and years. Apparently he was paid a lot of money for this job."

"Job?" Marah began to cry. Sophia squeezed her shoulders.

Marah wasn't the only one in shock. A fist to the solar plexis would not have come as more of a blow to Tess. She had heard nothing after the words "They arrested Rex Alexander."

We must see him, said a soft voice.

Yeah, face down the son of a bitch, said another, sharper one.

It's only way we'll ever be rid of him, she heard. *The only way.*

• • •

The Remington County sheriff's department and adjoining jail was a new, modern building. Ethan took care of the preliminaries while Marah and Tess sat in a small waiting area, nervously holding hands. Tess kept trying to take a deep breath, but her chest was too constricted.

They had extradited Rex Alexander from Midland and were holding him in a high-security solitary cell, awaiting Chandler's second trial, for which he was a key prosecution witness.

Ethan gestured toward the sisters, and they rose as one and approached a room which contained only a hard wooden table surrounded by a few metal folding chairs and a mounted video camera high in one corner. "He'll be here in a minute," said Ethan.

Tess turned to Marah. "Would you mind terribly—I mean, can I have a few minutes with him alone before you see him?"

"Are you sure?" Marah worried at a raw bottom lip.

"I think it's . . . necessary."

Marah peered at her. "This *is* Tess, isn't it?"

A weak smile flitted across Tess's face. "Yes, it's me."

Her sister relaxed slightly. "Okay. I'll wait out here. But just a few minutes. There are some things *I* want to ask him, too. I mean, I still have to face the fact that my own father is a child molester and a murderer." Her lip trembled.

Tess touched her sister's arm. "It's not your fault."

"I know that. But his *blood* runs through my veins!" she cried.

"Look, Marah." Tess took both her sister's arms. "Don't you ever forget that you're a Powell. You've got good, strong stock in you from way back. Papa would be proud of what you've been able to do with the ranch."

"Do you think so?" Marah pleaded with her eyes. "I've been working with the agricultural extension service and experimenting with new feeds and pasture rotation. We might even turn a profit this year."

Tess smiled. "I never knew you were a born rancher. I shouldn't be surprised, though. Mama inherited the ability from Papa, and you inherited it from her."

Marah nodded thoughtfully, gave her sister a sudden, impulsive hug, and left the room.

Tess sat down at the empty table. Her stomach churned.

Deadline

Let me handle this, said a low, growling voice from within. *I'll kill him for what he's done to us.*

"No," whispered Tess. "I have to do this on my own." Her hands began to tremble and she hid them in her lap.

A side door opened; Tess jumped. She could hear the slow, malicious rattle of chains.

The *clunk-drag* drew closer, breathing, it seemed, down her neck. A cold shudder crawled down her spine.

A soft *thud* signaled that the door had closed.

Slowly Tess turned and got to her feet, the accumulated dread of a lifetime crowding into her throat, choking her breath, screaming in her ears.

She saw him.

He was an old man, handcuffed, bound in leg irons and chained feet to waist. Bushy white brows glowered at her over rheumy eyes and a mottled face that bespoke alcoholism. Up close, in the merciless light of day, he was Rex, all right. But put him in a dark room backlit by the feeble glow from a bathroom light down the hall and add a terrified child hiding in a closet; it was easy to see how he resembled Ross Chandler. In fact, he looked like the evil side of Chandler.

His ice-blue eyes chilled her to the bone.

Two deputies let go of his useless arms and stepped back, standing guard by the door, watching his every move.

"How 'bout a hug for your old daddy?" he said sarcastically.

"You're not my daddy," she answered, holding her trembling hands behind her back and lifting her chin. "You never were."

He shrugged. "Finally figured that out, did you? You never were too quick."

After all these years, his hateful face and malevolent voice still had the power to make her quake from head to foot. For a few panicked moments, she was a petrified child again, trying to squeeze way down inside herself, into a ball so tiny he could never find her. An almost irresistible urge to crawl under the table and hide possessed her. With a titanic effort, she shook it off.

Forcing herself to stand to her full height—which, to her shock, brought her almost nose-to-nose with him—Tess drew on a lifetime of rage. So empowered, she gave a mighty, psychic heave; and broke free of her chains.

Then she gave him the same sort of glint-eyed grin he used to give her. After all, *he* was still bound.

Focusing her concentration on the situation from a journalist's point of view (he couldn't touch her anymore), she asked him why he had committed the horrible crime against the Chandler women and children.

He cut a glance in the direction of the guards and lowered his voice. "I had no choice. Loan sharks were after me. Old Ross, he needed a favor, and I needed a favor. *Quid pro quo,* as the lawyers would say." His lip curled.

"*How* could you?" She wanted to strangle him with her bare hands. For a moment, she gave in to the fantasy of making him hurt until he died.

"Get drunk enough, you can do most anything," he answered.

"No." She shook her head. "You could do it cold sober. Just like the things you did to me." Her hands clenched into fists. "I could kill you right now, and I'm cold sober."

He inclined his head. "You always were a cocky little bastard, just like your old man. He was into law enforcement, too, you know. Got off on that stuff just like you. The police chief, did you know that?"

She stared at him.

"Spineless bastard. Left town with your mama holding the bag. Took me to come along and clean up the mess."

"All you cleaned up was Papa's money."

He grinned. "Well, it's a dirty job, but somebody had to do it." With a wicked chuckle, he added, "You all grown-up and everything, you look just like your daddy. God, I hated him. He just *loved* to find excuses to throw me in jail. After he knocked your mother up and took his miserable ass out of town, I made sure he knew I married Nan." He curled his lip. "Made sure his wife knew all about it, too. Figured she ought to know, right?" He chuckled again, coughed, hawked, and spat on the floor.

Tess clenched her teeth, but she gave no ground. After a moment, she said, "I used to think you were frightening, but now I know that the only people who need to fear you are children and sleeping, defenseless women."

Deadline

"Why you—" Rex took a step forward.

"Stay back!" cried a deputy.

"I'll get you someday," he muttered.

"Oh, no," said Tess. "You can't get me. Not now. Not ever again." Her eyes blazed at him. "I'm too strong now."

With a final, disgusted glance, Tess turned her back and walked away.

"Mr. Foreman of the Jury, have you a verdict in the matter of Ross Chandler versus the State of Texas?"

"We have, Your Honor."

"What say you?"

"We find the defendant, Ross Chandler, guilty of conspiracy to commit murder of his wife, Libby Chandler, and guilty of negligent homicide in the deaths of his daughter, Amanda, and his granddaughter, Jenny."

And guilty of destroying the life of his other granddaughter, Annie, thought Tess as the courtroom erupted into chaos.

Ross Chandler remained standing stock-still between his attorneys, rooted to his place by shock. Obviously it had never occurred to him that he might lose, that he might be held accountable for his crime.

Tess found herself moving forward through the surge of press that surrounded the silent former governor and his lawyers, who were already squawking rapidly about appealing the sentence. Through that strange serendipity that sometimes occurs in life, the crowd parted momentarily and Tess suddenly stood in front of Chandler.

During all the times she had faced him, never once had *she* felt the power. Always it had emanated from him.

Until now.

Now they locked gazes. She noted fine beads of sweat between his brows.

She wondered if ghosts would haunt his prison nightmares.

"I'm . . . I'm innocent," he whispered feebly. No one seemed to have heard him over the din except Tess. "You've got to believe me." He clutched at her sleeve.

Shaking her head gravely, she pulled away her arm and said, "It's all over but for the crying, Gov." Then she gave him a brittle smile. "I'll send a copy of the book to your prison cell." She turned to go. "Oh, by the way . . . I'm dedicating it to Annie."

"Wait."

She looked back. One of Chandler's lawyers gave him a sharp look. He said, so softly she might have imagined it, "I never knew they were in that house, I swear."

By "they," she knew he meant his daughter and granddaughters. She pursed her lips. "It's too late," she said. "Too late."

He started to speak, but was warned to silence by his attorney.

She left him. At the door, she looked back through all the noise and confusion as two burly sheriff's deputies escorted a handcuffed Chandler out through a side door. Yes, it was just as she thought.

Already he seemed to be shrinking.

Pulling herself up to her full height, Tess lifted her chin, pulled her shoulders back, and walked out the door, down the stairs, and into the fresh sweet sunshine.

A warm, benevolent, early summer sun caressed the countryside as Tess pulled the newly washed Mustang over to the side of the farm-to-market road and parked. Placed right in the middle of rambling hills, its gentle swells a tangle of yucca, brilliant red Indian blanket, bright yellow huisache daisies, and sky-colored bluebonnets, the country cemetery dozed under a moist morning breeze, the desert flowers that littered it rejoicing from recent rains, which had greened and gentled the landscape.

The gate was made of iron pipe and had a simple chain looped around it with no lock. She let herself in and replaced the chain. For a moment, Tess stood and gazed around her. Craggy hills nearby stood guard over the cemetery. Peaceful cattle dotted a distant pasture. A mourning dove sent up a plaintive cry.

She wandered the tombstones. Unlike the sanitary "perpetual care" cemeteries of large cities, this was a place of nature's beauty, where simple country folk could rest. Many of the graves had little cedar trees planted at the head, as if the mourners had wanted to protect their loved ones from the relentless prairie wind.

Deadline

One grave marker was rough-hewn rock, with the message crudely scratched upon it: *Our little girl Amelia Hogarth; born 1922, died 1933*. At the foot of the same grave was a splendid marble tombstone, mechanically engraved with the same name and dates. Someone, somehow, had waited many years to make up for the hard times of the Depression.

There were a number of graves for infants, and one that read, *359 Batt., 19th Div., 1919*.

One long tombstone read simply, *Homer Smith and Wife*.

Weeds and wildflowers caught at Tess's ankles as she made her way around the little cemetery. Lots of history here. Tough, pioneering folks at rest now, who'd battled fierce Indians and powerful dust storms and rocky soil and the sheer, raw *loneliness* of isolation, to carve their marks upon the land.

One plain, gray slab caught Tess's attention and she stopped. For a long moment, she stood there, studying it. It read, simply, *UNKNOWN*.

With a sigh she turned away, and there it was, almost hidden under the undergrowth and tangled sunny primroses. The headstone lay flush with the ground. She had to stoop to clear away nature's clutter to read it in full: *Jonathan Rex Alexander, born May 10, 1963, died July 10, 1966*.

For a while, Tess worked, clearing away the weeds, but she left the wildflowers, especially the yellow primroses. Then she sat cross-legged by the small grave, listening to the call of the mourning dove and the cry of the heart.

Finally she said, "Good-bye, my sweet brother."

A voice inside said, *We're leaving, too. You don't need us anymore.*

She nodded sadly and thought, *Even Alexandra?*

Especially Alexandra.

But I feel like friends are dying.

No. We're just a part of you, and we'll always be here, inside, just like a part of Jonathan will always be with you, and a part of Mama, and a part of Papa. Even a part of Marah. You just don't need us to show ourselves anymore. You're strong enough now. You've become whole.

She pulled up a delicate primrose and pressed it against her cheek. *I'm scared,* she thought.

It's okay to be scared. You just don't need to run away from it anymore. Now you can stand and face it.

I'd like to find my real father someday.

And now you can.

The wind tossed her sandy hair playfully across her face and she shook it free. A cheerful mockingbird chattered nearby. Tess filled her lungs with fresh country air and listened to the total peace. Like Scarlett, she could gain strength from the land.

After a long time, Tess got to her feet, brushed off her jeans, and headed out to her heavily packed Mustang, carrying the primrose with her.

AFTERWORD

"*FIRESTORM*: SIXTEEN WEEKS on the *New York Times* Bestseller List," read the poster which hung behind Tess at the table where she sat, patiently signing stacks of boldly jacketed books in a crowded Austin bookstore. "A Chilling Story of a Writer Whose Own Life Was Touched by a True Crime of Shocking Dimensions!"

It had been a long day and the lines, even longer. Her back ached and her hand was growing stiff from all the signatures. She was grateful when things finally began to slow down near closing time. She was even tired of smiling.

"I think that's about it," she said to the jubilant store manager, swiveling around in her seat.

"Nope. One more," said the manager.

Tess turned back, blinked, and almost swallowed her tongue. "Ethan," she said, taking his copy of her book dumbly. She held it, staring at him, drinking in his tall lean body and craggy face. "What are you doing in Austin?"

"I live here now. Transfer came through."

Her heart jolted. "Oh, yes. The transfer."

"I'm going to close up now, sir," said the manager.

"It's all right, Mr. Peabody. He's with me," said Tess. "Here, Ethan, sit down." She gestured toward another chair the manager had used from time to time.

Ethan took his seat and pointed at the book she still held in her hand. "You did an incredible job," he said. "I didn't think you'd write the story once we arrested Rex."

"Are you kidding? My editor would have had me shot." She laughed.

"I still can't get over the fact that the jury convicted Ross Chandler in less than an hour."

She gave him a satisfied smile. "And gave him the full sentence."

He nodded. "Feels good when the system works."

"Absolutely."

There was a small pause, then Ethan cleared his throat and said, "I'm glad you didn't get into any of, well, that other stuff. The stuff we talked about with Dr. Frazier. I mean, you didn't shy away from Rex being your stepfather and abusing you and all, but I was relieved you didn't get into . . . the other." He seemed reluctant to say it aloud, as if to do so would automatically provoke a sudden, unpleasant appearance by Alexandra.

"Well, some things are just too personal to dump on the public," said Tess. "You helped. You could have released the particulars about my stabbing to the press. Thank God you didn't."

He gave her a lopsided grin that tickled her stomach. "Cops are good at hiding things from the media."

She nodded, running her hand over the smooth black and red book jacket of *Firestorm*. "Ethan . . . why do you think Ross Chandler called me in the first place? I mean, he knew full well he'd hired my own stepfather to commit the murders. Why would he ask *me* to write an investigative book about the crime?"

Ethan considered the question. "Ego, for one thing. Towering, colossal ego. It never occurred to Chandler that he would actually be convicted for this crime. Asking you to write a book vindicating him—which he was sure you would do—was like a game to him. And remember: he liked to exploit the weaknesses of others. I'm sure he figured that if you ever suspected the truth, you'd never publish it—not with your own connection to the murderer, and not with your own traumatic history. It was a form of control. But like most liars, I think he eventually began to believe his own lies. He was genuinely surprised by the guilty verdict."

She could hear the jingle of bells when the manager closed the front door. She didn't want to talk about it anymore. She knew only too well what lies the mind was capable of believing. "How's Josh?" she asked.

Deadline

"Great. Just great. He's enjoying getting to see his cousins and grandparents. He asks about you, though."

"I miss him," she said truthfully. After an awkward pause, she said, "Did you know my sister got remarried?"

"No."

"She married Jimmy Baker. She was dating him when we first met. He's an ex-rodeo roper. He loves the ranch and they're doing very well. I think maybe she might stick with this one."

"What about your mother?"

She sighed. "It got to where we just couldn't take care of her at home anymore. We were having to lie on top of her just to get her to sleep. And she was wearing diapers . . . Anyway, we looked all over and found a wonderful facility in Abilene." She smiled. "They have this walled-in courtyard, with ivy on the bricks, and a fountain and flowers—it's strictly for the Alzheimer's patients to wander around in. We thought she'd be happy there, at least, you know, as happy as she can be."

He nodded, reached out to pat her hand, and held it.

Little electric shocks buzzed through her body. She took hold of his fingers. "I'm whole now, Ethan. All that bad stuff is behind me. I'm not even in therapy anymore."

He nodded. "I can tell. You do look so much better than you did the last time I saw you. Stronger, somehow." He pursed his lips. "Hey, I'm sorry I kind of freaked out over what happened that day. I just didn't know how to handle it."

The fluorescent lights overhead flickered and dimmed.

"Don't worry about it," she said. "I'm not sure I did either, not at the time. And I probably needed this time alone to get myself together, so to speak." She smiled.

"I'd forgotten how lovely you are when you smile."

The store manager cleared his throat. "Um. Miss Alexander, we really need to be going."

"Yes. Just let me sign this last book." She picked up her pen.

"Hey."

She looked up.

"Think I could bring Josh out sometime to your lake house? He loves to swim."

Their eyes met for a long, liquid moment. She felt the heat spreading throughout her body.

"In the meantime," he drawled, "maybe we could get together tonight?"

Hiding a grin, Tess, thinking back to the first day they'd met, leaned over his copy of *Firestorm* and wrote: "To the sexiest, best-looking man I've ever met. See you in bed. Tess Alexandr."

She had to go back and add the "e."

"TERRIFYING, HEART-POUNDING SUSPENSE!"
—Mary Higgins Clark

BILLY

The chilling new novel by *New York Times* bestselling author

WHITLEY STRIEBER

He was a bright, well-adjusted boy...
Until a madman invaded his home...
And snatched him away from all that
he knew—and loved...

"AMAZINGLY GRIPPING...A KNOCKOUT!"
—Peter Straub

___ 0-425-12955-1/$5.99

For Visa, MasterCard and American Express orders ($10 minimum) call: 1-800-631-8571

FOR MAIL ORDERS: CHECK BOOK(S). FILL OUT COUPON. SEND TO:	POSTAGE AND HANDLING: $1.50 for one book, 50¢ for each additional. Do not exceed $4.50.
BERKLEY PUBLISHING GROUP 390 Murray Hill Pkwy., Dept. B East Rutherford, NJ 07073	BOOK TOTAL $ ____
NAME_____	POSTAGE & HANDLING $ ____
ADDRESS_____	APPLICABLE SALES TAX $ ____ (CA, NJ, NY, PA)
CITY_____	TOTAL AMOUNT DUE $ ____
STATE_____ ZIP_____	PAYABLE IN US FUNDS.
PLEASE ALLOW 6 WEEKS FOR DELIVERY. PRICES ARE SUBJECT TO CHANGE WITHOUT NOTICE.	(No cash orders accepted.)

"SANDFORD GRABS YOU BY THE THROAT AND WON'T LET GO!"
—ROBERT B. PARKER

NEW YORK TIMES BESTSELLING AUTHOR
JOHN SANDFORD

__RULES OF PREY 0-425-12163-1/$4.95

The killer is mad but brilliant. He kills victims for the sheer contest of it and leaves notes with each body, rules of murder: "Never have a motive." "Never kill anyone you know." Lucas Davenport is the clever detective who's out to get him, and this cop plays by his own set of rules.

"SLEEK AND NASTY...IT'S A BIG, SCARY, SUSPENSEFUL READ, AND I LOVED EVERY MINUTE OF IT!"
—STEPHEN KING

__SHADOW PREY 0-425-12606-4/$5.50

A slumlord butchered in Minneapolis. A politician executed in Manhattan. A judge slain in Oklahoma City. All the homicides have the same grisly method—the victims' throats slashed. This time, the assassin is no ordinary serial killer...But Lieutenant Lucas Davenport is no ordinary cop.

"THE PACE IS RELENTLESS...A CLASSIC!"
—*BOSTON GLOBE*

LOOK FOR SANDFORD'S *NEW YORK TIMES* BESTSELLER
<u>EYES OF PREY</u>. ON SALE IN PAPERBACK MARCH 1992.

For Visa, MasterCard and American Express orders ($10 minimum) call: 1-800-631-8571

FOR MAIL ORDERS: CHECK BOOK(S). FILL OUT COUPON. SEND TO:

BERKLEY PUBLISHING GROUP
390 Murray Hill Pkwy., Dept. B
East Rutherford, NJ 07073

NAME_____
ADDRESS_____
CITY_____
STATE_____ZIP_____

PLEASE ALLOW 6 WEEKS FOR DELIVERY.
PRICES ARE SUBJECT TO CHANGE WITHOUT NOTICE.

POSTAGE AND HANDLING:
$1.50 for one book, 50¢ for each additional. Do not exceed $4.50.

BOOK TOTAL	$ _____
POSTAGE & HANDLING	$ _____
APPLICABLE SALES TAX (CA, NJ, NY, PA)	$ _____
TOTAL AMOUNT DUE	$ _____

PAYABLE IN US FUNDS.
(No cash orders accepted.)

303a